THE DUCHESS AND THE HIGHWAYMAN

BEVERLEY OAKLEY

Created with Vellum

❧ I ☙

It was an evening like any other: dull, with a hint of menace and tension so thick, Phoebe imagined slicing a neat hole in it and disappearing magically into a new life.

Any would do.

The company had retired to the dim, close drawing room, gentlemen included, following a gluttonous dinner. By the fireplace, Phoebe worked at her embroidery, glad to be ignored though she knew that wouldn't last for long.

The reprieve was even briefer than she'd anticipated. Brutus exhaled on a shuddering snore truncated by a yelp as he chased rabbits in his dreams; this caused James the footman, who was stooping over Ulrick in the act of offering his master a drink, to jump in fright and deposit a snifter of brandy upon her husband's waistcoat. Not that it would concern Ulrick, who was snoring more loudly than Brutus and whose waistcoat was already stained with drool.

The footman cast the mistress a sideways glance as he unwound his lordship's stock and dabbed at the sticky mess, but Phoebe held her tongue and made do with a dispassionate look. She'd never liked James. She was certain he'd conspired with Ulrick on more than a few occasions to put her on the back foot and to tarnish her name belowstairs. Despite her obvious disdain, she was afraid of the power he wielded.

"That will be all, James." She rose with a dismissive wave and the rustle of silken skirts. "I'll attend to my husband. Please see Mr Barnaby and Sir Roderick out."

Sir Roderick, that most unwelcome of neighbors, appeared before her, bony and wraithlike; malevolent as ever. "I believe your dog needs more attention than Lord Cavanaugh." His thin mouth turned up in a parody of amusement as he wafted a fastidious hand about his nose, indicating Brutus's greater guilt than his master's snoring.

Phoebe offered Sir Roderick a cold smile. On the other side of the room, Ulrick's two other guests conversed in low voices by the window.

She inclined her head as she ignored his attempt at levity. "Good night, Sir Roderick."

Sir Roderick straightened his spare, weedy frame, which she saw trembled with suppressed outrage at being so summarily dismissed by the lady of the house.

Phoebe refused to turn away from his challenging gaze. Sir Roderick was another who couldn't wait until the doors of Blinley Manor were closed against her the moment Ulrick breathed his last. She'd offended his honor, having bitten his lip and kneed him in the groin six months before when he'd accosted her in a dimly-lit corridor, and suggested in lewd terms how he might assist in the creation of an heir for the already ailing Ulrick. An heir who would ensure Phoebe kept a roof over her head.

Ulrick stirred to wakefulness with a grunt but Phoebe ignored him.

"My husband is attempting, with the limited faculties yet available to him, to wave you farewell, Sir Roderick." She struggled to keep the acid from her tone. Sir Roderick was a powerful neighbor. He was also the local magistrate and self-proclaimed arbiter on acceptable behavior; not a man she'd have willingly chosen to cross. She bowed her head. "His strength is exhausted and I need to see him to bed."

Sir Roderick flicked a glance toward Wentworth and Mr Barnaby then pushed his skull-like head, which reminded Phoebe of an oddly-shaped mushroom sprouting some form of fungus, into her face.

"You'll be sorry—after your husband is gone—if you don't take advantage of the kindness I'm still prepared to offer you, Lady Cavanaugh." His thin fingers dug into her wrist as he all but dribbled down her cleavage, and Phoebe, icily composed until now, whipped her head around with a gasp but met only amusement in her husband's dull, onyx eyes as he regarded the scene.

She breathed in despair and exhaled on resignation. Although Ulrick could barely communicate these days, he was still more cognizant of what was going on around him than most people believed. But he would never champion her. He never had and he'd not start now.

Phoebe hoped he didn't hear the fear in her whisper. "I would rather copulate with an adder, Sir Roderick." It was an unwise response, though being blunt had to be better than a ladylike dismissal which might encourage him to repeat his predatory behavior.

Sir Roderick glanced over her shoulder, no doubt to ensure they remained out of earshot of the remaining two guests still conversing by the window. "You may discover some day, Lady Cavanaugh, that my bite is far more dangerous." His nostrils flared as he pinched her hand before releasing it. "Indeed, I'll ensure you rue the day you threw my kindness back in my face."

Kindness? "Good night, gentlemen." With a rustle of her skirts that hinted at the outrage more eloquently than Phoebe could put into words, she turned her back on the company and swept over to Ulrick's side. Her heart beat painfully as she rearranged his pillows, and the closing of the door on the last of their neighbors to leave offered only a small measure of relief. There was still Wentworth to deal with.

"The doctor doubts Ulrick will make Michaelmas." The lazy drawl of her husband's cousin punctuated the silence as Phoebe resumed her position in an armchair by the fire.

Wentworth raised his cut-glass tumbler to the light as he sighed in appreciation of Ulrick's best brandy. He took a sip and smacked his lips, meeting Phoebe's eye across her sleeping husband, whom she'd made more comfortable in his large leather armchair with the tasselled cushion Phoebe had embroidered to support his neck.

The odious creature could not help but interpret Phoebe's critical expression correctly, but there was no defensiveness in his tone as he chuckled. "The old bastard can't enjoy his riches when he's gone." His teeth were white; sharp and wolfish beneath his black mustache and Phoebe looked away, pretending concentration on her handiwork while her stomach clenched with revulsion and fear. She would not dignify Wentworth's grasping remarks with a response.

For a few minutes, Ulrick's wheezing, rattling cough and the hiss of the fire broke the silence. The harsh caw of a raven in the darkness made Phoebe jump, but she kept her fingers busy with her embroidery and her head averted from Wentworth's hard stare.

Tonight? Would Wentworth insist on claiming her tonight, with Ulrick so very ill and likely to need her?

Wentworth drained his glass, placing the empty vessel clumsily upon the low table beside him. *Empty vessel.* It's what she'd always been made to feel as Ulrick's wife. "Ulrick was always mean with his liquor. A good supply for his heir then, eh, Phoebe?" Ulrick's heir. Wentworth imbued the word with the disgust he'd always felt for the fact that *he* was not Ulrick's heir. It was hardly better than the reproach that had always hardened Ulrick's tone in the days he could speak, when he implied that Phoebe had failed in providing him with a son to continue the family line.

Phoebe glanced up and saw Wentworth's thin lips were pursed, observing fleetingly that he looked like a malevolent raven, his dark eyes glittering in the face she'd once thought so handsome. She tried not to show her fear.

"How long do you suppose it'll take my brother to drink the lot once he inherits?" There it was. The bitterness he didn't bother to hide.

"Hush, Wentworth. You'll wake Ulrick." Phoebe cast the sleeping invalid a nervous look.

"The doctor opines that our poorly Lord Cavanaugh will not last three months." Wentworth didn't trouble to lower his voice. "My guess is he'll be gone long *before* Michaelmas."

Phoebe could bear it no longer. She dropped her handiwork into her lap and sent her husband's regular and increasingly unwelcome guest an imploring look. "Please, Wentworth. He's not dead *yet*. Have the good grace to keep such thoughts to yourself. What if he hears you?"

Wentworth gave a short laugh. "What do I have to lose by my graveyard talk? It's not as if Ulrick's in any position to deny me what my imbecile brothers already have simply by virtue of them being *alive*."

How many times had she heard the same complaints? Phoebe forced aside her weary frustration and rose. "I'm going to bed."

Instantly Wentworth was behind her, his breath hot on the back of her neck as he gripped her hand.

"I thought you'd never say it, my sweet." He sucked gently at the hollow at the nape of her neck, twisting a tendril of her hair around his forefinger while Phoebe's insides clenched with revulsion. Once, though, Wentworth had thrilled her with his charm. She, who'd not known what it was to be wooed, had fallen for the oldest trick in the book.

"But Ulrick will need—"

"Ulrick looks comfortable to me." Wentworth moved her in front of him and tipped her chin to look into her eyes, his voice as thick as treacle. "Come, my sweeting. Let us do *Ulrick's* bidding."

Another rattling cough from the armchair was cut short by her husband's rasping, feeble voice. "Phoebe?"

Phoebe was for once glad of the chance to go to him. "Not tonight, Wentworth," she whispered over her shoulder, kneeling at his lordship's knee and arranging her shawl about him. "Ulrick needs me."

"Ulrick ne'er needed oo."

Phoebe's stricken look was met by Wentworth's satisfied grin. "Ulrick never needed you," he interpreted. "That is, he only needed you to provide him with an heir who wasn't an imbecile, which you failed to do." He bent at the waist and put his mouth to his cousin's ear. "My dear Ulrick, I was about to take your wife to bed; however, she appears to think *you'd* prefer her tonight."

"Never wanted her. Go!" The old man flicked a trembling hand in the direction of the door, and with a chuckle, Wentworth gave Phoebe a push as she straightened. She stumbled a few steps, regaining her balance only because Wentworth swung her round to face him, one hand gripping the back of her neck, the other her chin. Over his shoulder, she could see Ulrick snoring again, his head at an odd angle upon the cushion; dribbling his bile upon the handiwork which was all she'd ever been good for.

❧

PHOEBE USED HER LAST BARGAINING CHIP AS SHE SHRUGGED herself out of Wentworth's grip. They'd made it as far as the first guest bedchamber only to find the fire unlit, which was hardly surprising she tried to tell him. Still, Wentworth's desire was greater than his fear of discomfort, and as he ran his clammy hands over her, she tried another. "I think I'm with child."

He blinked owlishly and tilted his head as he pushed her against the bed.

"I'm late." She put her hand to her head and closed her eyes. "Please Wentworth, I'm very tired tonight."

"How late?" His voice was thick with hope.

Phoebe stared at the cherubs dancing above her on the plaster ceiling and tried to think quickly. She was not a natural liar. She'd been clutching at straws, but she felt no desire to play brood mare to yet another Cavanaugh stud. "A week. Oh, but see, there is no linen on the bed, Wentworth."

"Too early to be conclusive then." He ignored her reference to the unsuitability of their location, adding briskly, "No, my love. Both of us have a duty to Ulrick." He snaked his arms around her waist as she tried to make for the door. "A duty to ensure my imbecile brother Bentink does not succeed your wreck of a husband and bankrupt the estate within the twelvemonth. If you'd only listened to sense a year ago and not let your precious scruples intrude, there might already be a lusty son in the nursery." Pushing her backward, he flopped down next to her, the mattress dipping under his weight.

"Bentink will drink himself to death before he's likely to find a wife," Phoebe remarked wearily, trailing her hand over the velvet counterpane as Wentworth kicked off his boots from his supine position. She slanted a look across at him, lying beside her, wondering hopefully if he'd fall asleep before he got down to business.

Wentworth snorted. "And then there'll be Oberon to worry about. Lord, but if ever there was a pair of brothers to bring shame to the family name. I'm not the first, of course, to believe succession should be based on merit, not birth order." He looked at Phoebe as the second boot joined the other with a thud. "Come, Lady Cavanaugh. Surely I don't have to do the seduction routine and remove your clothes for you?"

"I...I'm not sure we should do this." Phoebe edged away from his seeking hand and slid from the bed. "What if Ulrick gets better?"

"Lord, Phoebe, of course he won't, and even if he does, you know he can never get it up for you." Not caring that his crudeness was offensive, not to mention wounding, Wentworth grunted as he removed his coat, adding on a pained note, "Never did know why he offered for you."

"A fine thing to say if you're planning to win me over."

"That's what *Ulrick* said."

Phoebe closed her eyes as Wentworth drew her to him and wrapped her in his arms, his right hand dipping into her bodice to fondle her breast. He chuckled. "If one likes their women small and dainty with not a lot to squeeze, *I* think you're rather a fetching little thing, though I'm sure if I'd been Ulrick, I'd have somehow risen above my aversion and managed the deed at least a few times in the faint hope of siring something to oust my brothers."

"Oh, Ulrick did his best," Phoebe muttered, trying to ignore Wentworth's mauling and to block her mind to memories of Ulrick's wandering hands, her husband panting and grunting and sweating above her, night after night in the early years. If the loss of Ulrick's function hadn't also meant the loss of Phoebe's security, she might have been overjoyed.

"Ah yes, the dutiful wife...and you'll be a dutiful mother, too." His breath was hot on her cheek as he slid his hands up her thighs. "If you're not already with child, my dear, it won't be for want of trying." His hand cupped her sex, and he grunted his displeasure, no doubt at finding little to indicate her interest in the act for which he'd regained enthusiasm. Phoebe slanted her gaze from the ceiling to the unwelcome man beside her. In the faint glow of the single candle upon the carved kist at the end of the bed, she could see his member straining against his breeches. Turning her head to the side, she tried not to cry as his words floated over her.

Was it a carnal sin to sleep with her husband's cousin when her actions were as much motivated by Ulrick's wishes as her own self-preservation?

"We just have to keep Ulrick alive long enough to fill his nursery with my seed," Wentworth panted as he divested himself of his breeches. "You're healthy, and my ability to sire a child is proven." He lay back down next to her, his fingers probing her while he stroked himself. Phoebe turned away from the sight, trying to block her mind to what was happening; and what *would* happen, while she imagined a different life.

"Only then will I feel my duty discharged to my cousin—and to you, my dear." He narrowed his eyes. "No need to remind you what a miserable widowhood you look forward to if you're not mother to Ulrick's heir. His legal and official heir, at any rate, which means we have to succeed at this before he breathes his last. Or at least within a fortnight of the sad event."

It was pointless pretending she had any means of preventing what Wentworth intended, for all that the thought of being possessed by him made her body and mind close in on itself.

She loathed herself for that fact that upon Ulrick's directions, she'd encouraged him all those months before, though initially she'd refused Wentworth's overtures with genuine outrage.

Wentworth, aware of what he had to gain now that Ulrick had drawn him into his perverse plan, had wooed Phoebe with all the charm of the Casanova he was, reminding her that begetting an heir was the primary responsibility of the dutiful wife, and in this instance demanded by Ulrick, who could no longer perform the deed.

A dutiful wife? For years, Ulrick had mocked *her* with her inability to provide him with a son, though they both knew it was the fact Ulrick had rarely been able to sustain an erection long enough to even *possibly* impregnate her that made him so bitter toward her.

She felt sick at the memories. A dutiful wife would fill the nursery, not make her husband a laughing stock. Ulrick's eyes had reminded her of raisins in his pallid pasty face as he'd spat the words; little black dots of malice.

A dutiful wife would use *any* means to ensure her husband's self-respect.

Even if that meant being impregnated by her husband's cousin.

Quickly, Phoebe sat up. She could not simply allow Wentworth to treat her any way he chose. She had her self-respect. Just because Wentworth had visited Blinley Hall every fortnight for the past six months with one objective didn't mean it had to continue.

"I will not submit like a harlot in an unmade bed and in a room as bitter cold as the grave." In the gloom, she could see her breath misting.

Beside her, Wentworth sat up. "You're right," he conceded. "I'll prove as poor a stallion as your pathetic husband unless we go where the fire's lit."

❦

IT WAS NOT WHAT PHOEBE HAD INTENDED. EMOTION CHURNED in her gut as Wentworth hustled her along the corridor toward the west wing. The maids she passed dipped a curtsy, respectful as always. She knew what they were thinking, and it made her feel ill and ashamed. While she had always received due deference from the staff, she knew the untruths Ulrick spread about her. The master was a man to be feared, and the mistress was a slut.

2

As soon as they reached her private apartments and the door closed behind them, he was on her, his breath hot in her ear, his hands, urgent and clammy, unlacing her, tugging, pulling, removing her clothes, so that within seconds rather than minutes she was beneath him, naked, her white limbs wrapped about his muscled, hairy, hard body while he thrust into her with no more preliminaries. But then, that's how it was with men. Ownership was very different to love though that's what she'd imagined—once, briefly—she had with Wentworth, illicit and shaming though though that was. Love. She'd thought disgracing herself would be worth it, when she had her husband's sanction.

As ever was the case during the unpleasant act of procreation, she transported her mind; this time, to the unhappy prelude of her current dismal situation.

She'd been an easy target. Wentworth had wooed her with honeyed words and she, a wife starved of kindness for five long years, imagined Wentworth saw her as she really was: a woman of hidden passions who longed for affection.

He'd made her forget her misery as an unloved wife with the

courtly, urbane, and respectful attitude he adopted to coax her out of the silence, which had become, for her, habit following her marriage. Ulrick was not a man who'd appreciated her opinions.

Or anything she had to say, for that matter.

Wentworth, by contrast, appeared entranced with her opinions, her desires.

For at least three visits, he'd elicited her thoughts on everything from what music she liked to what amused her. He'd hung upon her words during dinner, and then, as his visits increased in regularity, an enigmatic glance, a seemingly accidental brush of the hand, had suggested that his heart had been engaged.

Tormented, Phoebe had not known whether it was right even to go walking with him alone. She was a married woman, and the more she felt her own heart engaged, the more she feared the consequences. She belonged to Ulrick and would for as long as her frustrated, angry husband remained alive.

What torture it had been to say her demure goodnights to Wentworth, and then to have to submit to her husband's futile efforts to make love to her. Like the dutiful wife she was, she'd tried every trick she could dream up in order that he might harden sufficiently to pierce her. Dancing naked, she'd imagined her display was for Wentworth's benefit. When Ulrick forced himself into her mouth, she'd again withdraw into her own thoughts, feeling nothing but revulsion for her unkind husband.

She wondered, if it were Wentworth, would she summon the necessary enthusiasm. For then, wouldn't her heart be engaged?

It was not long before she found out. Ulrick became ill almost overnight. A loss of appetite, cramping in his gut, and then suddenly all physical activity was beyond him. Even the act of procreation.

When Wentworth had stepped forward to undertake the role her husband had forced upon her, and which Phoebe had found so distasteful for so many years, *of course* Phoebe had offered outrage, though it shamed her now to recall that her fragile heart beat wildly at the thought of being held by a desirable man.

But commit adultery?

No dutiful wife would do such a thing.

Unless her husband demanded it.

It hadn't been hard to take that first step, she had to admit. And the first time had been magical. Wentworth had caressed her limbs, smoothing, massaging, whipping her into unimaginable ecstasy with his hands, his mouth, his tongue.

It wasn't long, though, before her whimpers of ecstasy in a tangle of bedclothes were whimpers of fear in any corner Wentworth chose to force himself upon her. Wentworth liked to dominate.

Wentworth liked to inflict pain and humiliation.

Yet with Ulrick tonight as insistent as Wentworth that she submit like an animal, Phoebe had no choice but to do his bidding, taking refuge once again into her own imaginary world.

She was brought back to the present when her unwelcome lover suddenly withdrew and pushed her out of the way. Phoebe blinked open her eyes and saw with dismay that Wentworth still had a way to go before he was finished.

"Onto the floor," he demanded, eyes as black as the devil's. "Now!"

Oh yes, Wentworth liked to dominate, and there was no point in arguing though she burned with humiliation.

Tears sprang to her eyes and she tried not to whimper. "Please, Wentworth..."

The pain in her voice seemed to only excite him but he relented. Roughly he parted her legs, and thrust into her with a cry of triumph.

"If you weren't with child before, you certainly are now!" He was panting heavily, grinning as if he expected her to gaze at him with adoration.

Phoebe was not in the mood to pander to him. He'd hurt her physically, though the wounds to her soul and her dignity distressed her more, and she was trying hard not to cry.

But he was clearly angered that she turned her head away, her expression more sullen than was wise.

He gripped her chin and made her face him. "Ulrick is not destined to remain long on this earth, and you'll not be a widow long, either. Think on that, Phoebe, before you show me such lack of deference."

Suddenly, the idea of belonging to any man ever again was an abomination. Shrugging out of his grip she rose and faced him, eyes blazing. "You take a great deal for granted, Wentworth," she rasped. "It's true I look forward to being a widow. I also look forward to remaining one. No one can force me to become a wife if I do not choose it."

He stilled, and in the pale glow of candlelight, she saw the evil transformation of his features, as he rose into a sitting position and moved to sit with his legs hanging over the edge of the bed.

"You will be the mother of my child." His voice was low and dangerous.

"I will be the mother of Ulrick's child. The mother of *his* heir." She dared to whisper it. He could not, would not, hurt her when there was the possibility she carried such precious cargo. For one of the few times in her life, surely Phoebe could revel in a degree of power. Wentworth needed her far more than she needed him.

She bent to pick up her discarded chemise that lay in a tangle of stays, gown, and paisley shawl.

"You may go now, Wentworth." Though she was naked and her hair a tangle of gold that brushed her waist, she strove for dignity. "Our business is at an end."

He interpreted her meaning correctly for he had his argument ready. "If Ulrick dies without an heir, where will you live? Not here, in comfort, that's certain. You'll be the wife who failed to do her duty...failed to fill the nursery which was the only reason Ulrick married you. Unless you're mother to Ulrick's heir, you'll be cast out to live in the country in penury. Your father made a poor bargain when he signed the marriage contract. And don't think I haven't seen it."

He spoke the truth. Her father had cared little for her beyond her ability to provide him a reprieve when he was dunned. She'd had no say in this hateful marriage. With widowhood beckoning, her future was even more perilous. Had Ulrick made any provision for her in his will?

"There are others who can fulfill your role as well as you, Wentworth," she hissed, turning her back on him as she pulled on her chemise. "You've done little enough to win my heart, and to tell the truth, I desire marriage with you as much as I ever did with Ulrick."

When he rose above her, she regretted speaking with such bravado. He would make her pay for her belittling words. Fear bloomed, and she retreated, still only in her chemise, eyeing the door.

These were her apartments, and he was not going to vacate them, warm and comfortable as they were. But if she ran, she could find a refuge in some cold guest room and she could lock the door against him, surely?

An unexpected rapping on the other side offered salvation. Sagging against the four-poster, she called faintly, "Come!" without a thought for Wentworth in all his naked glory just a foot away.

"Ma'am! Terrible news!" Her maid, Barbara, hurried into the room, squeaking when she saw Wentworth. She brought her apron up to her face as she continued in a rush, "Oh ma'am, His Lordship's heir is dead!"

"My brother?"

Phoebe gasped and instinctively put her hand out toward him. "Oh Wentworth, I'm so sorry."

Ignoring her, Wentworth pulled on his breeches and shirt and pushed past Barbara. Phoebe ran after him as he strode down the corridor, down the stairs, his footsteps loud and determined before he burst into the drawing room.

Ulrick was hunched in his chair, his eyes slits from the reflection of the fire. "Terrible accident, Wentworth." He was properly awake now and holding out a letter which Wentworth snatched from his grasp and scanned quickly.

Phoebe felt the tug of sympathy at the shock on his face and wished she'd not been so harsh earlier. She took a step toward him, but he avoided her outstretched hand, the shock on his face increasing as he jerked up his head.

"By God, *both* of them? Both my brothers are dead." He stabbed at the letter. "The imbecile was driving. Why, the other's as imbecilic to let him take the reins and now they've both plunged to their deaths."

"A great shock, Wentworth," Ulrick muttered. "Changes everything, of course."

Phoebe's eyes widened at the implication. She gasped. "You're Ulrick's heir, Wentworth." She felt a wave of relief and nearly laughed aloud, so filled with joy was she that she need not have to suffer Wentworth's attentions ever again.

Casting herself at her husband's feet, she rested her cheek upon his knees. "Now you can rest in peace, Ulrick, though it's a terrible thing to rejoice in another's death." She took his bony hands in hers and began to chafe their papery backs. "We will mourn as is proper, yet it's the truth, my husband. Your worries about the succession are over."

"Unless you are carrying my child."

Phoebe glanced up, shocked at the blaze of anger that marred Wentworth's expression. Unconsciously, she put her hand to her belly. "I...I don't believe so, Wentworth," she said cautiously. And nor did she. She'd only suggested such might be the case to try and deflect his advances earlier this evening.

"But you may be now. As of five minutes ago, my angel."

It was no endearment. Phoebe stared up at Ulrick to gauge his reaction, but he was obviously in great pain; his eyes glazed with it.

"Then we've no choice but to wait and see," she whispered, her mouth dry though she forced herself to hold his angry glare. "We shall make the best of whatever we have done."

"We shall make the best of a badly done deal *now*." Wentworth's voice was frighteningly calm as he stepped forward.

Phoebe recoiled as she squeezed Ulrick's hand. "Ulrick, can you hear me?" she pleaded. "You must reassure Wentworth, if only for my sake."

Her husband breathed heavily. It was often thus in the evenings when the pain came down strong and hard.

Wentworth gave a mirthless laugh. "He's not long for this world, my dear. You can see it; the doctor says it. He's suffering. See how he suffers." And all the time Wentworth was moving closer, while Phoebe drew farther back against her husband, who would not help her when he was in good health and would not help her now.

"A dutiful wife would put him out of his misery, wouldn't she?" He'd picked up the paper knife from the escritoire settled in the enclave by the tasseled curtain. It was a slender, chiseled, and elegant instrument. Deadly.

"No, Wentworth." Her teeth chattered. She tried to get to her feet and run, but Wentworth's arm shot out and his hand gripped hers, forcing the paper knife into her grasp, forcing her forward. She tried to resist, tried to snatch her hand back, the sharp blade catching on the skin on the back of her hand, drawing a thin, instant incision that filled with blood.

"No, Wentworth! This is madness!" she cried out, flailing in his relentless grip as with merciless intent, he drove her hand forward, overpowering her with his strength—his evil intent. She'd never fought so strongly to preserve the life of the man she hated as much as Wentworth, but he was too strong, seizing her throat, holding her hand around the knife, forcing her to pierce her husband's chest with the deadly blade, neatly between the ribs and directly into her hated husband's heart. She heard the hiss of air as his lung deflated, saw his glazed incomprehension turn to wide-eyed horror in his final moment, and she screamed as the crimson lifeblood spattered her face.

The door was thrust open and two maids ran into the room.

Phoebe stared at the knife in her hand, looked down at her blood-stained chemise and then at the horror on the servants' faces before Wentworth pushed her and snarled, "Get out and summon help, both of you. Fetch Sir Roderick, the magistrate. Your mistress has just murdered the master."

Phoebe dropped the knife which fell soundlessly onto the Aubusson carpet.

"It's not true. You can't say that, Wentworth. I'll tell them the truth." Shock and horror made her voice thin and weak as the maids scurried out of the room, but Wentworth was entirely self-composed.

"And they may choose to believe you, or they may not. They may convict, and then you'll plead the belly." He shook his head; his lip curled. "Plead the belly because you'll say you're carrying Ulrick's child. His heir. No, I can't have that, Phoebe."

Terror froze her to the spot. Her legs refused to move as he advanced a second time, bending to pick up the knife that lay at her feet.

He gazed at her coldly. "The maids have gone to summon help, but you'll have seen the error of your ways before they return. They saw you drive the knife into Ulrick's heart. They'll understand perfectly why you'd choose to end your life rather than face the hangman's noose, my dear."

Realization of his intentions snapped her into action as the distance closed between them. In the recesses of her mind, she knew he would be too quick for her. He'd catch her, or one of the servants would. Death was certain, either way.

The only tiny possibility of reprieve was in flight. Phoebe ran for the casement, thrusting it open before hurling herself through the cavity.

And as she dropped through the dark and chill night air, she barely wondered if she were consigning herself to a death more terrible than the one Wentworth had in mind for her.

For nothing could be worse than the fate Wentworth intended for her.

3

Dazed, Phoebe lay in the soft mulch, staring at the star-studded sky for a critical couple of seconds before she heard shouting from the first floor. She was alive.

However, she'd not take much comfort in that if Wentworth caught up with her. Scrambling to her feet, she had the presence of mind to cast about for her shawl, which had caught on a tree branch, before spying Wentworth's carriage on the driveway. To her surprise, the coachman was on the box with, she saw, Jimmy, one of the grooms. She could hear them discussing the merits of the handsome equipage.

Dashing across the stretch of damp grass, she hauled open the door and climbed in, rapping on the roof as she shouted. "It's a mercy you're here. Make haste for we must fetch the doctor! His Lordship's condition is critical."

Thank the Lord the coachman was an unquestioning servant and had not caught sight of her blood-stained chemise, for he obediently and with all due haste, dismissed his appreciative audience and cracked the whip over the horses.

The carriage rolled over the ruts and headed onto the drive through the park with an impressive show of speed, though

Phoebe knew it wouldn't be too long before Wentworth saddled up a horse and overtook her.

For the moment, however, this was her best chance. If they could reach an obscure turn-off about half a mile distant she might lose him.

"Take the left!" she shouted when they were nearly upon it. She leaned out of the window to add, "The doctor's attending Mrs Proctor."

Mrs Proctor was a widow who lived another mile down the rutted road. If Phoebe could slip away when the coachman halted and make for another cottage down the slope whose occupants may be sympathetic, it was the best she could hope for.

Obediently, the coachman eased the horses into the narrow laneway while Phoebe put her head out of the window, straining for sight or sound of anyone following. In the far distance, twinkling through the trees, she could see Blinley Manor, but the coach was going at such a speed it was quickly obscured by the rise of the wooded hill. She allowed hope to blossom just a little more. Wentworth might disregard this road and continue on the main thoroughfare toward the town. He'd think she'd make for her closest friend, Ellen Cosgrove, who lived in the village.

It was not a road well suited to a sprung carriage. Frustrated, Phoebe watched her surroundings pass by at a snail's pace as the coachman carefully navigated the ruts.

The large, waxing moon did not favor her for it lit up the small valley with its sweeping vistas, making them a clear target to anyone in pursuit. If they could only make it to the thick woods on the other side of the clearing where the road was swallowed up by overhanging trees, she may yet have a chance. The widow lived just on the other side.

They were nearly there when she heard the harsh, guttural command terrifyingly close to her window before the carriage lurched to a halt, and the horses whinnied in terror.

"Stop, or I'll shoot!"

Phoebe was flung forward, covering her face with her hands as she hunched in fright. Dear Lord, Wentworth must have come up the back way and cornered her, realizing all along this was what she had intended.

Though her breath came hard and fast, she knew there was only one thing she could do. And that was run.

Tugging open the door, she leaped to the ground, dragging her shawl behind her. Perhaps it was that which held her up for the crucial second, for suddenly his voice was only a yard away.

"Stop! I swear I'll shoot!"

She had no doubt that he would. It was worth it to Wentworth to see her dead. He *had* to see her dead after what she'd witnessed. Oh God, and for all that she'd resisted, the truth was that she'd been a party to it.

She covered the wide, open expanse as fast as her bare legs could carry her, but mercifully made it to the thicker part of the woods before she heard him galloping hard, just behind her. Hurling herself into the sanctuary of a copse of trees, she began her scramble toward a dip through which ran a small stream. The terrain would be too rough and difficult for a horse.

Self-preservation was one thing, but there was also her dignity to safeguard. She'd spent long enough being the servant or plaything to men she did not love. Or respect. She'd not be slave or worse now, even if her only survival were to eke out the most pitiful existence. Life beat strongly in her. She wanted to live. She'd do whatever was required to live—as long as she could do so without being subjugated by a tyrant. Not Wentworth, and not in a prison cell waiting for the noose.

"Stop, I say!" Clearly, Wentworth had too much to gain by her death, but Phoebe did not intend giving up now. He'd dismounted and got a bearing on her, leaping through the undergrowth in pursuit a short distance behind her. She could hear the crackle of small snapping twigs, his labored breath, the squelch of mud under boots. "Stop!"

Only then did she realize the voice was not Wentworth's. The realization provided a measure of relief, though not for long.

Another villain who would do her harm? So he really was a highwayman, holding up Wentworth's fine carriage in the hopes of rich booty.

Well, that was just as much reason to flee.

Her lack of clothing made her surprisingly agile. She couldn't imagine achieving such speed in all the layers she was required to wear in her daily life, even though the fashions of the day offered so much more freedom than those worn by the previous generation.

But to be wearing only a chemise was to be all but naked. If her pursuer saw her as a serving girl so scantily dressed he'd think he could do anything he liked with her. A highwayman was beyond the law, a desperate man without honor, who'd capitalize on such an opportunity since the jewels of the carriage occupant he'd expected were not forthcoming.

Holding her aching side, Phoebe clung to an overhanging branch as she tried to gauge how far away he was. She couldn't see him, but his labored breathing was audible; and then she glimpsed his bulk just a few yards behind her, clambering over a large fallen log.

His head was bent, the lower part of his face obscured by a black handkerchief; a low-crowned felt hat pulled down over his brow. She could see the bulge of a pistol tucked into his waistband, and suspected he'd have no compunction either in killing or raping her. Well, she'd rather be dead in both instances—although how different was rape considering how she'd submitted with such reluctance so many nights since her forced marriage?

Her assailant had just navigated the log, and locking eyes with her as she turned, lunged forward. Phoebe screamed as she leaped over the stream before losing her balance on an unstable, mossy rock on the other side. For a moment, she flailed helplessly before she was plunged into the icy water.

Then, strong hands gripped her upper arm to drag her to her feet, though not for a moment did she give in to the inevitability of being a prisoner.

She lashed out, kicking him in the shins, though this proved an ineffectual act as he laughed, remarking that he was still a great deal cleaner than she was, and certainly not as wet. To her surprise, his voice was cultured in contrast with the rough tones and style he'd used earlier.

"I've no money an' I'll not yield without a fight, yer great villain," she snarled, breathing heavily and adopting the accents of a peasant. Tonight she could not be Lady Cavanaugh to anyone. "Don't ye dare touch me, sir, or I'll bite it off! Ye see if I don't."

His expression betrayed a flicker of incomprehension followed by an easing of his facial muscles, and when he laughed again, he looked quite pleasant she noted with the benefit of the pale moonlight that filtered through the interlaced branches above them.

"I have no intention of hurting you. I'm just after your master. The man whose carriage you are inexplicably occupying dressed in nothing but your...." His expression turned to one of disbelief as he took in her garments, and as Phoebe looked down, she saw she was covered in more blood than she'd thought.

"Oh my, a murder, eh? Well, I hope you've done away with your Master Wentworth and saved me the trouble. No, don't try to kick me again. You'll only bruise your toe and you look already to be in quite a good deal of discomfort. This isn't the way you usually deport yourself, is it? Who *are* you?"

Phoebe tossed her head, then quickly adjusted her posture. No need to advertise that she was lady of the manor. Clearly, in the dark with her wild hair and mud-streaked face, he'd not recognize her. Not that she recognized him. His accent was not of these parts and she'd not seen him before.

She stayed the haughty rejoinder that came naturally, working to broaden her vowels. The lady's maid. Yes, that would do for now. It could be helpful to her cause, in fact, especially if this man had a bone to pick with Wentworth; and now she really could show the fear and terror that she'd bottled up, and use it to her advantage. Covering her face with her hands, she collapsed upon the fallen log as she wept, "Might yer really be 'ere to save us from that madman? M'lady were set upon by the villainous Wentworth after 'e'd done away with 'is lordship. I were on me way ter bed when I 'eard the screamin' an' I dashed inter the room as he 'ad the knife raised ter do 'er in."

"Good God!" The villain, who now didn't seem nearly so villainous, steadied himself against the trunk of a large tree while he regarded her with an expression of compassionate horror. "Was her ladyship injured? Is this her blood?"

"No, 'tis Lord Ulrick's, sir. Lord Cavanaugh's, I mean. He ain't never comin' back what with so much lifeblood spattered upon me." She began to tremble. "Now Wentworth's after me."

"Wentworth? After you?"

She nodded fiercely. "I seen too much, I 'ave, and now I ain't got no one ter protect me." She sent him an appealing look.

Dubiously he looked her up and down. "I daresay I should get you indoors and warm and dry. You'll catch your death. But Wentworth is after *you*?"

She was astonished this man believed her story. She had no idea who he could be or why he had a bone to pick though, but suddenly he offered her salvation.

His mouth was set in a grim line. "First we must rescue the duchess!" He gazed out through the trees while Phoebe shook her head, alarmed.

"No, no, she's fled already. Yer don't want ter go back ter Blinley Manor where there's just Lord Ulrick, dead in 'is chair. Mr Wentworth will kill ye too. 'E's a murderer."

The man angled a glance down at Phoebe, who found her legs were not doing a very good job at holding her up. She gripped the tree branch by her head to haul herself up as the man muttered, "It's true I want Wentworth—away from Blinley Manor where it's just him and me, man to man. But are you telling me the truth? You *saw* him commit a murder?"

"'E...'e murdered Lord Cavanaugh right in front of me. That's why I 'ave so much blood on me." Phoebe couldn't bear to look down at the crimson testament to the horror she'd more than just witnessed.

The man appeared to deliberate. He took a step toward her. "I'm sorry we met at the point of a pistol. I'm more gentleman than highwayman, though I've been spoiling to have it out with that blackguard, Wentworth." A shadow crossed his face. "That will have to wait for another night. I daresay I have no choice but to do as you suggest: take you home with me. I'm new to these parts, but we'll have to find the magistrate."

"No!" Phoebe shook her head wildly. "I mean, of course, if the magistrate were in town we would 'ave to see 'im...."

The man raised one eyebrow. "You're happy to come home with me but not to see the magistrate?" He inclined his head. "Mr Redding is my name. Where's your family, lass? Surely I should deposit you with them?"

"There's none in these parts, sir. I 'ave an aunt in the north, 'bout a day's travelin'. No one else." She spoke the truth. Ulrick had brought her far from home and the few friends she'd had since childhood. He'd distanced her from everything familiar as he'd poured his energies into ensuring she fulfill the one important duty for which he'd traded her—her ability to provide him an heir.

She touched her belly and felt again the now familiar spasm of fear. If she were with child, would that save her, or sacrifice her to a life of endless misery, her life in danger until the cargo was birthed—if she managed to live that long? Yet if she were not with child, she'd still be in danger from the man she thought once had harbored feelings for her. She'd seen too much.

She looked over Mr Redding's shoulder and glimpsed through the dense forest the patchwork of fields that stretched endlessly to places she'd never been.

If he left her here, she'd have her freedom but not much else. With Ulrick dead and with no heir, she was penniless and homeless. The terms of her marriage contract were not favorable to her in widowhood. They'd hinged upon providing Ulrick with the son whom he desired more than anything else.

To her surprise, she gulped on a sob. She was not inclined to easy tears, but the shock of her stark situation was suddenly more than she could bear. If he didn't take her, where could she go? Tonight? Tomorrow? For the rest of her life?

"Are those tears real?" Mr Redding cleared his throat. "You really *were* fleeing Wentworth and nothing else? You weren't caught stealing the sugar?"

"I seen 'im kill 'is lordship!" Phoebe repeated with some heat.

Mr Redding sighed again. "I suppose I'll have to take you home with me if you really are as friendless as you say. Don't worry; I won't hurt you," he reassured her when she flinched away from him. "I'll have to find you clean clothes, of course. And then I'll have to feed and protect you from Wentworth...but I will do so only on one condition."

She slanted a narrow-eyed look up at him and he gave a laugh. "No, I'm not in the habit of taking advantage of serving wenches. You'll be safe with me."

"I am not a servin' wench, sir."

"A lady's maid. I beg your pardon. Yes, I can hear your tones are far more refined when you put the effort into it. And no, my condition is quite simple and one that is clearly in your interests." He regarded her again with that strangely unsettling stare of his, and in the moonlight, she thought that the eyes that bored into her from above the handkerchief he now removed were bright with intelligence. "I want you to give me all the information you have that would ensure justice for Wentworth. You know already that my mission tonight was to extract my own form of justice upon the man I despise above all others, but now you have the means to help me see him face a far more robust accounting."

Phoebe nodded, more than ready to have him lead her out of the woods and to his own dwelling. She couldn't imagine being anywhere safer right now, though of course she knew she was too trusting for her own good. Hadn't she believed Wentworth when he'd professed to love her? Just for now, though, she needed to believe there was kindness in the world and a single human being who would protect her.

She took the arm he offered her, as if she were the fine lady she was by birth and not the blood-spattered, undressed servant she pretended for her own safety. “I swear that justice fer evil, wicked Wentworth is me greatest goal also,” she whispered.

4

Once back at his small manor house near the village, Hugh removed his hat as his manservant opened the door, the old man's eyebrows shooting north as he took in the unlikely spectacle.

Hugh had covered Phoebe in his greatcoat so that her liberal spattering of blood should not cause comment, and now he pondered what to do with her as he led her to dry in front of the fire. She might be his greatest weapon in his quest to avenge his sister, but she was also an encumbrance, though his frisson of frustration was tempered by another quick glance in her direction. Acting as her protector for a few days would not be a complete hardship. The curves of her lithe young body had been impossible to ignore when she'd been pressed against him clad only in a chemise.

He forced away the uncomfortable recollection of his too virile initial physical response to her, giving what he'd intended to be a reassuring, fatherly pat on the shoulder before he left her to go to his writing desk. He was not a blackguard, and she'd obviously endured a great deal.

She slanted a wary look at him before her lips turned up into a pert smile, causing two charming dimples to pop out in her cheeks. In the light, she looked bolder. Saucier. Obviously, time would tell how she chose to act upon her good fortune in finding a protector such as himself, thought Hugh, wondering if her awareness of him was on a level with his.

Well, she should not get ideas, and neither should he, he counseled himself sternly as he sat down, pulling out a piece of parchment and opening the inkwell. That said, he was not averse to having a bit of fun with her to see how easily she'd be needled if he slighted her precious consequence.

Even walking the short distance between the stables and the cottage, she'd walked with the dignity of the lady born, assuming she should enter through the front door and no doubt be properly introduced. There was bound to be a battle of wills between the surly servant couple he'd inherited with the cottage, though Lord knew he needed some diversion after the lonely and fruitless week he'd endured trying to find a solution to poor Ada's woes. Though he never intended his sister to know it, it was on her account he'd rented the cottage from a miller and his wife who'd gone to London.

Mr Withins, still in the guise of butler, was shaking off the water droplets from Hugh's hat, his eyes boring into Phoebe as if he couldn't make head nor tail of her.

Hugh smiled as he dipped his pen into the ink. "Aye, Withins, you might well look at the fine baggage I picked up in the street, but once she's cleaned up she'll be fit company for you and me."

A disdainful sniff from Withins turned Hugh's amusement to regret. His sister would have flown at him for speaking in such an ungentlemanly fashion about anyone, and she'd have considered it unforgivable for him to have publicly denigrated an underling under such circumstances. Well, she *would* have torn strips off him in the old days. Wishing the words unsaid, he sent Phoebe a rueful smile as atonement before turning back to address his servant once more. "Ask Mrs Withins to rummage in the wooden trunk of the guest room and see if she can find anything suitable for the lass to wear. And fill a tub of water in front of the fire, please."

He saw the young woman blink rapidly as she took this in before she stammered, "'Ere, sir? In this room?" She looked about her as if she'd never bared her limbs in public. "Wot about me privacy?"

Her words dispelled his humor. He'd been on the hunt for days and so close to coming face to face with Wentworth. Yet all he had for his pains was responsibility for a young woman who looked likely to be more trouble than she was worth. It was all very well if she'd witnessed Wentworth's crime, but her obvious capacity for embellishing the truth, and her pretentiousness, would not go down well in court—for that's where Hugh intended seeing Wentworth. Of course, not a whisper would connect Wentworth with his sister, and nor did Hugh intend for Wentworth to make the connection.

He tapped his fingers on the parchment in front of him and sighed. "I'm not about to have the tub lugged upstairs to a private bedchamber, Phoebe. Even if you are a *lady's* maid."

She gritted her teeth, he noticed, and her whole body shook. If Hugh weren't so weary he might have been more amused as she all but hissed, "I am used ter a good deal more respect than ye seem to think, sir, though I thank ye for the offer of a 'ot bath an' clean clothes. That is indeed kind."

"*I* thought so. Now tell me your name. Your *real* name." Her determination to set herself on a higher perch than the one to which she was entitled needled him. He was not going to be taken advantage of, regardless of her plight.

Yet despite his best intentions, he could not ignore the quickening interest he felt each time she looked his way. Leaning back into his chair, he raised his candle. It was hard to tell if she were comely or not under all that mud.

"Lady—" She broke off abruptly, and he quirked an eyebrow, before she added with a haughty sniff, "Lady Cavanaugh's maid, Phoebe...Cooper."

"Well, Phoebe, I'm sorry we met under such circumstances. I promise you will be well treated while in my care."

She sent him a narrow-eyed look. "I 'ope I'll not 'ave to impose upon ye fer too long, sir."

Hugh was about to say he hoped not too, but he wanted to make up for his ungentlemanly manners of before, so he remained silent. He had no doubt the girl intended milking the situation to her advantage. *What lowly servant wouldn't?* he thought as he scratched her particulars onto the piece of paper that would form part of the inevitable investigation. He could see it in the worldly look in her eye, for it was usual for a servant who knew her place to drop a demure gaze to the floor when a superior addressed her.

What were the color of her eyes? He glanced up again. A very pretty blue. Unwittingly, he found himself examining her lips. Even caked with mud he could see they were rosebud-shaped. Very *kissable* lips. Annoyed at the direction his thoughts were taking him, he returned to writing up the location where he'd met Phoebe, and what she'd told him while he wondered to what extent the girl used her very kissable lips to her advantage. He'd have to be on his guard.

"That really depends on what you can tell me about this villain Wentworth." His tone was grim. He must make it clear he'd not be a soft touch. He put his pen down and tapped the paper in front of him. "Let me be plain. I want Wentworth's head on a platter, and I think you want that too. After all, he's the reason you're...homeless and friendless. While the servants draw your bath, let's make the most of what you remember while it's fresh in your mind. What were Wentworth's precise movements in the time leading up to this terrible event?"

"'Is movements...sir?"

"Yes, I believe he's a common visitor to Blinley Manor." Hugh cleared his throat. "Though I've not been in the area for long, it wasn't hard to learn the local gossip with regard to the peccadilloes your mistress enjoys with Mr Wentworth."

"How dare ye!"

Despite himself, Hugh laughed at her outrage. She rose, hands on her slender hips as she thrust out her bosom. She looked as if another slanderous word would unleash her little hand in a stinging slap across his cheek. Hugh was uncomfortably aware of a frisson of excitement at the thought. Instead, he raised a supercilious eyebrow as he said, "If only we all had such loyal retainers, Phoebe. You do Lady Cavanaugh proud. Now, where do you suppose your fine mistress has fled? Perhaps she and Mr Wentworth planned this vile murder together. It's the kind of thing clandestine lovers are wont to do—especially if the husband gets wind of the fact he's being cuckolded."

Her eyes blazed, and she trembled with visible anger though seemed unable to offer a coherent reply.

Hugh rose. "Into your bath, my girl. You are beyond filthy, I don't need to tell you. It's not necessary to fill it to the top, Withins. A couple of buckets are all that's needed to get the dirt off." When she began to protest he took pity on her. "All right, you can be like your lovely, sinless Lady Cavanaugh, just for tonight, and soak to your heart's content. Withins!" He recalled his manservant. "More water, then. No, don't look at me like that. I have to humor the lady if she's to furnish me with the information I need on that rogue Wentworth." Hugh rose and went to the door, opening it and bowing with a flourish. "And now, Phoebe, we will leave you to soak in private."

"Thank ye, sir." Her tight-lipped response followed him into the passage, as Mrs Withins passed him from the opposite direction carrying a bundle of white linen underthings and a full, bulky, gown belonging to the venerable miller's wife, a stocky creature who was about three times the girth of young Phoebe.

It was an incongruous thought that Phoebe, whom Hugh had seen sheathed only in her chemise with her prettily turned ankles peeking out from just below, would soon be thoroughly covered up by the thick woolen garments that were all the miller's wife seemed to have in her trunk. He'd been unwise to give in and allow her a full bath. Next, she'd be asking him to provide her with a new dress; though he shook his head as he wondered why he'd think such a thing. He'd only just met her, and he had no intention of being saddled with a wench on the make. Certainly, she'd be useful. There'd be a trial. There'd have to be if Phoebe was the witness she claimed and could testify against her mistress's lover.

The harsh smell of the tallow candles Mrs Withins had lit and placed in the candle sconces by each doorway, turned his thoughts to practicalities as he returned to the small room the miller used apparently for storage and writing letters, for it contained a deal table and chair. Aside from seeing to better quality fuel, he would need to expedite criminal proceedings. Surely the magistrate would be back in town if a murder had been committed at the manor.

As he lowered himself into the little wooden chair that was surely too spindly to support a man of the miller's girth, he mused upon relations between Phoebe and her master and mistress. Was she telling the truth? *Had* Wentworth killed Lord Cavanaugh? Would he recognize his lover's maid? Wentworth was a man who took advantage where he could, so Hugh would have to ask the question. Several men with whom he'd shared an ale at the local tavern had suggested the local lady of the manor and her lover had eyes only for one another. The Blinley Manor servants said Wentworth was renowned for incarcerating himself in his lover's salon for days at a time; an observation that suggested he had little interest in the underlings of his own household.

Hugh pushed open the casement window and stared at the starry sky above. Far in the distance, he could see Blinley Manor, a single twinkling light burning. He felt foolish now, imagining he could have forced Wentworth out of his carriage at pistol point in order to gain the satisfaction he needed. The truth was that red-hot fury had fueled his wild ride to this part of the world the moment Ada had reluctantly given her brother the name he'd hounded her to reveal.

But with Phoebe as his new ally, a far more sophisticated and effective plan was going to win the day. One that would ensure justice for Hugh's sister without Hugh having to dirty his hands.

A sound in the bushes below caught his ear. Instantly he was on the alert, tensing as he withdrew his head and snuffed out the candle while he peered into the darkness.

With a murder having recently occurred up at the manor and Wentworth no doubt on the run, who knew what characters were about? Quietly, Hugh slipped into the corridor and exited through the scullery and into the kitchen garden. He allowed himself a moment to get used to the darkness before moving silently around the ivy-clad walls, glad of his dark clothing. When he reached the casement of the front parlor, he rested the back of his head against the panes and strained his eyes for a sign of movement in the bushes that bordered the grounds. But only the soft sighing of the breeze through the leaves emitted any sound. He moved forward to begin an investigation deeper into the garden, when the muted splash of water within reminded him that, just inside, Phoebe was having her bath.

He turned, and felt a jolt of shock and something he was immediately unable to identify, as through the diamond-paned windows, he took in the startlingly erotic sight of a young woman with slender, milky limbs, and long ripples of golden-brown hair standing in a bathtub, reaching down to soap her thighs. Her face was no longer streaked with mud, and as she raised her chin, Hugh felt guilt and fascination in equal measure; topped with a large degree of astonishment. The girl was a beauty.

He turned away, uncomfortably conscious that his hatred of Wentworth stemmed from that man's disregard for the dignity of a woman. Hugh did not want to be compared. But as he took a step back toward the house, he felt softness beneath his feet and then the startled shriek of Mrs Withins's deaf and blind cat which flew at him with bared claws.

His last glimpse before he hurried back into the safety of indoors was confirmation that Phoebe's body was indeed goddess-like perfection, her waist tiny, her breasts full and tipped with two tiny pink rosebud nipples. Trying not to deny the effect of such a sight, he closed the door to the outside behind him and took the stairs, two at a time, to his room.

❧

DIPPING THE SPONGE INTO THE WATER AND WRINGING IT OUT, Phoebe looked about her for the usual accouterments that made bathing a pleasure. The bath salts? The scented oils? And that piece of rag...was that supposed to be the linen she dried herself with? It looked more like something the scullery maid would use to scour the bottom of the cooking pot.

A scullery maid? Mr Redding thought her little better.

She stood up, allowing the water to drip all over the floor while fear flooded her anew. What was she doing here? In a strange man's house?

And why, oh why, had she used her Christian name? She let the sea sponge fall into the water and put her hands to her face. There was little danger of Mr Redding associating her with the supposedly guilty Lady Cavanaugh, but what were Phoebe's choices? Where could she go? She had nowhere but here.

The shock seemed to be abating, but in its place came the familiar misery overlaid with panic. She balled her fists before bending to steady herself on the side of the tub as she closed her eyes. She could not let fear and despair get the better of her. She knew how to hold them at bay. Years of living with Ulrick, and then suffering at the hands of Wentworth following the truth of her girlish delusions, had forced her to develop ways to cope and survive. Now it was even more important to stay strong.

Her first priority would be to maintain the fiction of her identity and then flee to the safety of her aunt's cottage in remote Norfolk. Of course, she couldn't stay there. Her aunt would not welcome her for more than a duty visit, and nor did she have the means to support another mouth to feed—or two. If Phoebe were with child—oh Lord, it would buy her the time she needed to bring a case against Wentworth—she would be spared the hangman's noose, for now. Wentworth would do all he could to condemn her, but if she were seen to be carrying Ulrick's heir, she'd have time she might not otherwise have had to build up her own case regarding her innocence.

She just needed time.

She clenched her hands at her sides and took a deep breath. By God but Wentworth would pay for his treachery. Ulrick had not been a kind husband, and Phoebe would not pine in widow's weeds, but he did not deserve to die at the hand of a dagger. No, not even a dagger. A paper knife wielded by his cousin.

She reached for the rough piece of linen as she stepped out of the bathtub and onto the hearthrug, soft and welcoming beneath her feet.

It was some consolation that this handsome gentleman hated Wentworth with a similar passion. Phoebe had no idea of the nature of Mr Redding's grievance, and while the gentleman upheld such a low opinion of Lady Cavanaugh, she could not reveal her identity. But the realization of how the common folk spoke of her made her sick to the stomach.

Still, this man offered her the greatest chance of escape from the rough justice that Wentworth no doubt had in mind for her.

She shuddered—this time in disgust rather than fear—as she picked up the voluminous garments she was lucky enough to be loaned to replace her bloodstained chemise. They were an abomination, but nothing compared to the knowledge that Mr Redding thought the mistress of Blinley Hall a harlot and in all likelihood in collaboration with Wentworth. She'd have to tread a fine line to see how it was possible to save her neck through working the situation—and Hugh Redding—to her advantage.

He liked a pretty face. She'd not missed the flare of unguarded interest when he thought he was being dismissive. Well, Phoebe had spent enough time balancing a tightrope with Ulrick and Wentworth to know how to play men. If she were to survive Wentworth's determination to see her hang for his crimes, she had no choice but to court Mr Redding's interest. He wanted Wentworth to face the law, and she wanted Mr Redding as an ally in her own quest.

As she pulled the chemise over her head, and then the bulky gown, dispensing with the stays which would have slipped over her hips, even with the tightest lacing, she wondered how she ought to model her behavior. She'd always had to think before she addressed Ulrick. He'd well and truly snuffed out her propensity for impulsiveness when he'd married her on her seventeenth birthday.

How she hated play-acting but she could see little alternative. Wearily, she put her mind to the task at hand.

A lowly maid with ideas above her station would be a trifle flirtatious and eager perhaps, though she'd have to be careful not to give him too many ideas. Phoebe needed Mr Redding on the end of a string. A very carefully tensioned one.

Cramping pain made her abdomen contract, and she put her hands to her stomach, her mind roiling with disappointment as she recognized the signs.

No, she was not with child.

Not only that, she was once against forced into pretending to be someone she wasn't.

5

The next morning, dressed in the voluminous gown of brown and gold wool that Mrs Withins had brought her, and with nothing to cover her hair, Phoebe sat on a chair by the fire in the little parlour and waited.

It had been well after midnight when she'd been shown to a spare bedchamber and she'd been too exhausted to even think about turning the key in the lock.

Now it was nearly midday and she had no idea what the terms of her protection would be. Or what kind of man Mr Redding really was.

She was still pondering her uncertain future when Mr Redding walked into the room and as she stood up and nearly tripped upon her too-long skirts, he laughed.

"Methinks Goodwife Miller and you differ a little in size." He regarded her with interest as he half circled her then went to his writing desk where he sat down. "Still, a good wash has been transformative."

It was certainly not a compliment but, as she inclined her head, she was conscious, once again, of his admiration, which he clearly wished to hide. Phoebe knew that men found her attractive. As a girl of seventeen about to embark upon her first season, she'd dreamed of clothes and handsome suitors, having enjoyed considerable attention at the local Assembly dances over a few short weeks.

But then, her father had reeled in Ulrick. Ulrick who had no interest in her beyond her ability to procreate but who, in her father's eyes, was too great a catch to let go. Decades older than herself, Ulrick lived an almost hermit-like existence with—as it transpired—a reputation for cruelty and a vicious scorn for women.

Her father and his ally—Phoebe's governess Miss Splint—had told her Lord Cavanaugh would make Phoebe a duchess. They'd rubbed their hands with glee, congratulating themselves on a fine piece of match-making that meant there was no need to spend money on a wardrobe for Phoebe to participate in London revels to catch a husband.

Emotion thickened her throat. At least, having had a father who'd shown her so little affection, Phoebe hadn't had high expectations of her husband.

She picked up her skirts and carefully sat down again as she contemplated how far short of the life she'd once envisaged she'd fallen.

She wouldn't deny that it was a relief that Ulrick was dead and she need never fear the lash of his belt or back of his hand, again.

But while she was free from the constant fear of physical violence and coercion, she needed to keep up her charade if she were to remain free in the eyes of the law. Without the right clothes, she was as much a prisoner as she'd ever been. She sighed. "I wonder 'ow I'm ter walk out of that door an' not cause tongues ter wag wearing this."

"Is that your way of asking me to fund something for your own wardrobe before I return you to your single relative? A new dress at my expense, eh? Something you can wear in a magistrate's court?"

That was the last place Phoebe wanted to think of being right now. "That mayhaps be some while, sir. I was thinkin' of 'ow I might present meself ter be useful ter ye since I can speak like a lady when I needs to."

"You already owe me your life since, according to you, Wentworth would have killed you if he'd found you. As for a new gown, no doubt you're thinking of something that would be more than you'd earn in two years of wages, eh?"

Phoebe's outrage was a mixture of acting and the real. Mr Redding, seemed to take pleasure in needling her, with a pair of engaging brown eyes that could be serious one moment and twinkling with devilry the next. Well, she would have to work hard to make herself immune to both his barbs and his cajolery. No doubt he was like all the rest. A woman was a plaything, and a penniless one would be expected to dance to a rich man's tune.

She wondered what a cheeky maid would say. She'd whip up the flirtation perhaps, holding back while suggesting more. So she plastered a smile on her face and put her head on one side. "If ye want ter barter, sir, I will...give ye a kiss on the cheek." With mock severity, she added, "I 'ope that's all ye expect, Mr Redding 'cause let me assure ye, I'd rather go naked than barter me only asset."

"Your only asset?" He was mocking her now, a smile playing about his lips as he looked up from his writing desk. "And pray, what do you suggest is your only asset?"

Heat burned her cheeks. Her only asset had been bartered for a good marriage, and then she'd bartered it again at her husband's behest—with a man who at the time she quickly grew to detest—in the hopes of an heir.

Oh, Wentworth, she thought with a pang of despair. *Did I ever love you?*

She was ashamed she could transfer her heart so easily. Wentworth was worthless, and yet she'd been taken in so easily. Why? Because Ulrick had exerted pressure. She had to cling to the defense that her adultery had been driven by the knowledge that without an heir, she'd lose the only home she had. Surely any other woman, even a decent, God-fearing one, would have acted as she had?

And yet she was still going to lose her home; her life, even, if Wentworth had his way.

Mr Redding looked at her with amusement, not ready to let the topic go. "The way you're blushing suggests you lost your only asset a long time ago." He rose and took a few steps towards her. "No, don't strike me when I was only going to take you up on your offer of a kiss."

He stopped a foot from her but instead of swooping to kiss her, gently touched her cheek. His smile was very warm. "I like you, Phoebe. And the look in your eye suggests you more than like me. But are you really that bold? What if I called your bluff?"

Was she that transparent? Yes, she did like him, but it was ungentlemanly of him to say so and unladylike for her to show it. Indignation powered through her, and before she could stop herself, she'd slapped him soundly across the face before realizing the foolishness of her behavior when this man was the only person in any position to aid her.

Flinging around, she brought her apron to her face. "Jest like Mr Wentworth ye are! Thinkin' ye can take yer pleasure just 'cos I'm only a lowly servant, an' no doubt thinkin' ye can force me inter what I says no to."

When he didn't grab her, or shout, she lowered her apron to find him contemplating her.

He stood, resting against the back of the sofa. "It's rather sobering to be compared to a blackguard like Wentworth." He held up his palms in a gesture of supplication. "And I had rather taken your previous words to be an invitation." He shrugged, and half turning, indicated the door. "You must be tired, Phoebe. And overwrought. Go and walk in the garden for a bit. The weather is fine and there is no one about. I have some work to do, not least of which is deciding what is to be done with you. I can't send you back to Blinley Manor, can I?"

She was unable to hide her terror, which, for some reason made him laugh—although that was perhaps because she tripped on her overlong skirts again and was only saved from falling to her knees when he gripped her elbow to steady her.

"Deftly executed, Miss Phoebe. I see how anxious you are to reinforce to me how ill the dress fits you—indeed, a health liability. Now," he waved her to the door, "off you go! Mrs Withins can give you something to eat which you might want to take into the garden."

"You've had luncheon, sir?" she asked, only realising her mistake when he looked at her, curiously, and replied, "I dine at two."

Of course, he'd hardly expect her, a mere servant, to join him. Phoebe lowered her eyes. She'd have to make sure she didn't a similar mistake that might cost her the freedom she was at such pains to protect.

❧

AFTER A LONELY AFTERNOON AND A CHILLY RECEPTION IN THE kitchen as she'd eaten her dinner with Mr and Mrs Withins, Phoebe climbed the stairs to her room, wondering how long she'd be living this half life. Mr Redding did not intend spending more time with her than necessary while the servant couple clearly despised her.

The cramping she'd felt earlier had returned, so she was glad to be able to lie down. She knew the signs well. In another ten days she would bleed, and there would be no child. No heir for Blinley. No cargo she must carry on behalf of her late husband. She was, as ever, redundant.

Wearily, she lay down, still in the ugly round dress, not bothering to put on her nightrail. She needed a plan to get her out of the danger she was in.

She needed Mr Redding's protection, and continuing her

charade as a servant increased her chances of remaining beneath anyone's notice. Wentworth would have wasted no time eliciting every local yeoman and servant in the area to search for the murdering mistress of Blinley.

Huddled beneath the musty covers of a strange bed, Phoebe realized how carefully she must orchestrate the coming few days.

Without money or clothes, she could go nowhere. She wasn't afraid that Mr Redding would cast her out. He wanted her to testify against Wentworth and she'd do it—though not until Mr Redding had ensured Wentworth was properly charged with his crime, and Phoebe could try and find someone who would uphold her version of events. She dashed away the tear that trickled down her cheek. The servants had seen *her* with the paper knife—the instrument of death—in her hand. There was no evidence more damning than that. She needed to find someone who would affirm that Phoebe was of good character, a dutiful wife, and that Wentworth was a master manipulator.

But who?

As she buried her head in the pillow she thought of the risk she ran in going out in public where she might be recognized. Really, she was much a prisoner here, in Mr Redding's house, as she had been at Blinley Manor.

She must have been just drifting off to sleep when she was woken by the sound of heavy pounding on the front door. Terrified, she threw back the covers and ran to check that her door was locked before going to the casement which was slightly ajar. She could hear voices below, and when she glanced into the distance was horrified to see, in the fading light, Sir Roderick's carriage.

Voices floated up to her from the portico. "No sign of Lady Cavanaugh, then? We've had our men scouring the countryside."

Phoebe strained to hear Mr Redding's response, the sweat tickling the back of her neck as his considered response stretched out in the silence.

"Murder? Is Lady Cavanaugh in danger?"

"In danger from the noose!"

Phoebe flinched. Did Sir Roderick despise her *so* much for rejecting him? Surely he could not believe Wentworth's version of affairs?

"Good Lord, pray elaborate!"

Mr Redding put on a good show of ignorance. Well, at least that augured well for Phoebe. He had no idea of Phoebe's true identity, and she intended to keep it that way.

Phoebe couldn't see Sir Roderick, but she could imagine the pugnacious stance he'd be adopting right now. His voice dripped with salacious glee as he recounted the morbid details. "She pierced her husband through the chest like a stuck pig before running off with her lover. We're looking for both of them."

"Lady *Cavanaugh* has killed her husband?"

"And escaped with her lover. Or one of them." Sir Roderick's laugh sent shivers down Phoebe's spine. "She's not discriminating."

"Can you give me a description of Lady Cavanaugh and her lover?"

"The kind of looks that'd make a man drop his breeches if she crooked her finger—which is what she's done too many times. Not that I want to say more for the sake of his poor, departed lordship."

"Sounds quite a piece." Phoebe heard Hugh laugh, and felt like crying. "And were you so fortunate, Sir Roderick?"

There was a pause before Sir Roderick answered peevishly, "I am a married man, Mr Redding. I made it clear to Lady Cavanaugh that I was not one to make overtures to. That put her in place, so to speak, not that she didn't try her lures again. Thought she could make me another of her conquests...."

Phoebe shuddered at the memory of the occasion to which Sir Roderick alluded. Each time she'd passed through the lonely passage where he'd accosted her, she was assaulted by the memory of his brandy-soaked breath as he'd pushed her against the wall and slurred that he would be eagerly awaiting a quick tumble in the storeroom the moment she could extricate herself from her hostessing duties. That he'd heard he'd not be the only one, other than her husband, to enjoy her favors.

Phoebe cringed at the memory of the night she'd gone from being the faithful wife of an abusing husband, to the lover of a man who proved to be even crueler than Ulrick.

What had Wentworth told Sir Roderick and others about their affair? Why would Sir Roderick have tried to force himself on her, using the words he had?

Clearly, he was now determined to be avenged for her dismissal of him, and he would win. He was the magistrate.

Her heart was in her mouth as she waited for the spiel that would instantly make it clear to Hugh that Phoebe was, in fact, Lady Cavanaugh, the woman they were looking for, but to her surprise, Sir Roderick's description of an uncommonly handsome woman with a haughty bearing and a crown of golden hair had rung no bells with Hugh.

Haughty? Phoebe felt quite indignant at the word. She was not haughty. She was terrified.

She turned back from the window, expecting to hear Sir Roderick take his leave and get back in his carriage. Instead, to her horror, Hugh Redding's pleasant voice could be heard inviting Sir Roderick indoors.

Phoebe ran back to the bed, put on her nightrail and dived under the covers where she lay, shivering with terror as she wondered if she were to be dragged from her bed and brought before her neighbor to give her account of the story. After all, Mr Redding knew she had witnessed the murder.

The vulnerability of her position was as stark as ever. Mr Redding thought he could use her to entrap Wentworth for his own reasons, but what would he do when he discovered who she really was?

Presently, she heard a soft tread upon the staircase, but to her relief no turning of the doorknob.

Yet even though it was apparent Mr Redding had passed her bedchamber door, the horror of what might unfold in the very near future continued to disturb her much-needed rest until she thought of a new tack.

She must make herself valuable. Mr Redding was a bachelor living a simple existence. Phoebe would have to show him how much more comfortable it was having her around.

6

"Good mornin', Mr Reddin'." Phoebe looked up from her chair at the dining room table as her rescuer—or host, or the man holding her prisoner until she'd proven her use to him in apprehending Wentworth—slanted her a look of surprise as he entered the room.

"I've organized breakfast." She smiled pleasantly. "Obviously ye've not been a resident 'ere fer long. Ye certainly don't know 'ow ter order yer servants around."

His initial wonder at seeing her dressed, her hair done as best she could under the circumstances, was almost comical. Just as Phoebe was silently congratulating herself on having produced such a response, she was highly indignant when he burst out laughing.

"Oh my, but it's *Lady* Phoebe is it, to be sure?" He swept her an exaggerated bow. "A rather fetching effect, I might add, since I can't decide whether you look more like a burgher's wife or a schoolroom miss playing dress-ups." He cocked an eyebrow. "It's true I could do with a woman about the place. A housekeeper would do well enough. A bit 'o muslin would be my preference." He quirked a playful smile over one shoulder as he went to the sideboard, adding, "But not a wife, Phoebe my dear. I could lead you a merry dance, of course, and make you believe that I had honorable intentions; however, I'm not a liar."

Phoebe tugged at her lip with her teeth. She'd gone through every tactical alternative, and decided that her best course of action was appealing to the fact that Mr Redding admired her as much as he hoped to profit by her. Now she wasn't so sure.

"Mr Reddin', why didn't ye tell the magistrate that I was 'ere when 'e came ter the cottage last night?"

Mr Redding took a seat opposite, looking surprised. "Sir Roderick? Were you eavesdropping?"

"I 'eard 'im from me casement. I couldn't 'elp it, 'e's such a loud..." She left the sentence hanging, letting her expression make it clear what she thought of him.

Mr Redding sent her a level look as he picked up his knife and fork, closing his eyes in brief appreciation of the aroma of streaky bacon.

Thoughtfully, he said, "I remembered your distrust of the man, and I own, there was something about him that didn't sit well with me." He shrugged. "I should, of course, have brought you downstairs to give your account. I don't know why I didn't since it was only delaying the inevitable. He's investigating the murder and the disappearance of Lady Cavanaugh, and you know more than any of us." He paused, heavily, "Don't you, Phoebe?"

"Did 'e say anythin' 'bout...the murder?" Phoebe felt lightheaded just asking the question.

Mr Redding speared another piece of bacon. "Of course. What else do you think brought him here? Naturally, I invited him in, and he told me that immediately after she'd dropped the murder weapon, Lady Cavanaugh threw herself out of a window, leaped into Mr Wentworth's carriage, and disappeared into the night."

He finished his mouthful. Now he stared long and hard at Phoebe.

A great whooshing sensation rushed through her. So this was it, the inevitable unmasking. Mr Redding was playing with her. He knew very well that he was seated across from the woman who'd fled the scene of the murder—Lady Cavanaugh.

"Well, Phoebe, what do you have to say for yourself?" He put his head on one side. "Perhaps the truth would be a good start."

Phoebe clasped her hands together and leaned across the table. "I...it's true I—"

"Yes, that you and Lady Cavanaugh fled the scene of the crime together. But what became of her between the time you left Blinley Manor and when I intercepted you? That's what we'd all like to know, and it's what I should have had you tell Mr Roderick for yourself. Well, you will in due course, but I want to know *now*."

"Ye...want ter know what 'appened ter Lady Cavanaugh? Ye want ter know where I put 'er out of the coach so I could continue drivin' an' so draw attention away from 'er?"

Mr Redding nodded.

Phoebe couldn't believe her reprieve. She thought quickly before lying—for lying seemed the only way to keep herself safe—"The stage ter Bath were passin'. She leaped aboard at the last minute an' I carried on."

He seemed to accept this, completely.

"You'll have to tell Mr Roderick everything, you do realize."

Phoebe put up her hands in entreaty. "Mr Roderick is not ter be trusted. I'll not reveal ter 'im Lady Cavanaugh's whereabouts. 'E tried ter push 'imself on me mistress. 'E's a terrible man!" She worried her lip even more. "An' 'e's tellin' lies 'bout me mistress bein' responsible fer Sir Ulrick's death. She didn't kill 'im, I told ye that. Mr Wentworth did. 'E forced me mistress's 'ands around the knife an' with 'is own strength behind, drove in the blade."

Phoebe stared down at her skirts as if expecting to see them suddenly crimson with blood. She knew there was a limit to how much Mr Redding would believe, and how long he'd shelter her if she either refused to tell her account to the magistrate or proved of no use in bringing Wentworth to account.

He frowned. "I say, that's a rather different slant on your story of last night. Nevertheless, the truth will be for the magistrate to decide—once they've heard the witnesses. And one of those ought to be you."

She closed her eyes. This was terrifying. "Mr Wentworth is after me blood, sir," she whispered. "If 'e learns where I am I won't live ter testify."

Mr Redding sighed. "So he knows how loyal you are to your mistress, and he's afraid of what you saw. Is that it?"

Phoebe thought quickly. She dare not be recognized by anyone. If Mr Redding thought to introduce her to someone in the locality as Lady Cavanaugh's maid, she'd be revealed in an instant.

"The truth is, I'm as afraid of Sir Roderick as Mr Wentworth," she murmured. "'E tried ter force 'imself on me an' when I kicked 'im where it 'urt, 'e said I'd live ter regret it." It was the truth and surely he'd not force her. "Sir Roderick is jest like Mr Wentworth. They'd fondle the rumps of any servin' girl an' I were no exception. I can't tell Sir Roderick me story. Surely there's some other way I can 'elp yer get ter Mr Wentworth?" She rose and went around the table to put her hand on his shoulder. Dangerous and familiar, but it was the only way she knew how to beseech him. "Ye 'ave yer own argument with Mr Wentworth, an' I 'ave mine. I'll 'elp ye all I can, fer I am familiar with 'is 'abits, bein' as 'ow me lady talked often 'bout 'im. An' not in any flatterin' way, I can tell ye." She swallowed with difficulty, then added. "'T'was 'is plan 'atched with Lord Ulrick that meant me lady was forced to enjoy the...attentions of Lord Cavanaugh's cousin 'cause me lady's 'usband were so desperate fer an 'eir."

Mr Redding made a choking noise. "Lord, Phoebe, you can't run around spreading rumors like that if you claim on the other hand that your mistress is as pure as the driven snow."

"Well, mayhaps not the driven snow, but she's a good an' virtuous lady an' she 'ad no wish ter do the things 'is lordship commanded 'er ter do an' yet she's painted as...immoral. She was actin' on 'er 'usband's orders."

Another waft of some delicious cooking aroma made Mr

Redding turn with an appreciative sniff as Mrs Withins entered the room with more bacon.

"Did you really organize this by yourself, Phoebe?" He looked impressed. "I confess to being somewhat distracted by matters other than my stomach, and am the first to own I am not terribly efficient at organizing the servants. I caught them playing at cribbage last night when I went in search of food." He loaded up his plate once more, adding when the door had closed behind Mrs Withins, "But let us turn back to the topic at hand, Phoebe, now that we are alone." He chewed on the crispy meat then smacked his lips. "I daresay I'll have to concede your victory in this instance. You'll need a new dress if you're to sit at table with me like a real lady, for that's what you're intending, isn't it?"

Phoebe was both jubilant and full of ire as she watched him devour his plate of food. She hated being treated like a servant, but she *had* to get a new dress if she had any chance of getting out of the area without coming face to face with Sir Roderick.

AND AS HUGH HELPED HIMSELF TO YET MORE BACON AND EGGS, he thought how pleasant it was to enjoy the niceties of life without having to be responsible for organizing them. The household was a woman's domain, and Hugh had not the energy or inclination to get the servants to do what they'd done under Phoebe's direction. Clearly, young Phoebe the lady's maid was adept at more than just arranging her mistress's hair. If she contributed to the comforts of the next few weeks he had the lease of the cottage, then she'd want and need to be more ornamental than she was in the bulky homespun of the miller's wife's clothes. Yes, a new dress would be fair recompense.

"Is there something you require, Phoebe?" Her breakfast finished, she'd risen but was now standing in the doorway.

"Jest an assurance that ye'll not let Mr Wentworth get away with the wrong 'e's done ye. I want atonement fer me mistress."

Her shoulders slumped. "I worry fer 'er an' 'ope she 'as found sanctuary. She 'ad few friends in the area."

"I'm sure she's quite safe. It certainly sounds as if she knows how to look after herself. And let me assure you that Mr Wentworth's day of reckoning is almost upon him." Hugh felt the warmth of his mission feed through his veins as he sat back in his chair, gazing upon the lovely face before him.

Dressed like a lady, he thought, *and with her ability to ape her betters, coupled with a sharp intellect, he might really find young Phoebe an asset in a multiple of ways. It was quite clear she felt an attraction for him.* He shifted in his seat. He'd imagined a lonely, solitary time out here in the wilderness, but suddenly he felt quite fired up. He'd rescued Phoebe, and while he had no intention of taking advantage of her, the looks she slanted at him suggested she'd not be averse to his overtures.

"Well, Phoebe, if you're so inclined, you can ask Mrs Withins about the local dressmakers. Perhaps we can set you up so you don't look quite like a stout burgher's wife. *I'd* certainly like that."

7

A new dress was essential. After a wander about the gardens, keeping out of sight, Phoebe had nothing else upon which to concentrate her mind than the ugly, ostentatious, and overlarge gown she wore. Her agitated pacing from one boundary to the other had strengthened her determination that one day she'd assume her rightful status. Of course, her new gown could not be of the style she might have chosen had she been Lady Cavanaugh. That was too dangerous. A spasm of utter wretchedness gripped her. When might she ever resume her rightful status? When would she be a free woman again? *Would* she ever be free again?

At least she felt safe in Mr Redding's house. She'd never felt safe in her own.

She rested her head against the rough bark of a crab apple tree and closed her eyes as she breathed in its heady perfume. Suddenly she was back in her own garden, a child again, secure in her mother's love, if not her father's.

What she wouldn't give to have her mother to advise her, comfort her. Tell her she would have some small say in her destiny. But her mother would have been too afraid to have voiced any opinions. She'd have counselled Phoebe to obey for it was the men in this world who held the power. Her mother was another abject example of how little charge a woman had over her own life. Phoebe's father had shown her mother as little consideration and respect as Ulrick had shown Phoebe.

Which brought Phoebe's mind back to the bargaining she would need to do in order to get not one, but two gowns if she were to make the most of her opportunities.

A simple, muslin gown and a serving maid's print gown and apron would be essential in case she needed to flee suddenly for who knew when Sir Roderick would come knocking or Wentworth would learn her whereabouts. No one would question a poor woman alone, but they certainly would if she were in silk and lace, though Phoebe doubted Mr Redding would be ready to expend that kind of largesse upon her. She was a means to an end. He was a man, after all, no doubt thinking of little beyond his own comfort. Men were like that.

She ran her hand down the rough trunk of the tree. What would she do for funds if matters didn't turn out well for her under Mr Redding's roof? She'd always been kept short of pin money by Ulrick, but she did have her jewelry. Sadly, she had none with her. Not even her rings. They were all in her dressing room.

She returned to the house, no longer feeling the ebullience she had when Mr Redding had complimented her on her housekeeping abilities. In the parlor, she stared through the window, up at the hillside. Blinley Manor would be less than an hour's walk, but what was the possibility of eliciting the help of the only person likely to speak in her defense, her lady's maid Deborah? The estate would be swarming with potential informers. Wentworth was the new heir, and if Sir Roderick were to be believed, there was no doubt in anyone's mind that Lady Cavanaugh had murdered her husband.

Her word would never be believed against his.

Mrs Withins entered with a scowl and asked Phoebe her business, adding with a glance up at the manor on the hill, "Poor, murdered Lord Cavanaugh. I 'ope they find 'is wicked faithless wife soon, fer let me tell ye, I'll be right there when they light the first faggot."

"They 'aven't burned a woman at the stake fer thirty years," Phoebe muttered as she left to go to her own chamber. No one, it seemed—not even Mr Redding—questioned the rumors that painted Lady Cavanaugh as the cuckolding wife who'd committed murder to be free of her husband's yoke.

A woman's lot was fraught, she thought, throwing herself upon the bed. Regardless of where she was born on the social scale, freedom and independence of choice were virtually unobtainable. No wonder the fairer sex had a reputation for cunning when salvation lay in courting the affections of those upon whom they depended for their very lives.

Right now, Mr Redding was that man. He'd unwittingly stepped into her life just when Wentworth was on a mission to destroy it. That meant, feelings aside, she had to court Mr Redding's kind offices so he'd protect her. Perhaps he would develop some real affection for her so that he'd champion her if she found herself in any greater danger. Such as if Wentworth found her and dragged her before the courts.

But what did Phoebe have that Mr Redding might desire? She buried her face in the pillow. The usual fare: her body, her looks, fortunately unmarred by age or Wentworth's brutality. There was little else in her favor other than a fierce determination that she would not be charged for a crime she did not commit.

She was the rightful mistress of Blinley Manor.

A sob erupted from the depth of her being. No, she wasn't. Without an heir, she could no longer inhabit Blinley Manor. Her new home was the dower house at the end of the driveway of... *Wentworth's* new estate.

She began to cry in earnest now. The truth was, Lady Cavanaugh was entirely dependent upon Wentworth's charity for her survival.

And Wentworth didn't want her survival.

And Phoebe the maid was entirely dependent upon Mr Redding's charity.

Tears were pointless. Action was needed. With great determination, she rose and went into the hall where she called for Mrs Withins, who appeared from one of the rooms with a look of indignant inquiry upon her face.

"I need a dressmaker from the village to attend me as soon as possible," Phoebe said, using the polite but authoritative tones she'd normally employ in such a situation, especially when her mind was occupied.

Phoebe only realized her mistake when Mrs Withins put her hands on her ample hips, lifted her chin and said with calculated derision, "Is that so...*madam*? An' who's goin' ter pay fer this dressmaker? Is it Mr Reddin', mayhaps?"

The housekeeper looked Phoebe up and down as if she were no better than a common doxy aping her betters and bartering her body—which is what Phoebe realized was the role she was playing.

"I'll take me orders from Mr Reddin', thank ye," the woman added when Phoebe didn't reply. She turned on her heel and swept down the passage.

Enraged and embarrassed, Phoebe immediately went in search of Mr Redding and found him poring over a map in the parlor.

"If I am ter 'elp ye bring Mr Wentworth ter justice, I need a new dress, sir! Several in fact, an' in great 'aste," she added, not caring what he made of her. The only way to prevent herself from crying was to turn her recent humiliating exchange with Mrs Withins into indignant self-justification.

He turned his head and said mildly, raising his eyebrows, "I don't quite understand your demanding tone, Phoebe, since that is just what I have sanctioned."

"Well, then ye must tell Mrs Withins 'erself that this is what I need an' that *she* must send fer the village dressmaker." Phoebe's own dressmaker did not live in the local village.

Mr Redding straightened in his chair. "Ah..." he said slowly. Phoebe felt a slow blush spread over her face. Mr Redding had just deduced what had happened. She hoped he'd spare her the indignity of putting it into words.

He did not.

"So, Phoebe, the lady's maid, has offended Mrs Withins by assuming the airs of a lady." He chuckled. "I'd heard that distinctions of rank are just as important to the lower classes. Well, Phoebe, since you want a dress dreadfully badly—"

Rudely she cut in, "An' ye want Wentworth an' I promise ye shall 'ave 'im, but ter do that I need ter be properly clothed. I need two gowns that befit me station, sir."

"The station to which you'd *like* to be elevated and which you are currently doing an admirable job of emulating." He narrowed his eyes. "So, it's two now, is it. And how might I benefit from my generosity since you refuse to speak to Sir Roderick? If I tell Mrs Withins to send for a girl to fit you for *two* dresses, I'll want some enjoyment for doing it." His mouth quirked and his voice thickened. He was, of course, like any other man playing with her, only right now she found the experience more entertaining than frightening. With Ulrick and Wentworth, she'd had as much free will as one of the butterflies in their collection. But in no way was she bound to Mr Redding. She could leave at any time. It would have been a liberating thought if she'd had anywhere to go. "Just *how* much do you want a new dress, Phoebe?"

Phoebe assessed him with equal interest as his eyes raked her body. She took in his highly polished Hessian boots with their fashionable tassels into which were tucked buff riding breeches. Riding breeches which clung to his shapely, muscled, thighs as if they'd been painted on. She pursed her lips as her eyes traveled north, lingering on his groin which, before her very eyes, began to show the obvious signs of pleasure at her interest.

Shocked and embarrassed, she tore her eyes away with a gasp, the heat burning her cheeks as his mocking laugh rang in her ears.

"A bold miss you are, to be sure." His voice had the consistency of treacle, and the smooth assurance that he would have what he wanted, but he was enjoying the process of bending her to his will.

The reflection, coming so soon after her confidence that she held the upper hand, made her thrust out her chin and declare angrily, "Ye want Mr Wentworth? I'm not askin' fer much. Jest somethin' decent ter clothe me, sir. Ye insult me if ye think I'll..."

She might have bartered her body for her husband, for Wentworth, but she was still enough of a lady to be ashamed to put into words the baseness of what they were negotiating.

"...You'll what, Phoebe?" He rose slowly, the humor just beneath the surface, and it riled her.

"A kiss fer a garment that will aid *yer* aims, sir!" she ground out, stepping forward and thrusting herself into his arms, twining her arms around his neck and closing her mouth over his.

She felt his surprise as his body reacted, first with a ripple of defense at her suddenness, then with a flare of something else—a different kind of surprise. A surprise that emulated hers, as his arms went around her, and he pulled her against him with a sudden movement that belied his mocking humor of earlier.

Her immediate thought had been that she *would* make him enjoy this. Yes, for once she would be in charge. And then, without warning, something extraordinary happened. Heat filled her, a slow, mesmerizing sensation that first curled lazily through her body, then fired her senses as it powered through her groin, twined through her heart, and snapped at her nerve endings.

She took a shallow breath as he deepened the kiss, his tongue breaching her first line of defense: the portcullis of her teeth that she'd intended would keep him at bay.

But as his tongue began to explore the inside of her mouth which unthinkingly, wantonly, she opened to give him greater access, she found herself pushing herself against him, her body flowering with willingness while he too showed every sign of being equally enthralled.

A brief kiss. That's all it should have been. A kiss to show that she had what he wanted, but would withhold it.

That this was a business transaction, that was all.

And yet, it was enslaving. Euphoric. Her head swam, and moisture heated her inner thighs. She should push him away, but as he continued to plunder her mouth, and his hands roamed over her body, she was his slave.

He now had her back arched over the back of the sofa.

"By God, you're a vixen, Phoebe." His breath thrummed against her lips. She felt his hands grip the bulky wool of her skirts, pushing them up past her thighs while he pressed more heavily against her.

He thought he had her acquiescence.

He did not!

"I said a kiss!" She tore herself out of his grip, angry now. Angry at herself as much as him for taking such liberties. "If ye think I'm so cheap as ter barter me body fer a mere dress, then ye can think again, Mr Reddin'."

He looked shocked and surprised. At himself? "I've insulted you, Phoebe," he muttered, raking his hands through his hair. "I'm sorry."

"Ye have." It was foolish to allow herself to succumb to tears. She was stronger than that. Still, the disappointment ran deep. He was just like any man. He'd take what he could and damn the consequences. She was a servant. Below him...she didn't matter.

Yet wasn't every man just the same, and hadn't she led him on? He'd push for what he could get. Men were like that.

She shrugged off his placating hand on her shoulder. When she glanced up, she could almost imagine she saw genuine contrition. She sniffed. "I s'pose most men don't apologize. Wentworth didn't."

Now he looked truly mortified. "He...*really* tried to force you?"

"Ha!" Her lip curled, and she put her hands to her face. "Didn't I say? Wentworth took what 'e could get an' pushed fer what 'e believed 'e were entitled to. Most men believe they're entitled ter whatever they wish fer." She stopped, caution screaming in her head. She mustn't confess. But she could give him some of the truth. She rubbed her hand across the back of her eyes. "'Tis not a kind world fer women. But then, what would ye know 'bout that, Mr Reddin'? Ye're a man, an' a wealthy one ter boot. Ye'd know little of what it is ter be vulnerable to the desires of others."

She stopped when she saw he was staring at her in some amazement. "You should be on the stage, my dear, reciting that perfect piece of prose in such ladylike tones. "*You'd know little of what it is to be vulnerable to the desires of others.* Are you parroting your mistress?"

Phoebe gave herself a mental shake as she prepared her answer. "My mistress and I were...close," she whispered.

"And where do you suppose your mistress has gone now? She murdered a man. She has good reason to fear for her life."

"Mr *Wentworth* murdered Lord Ulrick...I mean, Cavanaugh. Is there really a distinction when 'e used 'is far greater strength ter force me lady, strugglin' ter drop the knife yet 'e used *'is* power ter drive it in, with 'er as 'is instrument, weepin' all the while ter stop?" Angrily, Phoebe flung around. "A woman is the weaker vessel 'an she is powerless when a man decides she's useful fer something. Such as murder."

"So you *truly* assert that Wentworth is the murderer of your mistress's lover?" He snatched at her wrist and pulled her back, gripping her shoulders so he could look at her.

"'Ow many times do I 'ave ter say it, Mr Reddin'? That's why ye can't throw me ter the wolves once ye've 'ad yer fill of me, ter put it crudely. Mayhap no one will believe me, but I know what 'appened 'an I could convince any magistrate—other than Sir Roderick—who chose to look at the case with an open mind. But if ye cast me out an' Mr Wentworth or Sir Roderick found me, believe me; I might as well be dead."

He dropped his hands and turned upon a sigh. "Send Mrs Withins to me, and I'll have her arrange for the village dressmaker. Perhaps we can find a couple of secondhand gowns which she can remodel for the various occasions you'll require a different wardrobe. Ladies of fashion are expensive, but you'll have to temper your desires to become one of them. I'm not a rich man."

"I jest need *one* gown that's—"

"That's what, Phoebe? In the first stare, so you can ape your betters? What are you really planning?"

She wasn't sure. It wasn't safe to parade herself as Lady Cavanaugh might have done. There were subtle distinctions. A lady's maid was too much beneath her. Coarse homespun would hardly answer if she were to launch herself into the world given the first opportunity. Perhaps a respectable companion in her mistress's two-seasons-old castoffs. She supposed that would do.

"I don't mind a made-over gown, sir. 'Tis not as if I'm not used ter wearin' me mistress's from the year afore last. Jest so long as it fits."

"And where do you plan on being seen?"

"Wherever it's ter advantage. Maid or mistress." She smiled and affected a look of coyness. "Though I reckon I deserve better'n coarse cotton."

"Yes, I am aware that you have aspirations above your station, but I've warned you that saving your life won't lead to my making you my wife."

"But ye're payin' fer a new dress, sir, an' I can be more 'elpful to yer with a couple of 'em. Cotton print for a serving maid..." She pushed back one shoulder and looked him in the eye, adopting the perfectly cultured tones that were her own as she added, "and one for a lady so I can seek out those witnesses from both below and above stairs who will attest to Mr Wentworth being Lord Cavanaugh's killer."

"Do you truly believe you can pull off being a lady without embarrassment or endangering us both?" He'd not admitted to admiration, but it was clear by the short, surprised pause that preceded his question.

"You don't have much faith in me, sir." Riled, she determined that, forthwith, she would only speak as a lady. "Just listen to me and you shan't be disappointed."

He gave her a searching look and murmured softly, "I'm gaining greater faith all the time in your ability to secure what you really set your mind on, Phoebe. All right, you shall have one print cotton dress and one dress in the first stare so you can gain admittance to the right places, though I don't know what help that'll be when I haven't promised to take you anywhere, and since you say you're afraid Wentworth will recognize you."

"Then if you're so skeptical why would you grant me that, sir?"

"Because I rather fancy *my* chances of what you might grant me, Phoebe, were I to satisfy sufficient of your venal wishes."

Phoebe looked at him askance. "You do have a fine opinion of yourself, sir."

"And I do wonder at the value of funding a gown that will cost me an arm and a leg, unless it's to show off to your friends the fact you've weaseled a new gown out of a credulous gentleman without giving him anything in return."

"I gave you a kiss," she said hotly.

The expression on his face changed. In fact, he looked quite uncomfortable, and she noticed that he shifted a little, before he began to pace.

"And might I ask, Mr Redding, what *is* your interest in Mr Wentworth?"

At the wooden desk beneath the window he turned, his expression grim.

"Mr Wentworth seduced my sister."

Phoebe cocked her head. "Seduced? Then she was a willing party? I'm sure Mr Wentworth has seduced many an innocent. You are an unusual man if you do not blame *her* rather than Mr Wentworth."

"I know my sister's character, and she is not cheap, Phoebe," he snapped.

Phoebe acknowledged this with a slight nod. "I hope I didn't infer that she was. I just have observed that whenever there is wrongdoing between a man and a woman that it is always the woman whose reputation is smeared. Take my mistress, for instance. She's not cheap, either."

Mr Redding shrugged, staring down at the parchment on the desk. "I hope I'm fair enough not to judge one way or another, not knowing the lady in question. But we were talking about my sister. If you knew her, you'd understand. She's sweet and innocent, and she believed him when he promised he'd marry her."

"Then why does she not file a suit?"

Mr Redding made a noise of frustration. "If only she had. Instead, my sister went into a deep abyss of solitude. I had no idea of her involvement with Wentworth, whom I'd earlier warned her off, until it was...too late."

Phoebe drew in her breath. "There were consequences?"

She saw the fiery hue that precluded the need for him to reply.

Phoebe sighed. "Your poor sister."

"She went away for a while, and I'd hoped the matter was finally laid to rest. Until recently, she refused to divulge the name of the man. Now she lives with an aunt, quietly, but greatly altered in disposition." He scowled. "I need not remind you that I rely upon your discretion."

"Oh, you have that. I'm a woman, sir, and very mindful of the fact that your sister is fortunate enough to have family who can ensure no shame attaches to her. It sounds like she pays for her crimes of credulity every day. I don't envy her."

"I'm very close to my sister," he said softly. "I do not condemn her."

"Perhaps her father does? Her mother too, because she must step in line with the politics of shame. So that is your argument with Mr Wentworth." She frowned. "I must say, trying to accost him at pistol point was rather extreme, if I might say so myself, sir."

"It is not your place to make comment on how I choose to conduct myself or exact revenge from Wentworth!"

"No need to react so hotly, sir; I was just remarking that I'd have thought a more subtle yet more damaging approach would have been more effective." She put her head to one side. "Like taking away what Mr Wentworth wishes for most in this world."

"And what would that be?"

"His newly acquired title and estates."

Mr Redding laughed out loud. "And how do you suppose I might manage that? I'm not the Prince Regent. No, Phoebe, you really have no idea how to approach this from a logical point of view, and there's no need to look at me like that. I'm not being insulting. For all that you know how to string words together to sound like a lady—and I'll grant you are an impressive mimic—you are a servant with, I'm sure, a good and faithful heart, but you cannot begin to understand the complexities of such a thing."

Phoebe offered him a respectful curtsey before turning on her heel. *Oh, I know exactly how it could be done*, she thought. But divesting Wentworth of his estates and title could only be achieved if there were another contender for the title: an heir produced by Ulrick's widow within a conceivably acceptable time of Ulrick's death. It didn't leave much time, and Phoebe was not one to barter her body for a dress, but she'd do so if it meant Wentworth had no claim on Ulrick's title. Yes, she might be unsuccessful in convincing a magistrate of her innocence, and she may yet die for a crime she did not commit, but if she could prevent Wentworth inheriting what he'd murdered to lay claim to, it would be some consolation.

At the doorway, she looked over her shoulder. "I'll ask Mrs Withins to attend to you, shall I, sir? So you can talk to her about summoning a dressmaker from the village," she added in response to his questioning look.

❧

HUGH STARED AFTER HER, AND WHEN HE'D REGAINED HIS senses, he found he was unconsciously touching his mouth with the fingertips of his right hand.

Damn, but she'd taken him by surprise with that kiss of hers. Even still his lips were burning.

At the window, he gripped the sill and stared down the modest drive that led from the cottage to the road.

She'd asked him what he'd hoped to achieve by accosting Wentworth at pistol point. Honor for his sister. Yes, it had been rash, but he'd been in his cups when he'd come up with the plan to prove to Ada that not all men were smooth-talking confidence tricksters who led vulnerable women down the road to ruin.

There was also the small chance of exacting some retribution from the man. A marriage proposal had been his ultimate aim, though when he'd confidently told Ada he'd ensure Wentworth did the honorable thing, she'd burst into tears and said she'd not marry him if he were the last man on God's earth.

Well, Hugh didn't much fancy Wentworth for a brother-in-law either, but he did love his sister exceedingly, and surely marriage was better than ruin or the convent, as Ada had at one stage desired.

And contrary to what Phoebe believed, he and Ada had grown up without a mother, and Hugh had had a more than usual guiding influence on his young sibling which was why'd felt Ada's failure was somehow his.

He fingered the scar on his wrist, sustained during a childhood show of chivalry on behalf of his sister's honor. Phoebe's talk of just now had unleashed a veritable storm of emotions. Surprisingly, her talk about exacting retribution in the form of depriving Wentworth of what he most wanted kept replaying itself in his head.

She'd sounded so confident, but what could a maidservant know about exacting retribution from a man like Wentworth? Who was she really? A village child born in some humble hovel? Her beauty had no doubt opened a number of doors. Could she have had a noble protector who'd left her to slide back into servitude? Is that where she'd learned to speak and act like a lady?

He touched his finger to his lips once more. Ha, that precious innocence of hers for which she'd not barter a dress was a tall tale. Only a woman experienced in the ways of men would have been so bold as to plant a kiss like the one she'd given him. A woman used to being paraded and feted by a gentleman.

Perhaps, as she claimed, she *could* be useful to him.

But she'd need a little coaching. He couldn't afford for her to embarrass them both by proving her low birth during an unguarded moment.

He smoothed back his hair and regulated his breathing. Yes, he would take Phoebe in hand and teach her how to be a lady.

Then he'd make her his mistress, and she could have all the gowns she chose, within reason.

8

"Some fabric was left over from a polonaise Lady Colchester bought from Paris and the feathers...."

Phoebe stared from the beautiful gown that clothed her to the little woman in front of her. Truly, this was a clever artiste. And Hugh was a clever man for finding her.

He looked smug as now he shifted his attention from Phoebe to the dressmaker who'd just packed up her pins and started to leave, having received payment and praise obviously sufficient to her needs. Offering Phoebe his arm, he led her toward the window.

"Miss Lavendar has traveled some distance today, but I felt it was justified to employ the talents of someone I know could be trusted."

Phoebe looked from where her hand lay on his sleeve, then up to his face, which caught the sunlight that slanted through the diamond panes and felt a surge of something that was not gratitude snake through her heart before traveling disconcertingly to her loins. She wanted to rub her hands over the short stubble of his chin.

Instead, she inclined her head. "You obviously hold great store by your sister's opinion," she remarked and then saw the shadow that crossed his face.

"My sister is a remarkable young lady." She could tell it was not lip service either. When he spoke of her, he was altered. When he was flirting with Phoebe, the maidservant, he was as louche as any man. The contradiction riled her, but she was also impressed by his loyalty. How nice if any man had ever championed *her*.

"I think she must be a lucky young woman to have a brother like you."

"Alas, I failed her as a brother when I did not observe the nature of the man to whom she was losing her heart." A flare of anger darkened his gaze.

Wentworth, of course.

Phoebe looked at him inquiringly. Perhaps now, in this moment of intimacy, he would make a confidante of her. Maybe, dressed as she was, he'd forget she was supposedly a lady's maid, so far beneath him.

It appeared he did. "About eighteen months ago, Wentworth was a visitor to our district. Ada met him at the Assembly Rooms."

Phoebe felt grateful for his trust. "And he swept your sister off her feet, like he did my mistress? Mr Wentworth can be a very charming man when he wants to be."

"Clearly, he was charmed. Ada was young and unused to the attentions of gentlemen, and she was offended when I tried to counsel her on the need for caution."

"Oh dear, she was rebellious?"

Mr Redding rolled his eyes. "Back then she was although it was a long time before I realised just how far she had strayed, and indeed that Mr Wentworth was in fact the devil I now know him." He sighed. "How I would wish to see a return to her wilfulness from those days though, for all the fire and life has gone out of my sister now."

"Poor Miss Redding. But surely a young woman with spirit would want revenge against a blackguard like Mr Wentworth?"

"And how would a gently reared young woman exact revenge?"

Phoebe tossed her head. "My point exactly. I hoped you'd see the impossibility we women face every day of enjoying the justice so often denied us." She touched his arm. "We need to employ clever men as our conduits. Your sister and I are lucky to have you, Mr Redding."

She was astonished by the stab of feeling his amused and interested gaze unleashed within her. Her nipples hardened, and again she was aware of the heat in her lower belly that surely wasn't just gratitude for the dress he'd paid for. Tempering her smile, she looked away. It was a relief she was still capable of warm feelings for a man, but she mustn't allow herself to grow too fond of him. She was poised for escape at the first opportunity. She knew it was too dangerous to return to her aunt in Norfolk for that's exactly where Wentworth would look soon. But soon she'd need to leave here and go far away.

"Well, together we shall prevail, Phoebe." They'd reached the window embrasure where he put his finger beneath her chin and tipped her head. "I was thinking long and hard about what you said the other day." At her inquiring look, he added, "That the way to bring Wentworth down would be to discover what he most wanted."

"I already told you what he most wants. The estate he's inherited through murder."

"And you plan to return to Blinley Manor to spy on him, is that right?"

"I can't possibly go into company where he might recognize me."

Mr Redding frowned. "But the new dress. I thought that was your very intention. I thought you planned to pretend to be a lady—"

"A lady, yes, but not ..." she trailed off, miserable and fearful.

"You are very loyal to your mistress, aren't you, Phoebe?" His tone softened. "Yet, despite your boldness, you're doubting your courage and ability not to make a misstep, aren't you?" He drew her unexpectedly against him, and his hands contoured her curves, skimming up and over the fine muslin before cupping her face. "Don't worry, Phoebe. I shall be your tutor."

"My tutor?" She pulled away, not liking the change in him. "I hope you mean in your endeavors to turn me into a proper lady. I am not as easy as you might suppose, Mr Redding," she ground out, fighting the urge to cry. Just when she'd begun to like and trust him, he'd reverted to type.

He put his hands on her shoulders. "I'm curious. You pretend you're an innocent, but you clearly have experience of men. You speak and behave like a lady. Who are you really, Phoebe?"

She wasn't ready to confess her identity when she wasn't sure enough of him.

"Were you trading on past experience to be so beguiling when you desired a new dress? Were you a rich man's mistress, perhaps?"

Phoebe hung her head. That's exactly what she'd been, and her silence seemed to confirm it in Mr Redding's mind.

"So, once you had a rich protector, but now you're a lady's maid?"

Unable to look him in the eye, she nodded, tears threatening.

"And now I am your protector and am funding a new wardrobe?"

Slowly, she raised her head. "So this is when you ask me to sleep with you?"

He seemed to be thinking, staring out of the window with a troubled frown. "I had no idea my wild adventure to apprehend Wentworth would lead to this." He returned his look to her. "To rescuing a beautiful woman and keeping her safe." He appeared to resolve upon something for he added, "But gallant gentlemen rescue maids in distress. Opportunistic blackguards seduce them." His sudden smile took her by surprise, sending her heart into freefall. "Have no fear, Phoebe. I shan't make uncomfortable overtures and trade on my good fortune in adding an accomplished, entertaining, and exquisite-looking woman to my household. Not if the idea is so repugnant. No, I promised a fair trade: your information to bolster a case against Wentworth." His voice dropped as his eyes traveled over her, lingering on her décolletage which, for the first time, was shown to best advantage thanks to the stays the dressmaker had procured in a hurry. "Perhaps one day I might persuade you of my inherent charm. But you will have to make it clear you're...in the market."

"I may have lost my virtue, Mr Redding, but not my dignity." This was uttered in a less convincing tone. Phoebe slanted another glance at him. He was a fine-looking man. And a gentleman; not a blackguard. How many men would not take advantage where they could?

He put out his hand slowly, and Phoebe watched his seeking fingers gently skim the puffed roulade of her sleeve before advancing across her shoulder toward her bared skin. Anticipation rose, and she sucked in a shallow breath as he slowly contoured the edge of her gown, skimming the top of her breasts.

"I know you've felt more than just a passing interest in me, from the moment we met, Phoebe," he whispered. His fingers were so close to dipping beneath the fabric of her bodice, but he restrained himself, and Phoebe felt a tugging, yearning feeling from the depth of her being and was unsure if she were relieved or otherwise.

By God, but he was making this difficult. She'd wanted any encounter of a physical nature to prove she was not the weak creature she'd always been with Wentworth. Yet she wanted only to step into this man's embrace and see where it took them.

Swallowing, she suddenly pulled away, saying in an as disinterested a voice as she could manage, "What news of the murder at the manor? You were out on horseback in the village this morning, were you not?"

He remained where he was, matching his tone to hers.

"A dozen more men have been scouring the countryside looking for Lady Cavanaugh, but there's not been so much as a sighting. Someone suggested she is so filled with shame and mortification she's thrown herself down a well."

Phoebe snorted. "I don't think Lady Cavanaugh is one to be cast down by mortification for something she didn't do."

"Well, there's no one standing in her defense except you, Phoebe."

She swung around quickly. "*No one?* Well, I'm sorry to hear it, but I'll not speak up and be the only one if it's my word against Wentworth's."

"You might just have to since it would appear you are the only one to have witnessed his crime. There's no doubt in anyone's mind that Lady Cavanaugh is her husband's murderer." He gave a sigh of frustration. "Are you sure there's no one else who'd speak up in your mistress's defense? That's if she truly is innocent as you claim."

"She *is* innocent," Phoebe muttered sullenly. "But it appears Mr Wentworth is going to get away with his crime, after all. Doesn't it?"

"Indeed. And in the days since the murder, you are I are no closer to achieving what either of us had hoped."

Yes, only a few days had passed, but already Phoebe was growing weary of the lack of respect, bathing water, and other comforts she was used to. The servants in the house were barely civil to her, believing her to be Mr Redding's mistress already, no doubt.

"So what do we do now, m'lord?"

He chuckled, reverting to the playful, slightly condescending tone he'd adopted prior to assuring her of his gentlemanliness. "I keep forgetting you're a consummate actress, Phoebe, but although you're adept at playing the lady of the manor, it only takes one misstep to be revealed for the imposter you are. No need to look so indignant. I am a gentleman; therefore you cannot refer to me as m'lord." He put his arm about her shoulders and led her to the window embrasure, talking all the while as if tutoring a student. "But you are good, I'll grant you that. Why, if the fancy took us, I do believe it would be quite a lark to take you somewhere I'd not be recognized and pass you off as my wife."

Phoebe raised an eyebrow. "As your wife, sir? Why, you speak of a lark for the future which almost implies I was already your mistress. What was all this talk about just now, then? You do take a lot for granted."

Mr Redding laughed easily once more, and Phoebe noticed the dimples among the smattering of freckles on his cheeks. He really was a handsome and good-humored man when he smiled. Phoebe couldn't remember when lightness and easy humor were a feature of her endless days with either Ulrick or Wentworth.

His eyes narrowed but again with humor. "Oh, I think you'll enjoy it, Phoebe. You like a challenge; I can tell."

"I like a challenge, it's true, but my greatest challenge right now is convincing you that my honor is greater than my mercurial desires."

"You intend to see how much I'll give you without you giving me anything in return?"

"I'm giving you amusement."

"There'll soon come a time when that's not enough."

"Spoken like a true male. Why, then, am I disappointed? Perhaps it's time for me to move on, since my *true* value—that is, getting you Wentworth—has proven not such a great asset since I'm not going to speak to Sir Roderick and risk my neck for anyone."

He sobered a moment, then laughed again, though less convincingly. "I never pretended to be better than I am. Perhaps I'll just call in that kiss you promised, especially if I'm likely to find you gone in the morning and nothing more on offer, given our last conversation." He pulled her back into his embrace, murmuring with his face inches from hers before he kissed her, "See if I can persuade you to stay."

She was easy to win over, she knew. The touch of his lips upon hers, the sensation wrought by his fingertips upon her heated flesh was incendiary. She had no shame or compunction in surrendering to the moment, albeit briefly. She'd had little enough warmth and affection in her life.

But they were in the parlor. Mrs Withins was quite likely to enter without knocking, and Phoebe was not going to compromise herself to such a degree.

"By God Phoebe, but you know how to send a man wild with wanting," he ground out as he kissed her neck.

"I'd...best place a chair against the bedchamber door tonight then, sir." Phoebe tried to make her breathing soundless as she watched Mr Redding gazing at her with a mixture of desire and frustration after they'd broken apart. She was aware she was nearly at the point of doing something unwise, and her head spun as she gripped the table ledge for balance. She must ensure he did not notice her discomposure. Let him think she held all the cards. The moment he realized the extent of her attraction toward him, then her power was heavily diluted.

She cocked her head in the direction of the passage, smiling brightly as Mrs Withins entered the room. "Ah, perfect timing, Mrs Withins, as I needed someone to admire my new gown. Do you like it?"

She cast an impish look at Mr Redding and saw that he appeared as breathless as Mrs Withins though did not have the excuse of having climbed a set of stairs.

"That's a gown fer a lady, and though it mightn't be me place ter say it, reckon people are goin' ter wonder 'ow ye came by such a thing, Phoebe," she muttered, swinging around to present her with her back and to ask her master, "I take it ye'll be dinin' alone this evenin', sir?"

Mr Redding looked past the red-faced retainer and licked his lips as he contemplated Phoebe.

"There's been a dearth of ladies' company to enjoy, Mrs Withins, and as you rightly point out, young Phoebe here is doing a fine job of pretending the role and now even looks the part. I think I might indulge her just this once and see if she knows how to hold a knife and fork. I suspect her deficiencies might mock her if I put her through her paces."

Mrs Withins gave a short nod. "Aye, well, if ye want entertainment, I'm sure Phoebe don't 'ave any scruples that'll get in the way, sir."

Phoebe gasped as she positioned herself in front of the rude servant. "I demand an apology this instant!" she said in her most cultured accent. "Mr Redding?" she entreated when no apology was forthcoming.

Mr Redding shrugged his shoulders as he sent her a look of shame. "I rely on Mrs Withins to feed me and keep me in comfort, Phoebe. I wouldn't dare. As for you, I've funded a new dress with nothing in return."

At least he made this point clear to his housekeeper, thought Phoebe, though the housekeeper looked skeptical. To push it home, Phoebe added, "Yes, you rescued me, and I'm grateful. I shall have to consider what recompense is appropriate."

Mrs Withins put her apron up to her face. "What a den of vice the good miller's house 'as become. If I 'ad anywhere else ter go I'd be packin' me bags on the instant. In fact, it mayhap'll come ter that if that baggage ain't gone soon!" she added with a baleful look at Phoebe.

Phoebe watched her scurry out of the room, transferring her despairing look from Mrs Withins's departing back to Mr Redding's amused face.

"Well, you made your intentions very clear to the servants, didn't you, Phoebe, promising me I'll soon get what I want in return for your fancy finery."

"She thinks I've already bartered my soul for a new gown." Phoebe shrugged. "Perhaps I have."

9

"I have nowhere to go, Mr Redding. Certainly not while Mr Wentworth is on his murderous rampage." Phoebe took a sip of the wine which a mutinous Mrs Withins had been prevailed upon to serve Phoebe at the dinner table. "But this afternoon, I've come upon a plan."

"I imagine you'd always have a plan, Phoebe. And another plan in case the first one failed." Mr Redding raised one eyebrow, but Phoebe could see he was intrigued. Intrigued by her or intrigued by her potential plan? Preferably both. Phoebe needed some security to know he was not going to suddenly evict her or, if he chose to take a more gentlemanly approach, deposit her in the village she professed to come from.

"Pray, do not keep me in suspense."

"I know things about Mr Wentworth that my mistress told me and which I believe the magistrate—no, the government—would be interested to know about."

"Why didn't you say?"

The truth was, Phoebe had been dismayed by her lack of knowledge regarding anything along these lines, though she'd trawled through her memory in case Wentworth had mentioned anything that might constitute felony.

Mr Redding needn't know this though. He just needed to think she knew enough to be useful, so he'd keep her safe until she'd somehow come upon a solution to her terrible conundrum as to where she could possibly go when she had no money and only one dress.

When Phoebe glanced up, however, she saw though that his look was not nearly as interested as before. He snorted.

"You don't know anything, do you?" Shaking his head, he topped up her glass. "Ah well, I'm a philosophic man by nature, so I'll just have to try and console myself with the fact that it's not a wasted evening to enjoy dinner with a woman as easy on the eye as you are, my dear." He sent her a rueful look. "I think I must be soft in the head to let you talk me into giving you such latitude. Mrs Withins asked me before you entered... 'Where will it end, sir?'." He shrugged and sent her a piercing look across the table. "Where *will* it end, Phoebe?"

His voice had dropped. The light was fading outside, and the candle in the center of the table sent long shadows dancing on the wall.

Phoebe finished her second glass of wine and noticed with a surge of appreciation how well he looked in evening clothes. His snowy stock was pristine. He'd shaved, and the smoothness of his skin was suddenly intriguing. She had a ridiculous urge to feel the soft linen of his stock drift across the back of her hand before she twined her fingers up through his hair and caressed the smooth skin of his newly-shaven jaw.

Goodness, he was a handsome man. His eyes were somewhere between green and brown, though in some lights she would describe them as...tawny. She'd never seen eyes like his. His light brown hair was fashionably styled; angular sideburns followed the line of his sharply-delineated cheekbones. When he was amused, he had one dimple that popped out, but when he was angry, his mouth was set in a hard, uncompromising line.

Now, however, the rhetorical question clearly both perplexed and amused him.

Phoebe pushed back her chair and slowly stood up. The wine had emboldened her, and she had a position to maintain. In this man's eyes, she was for all intents and purposes a doxy; and one who'd failed to give him any return on his money, at that. The money he'd spent on a fine dress which *she* hoped would come in useful for effecting her escape some day.

She took a couple of steps toward him, and her calculated thoughts were entirely a separate matter to the heat that swept through her core. She needed this man, it was true. Thank God she *wanted* him, too.

"Where *will* it all end, Mr Redding?" Her voice was low and husky as she stood behind him, lowering her head so that her breathy tone ruffled the curls behind his ears.

She noticed how he tensed, thrilled that her ploy really did seem to put his nerve endings on notice.

Gently she laid a hand on his shoulder, and slid her other down his waistcoat, lingering on his breast before snaking down toward his groin.

He startled, but beyond that was still. Phoebe was in charge.

In charge and charged with lust. She didn't believe she'd wielded such power. Certainly not with Ulrick. She doubted with Wentworth, even in the early days.

But this man had been attracted to her from the start. She'd seen it in the first interested flare during their heated exchange in the woods when her face had been smeared with mud.

Well, that was only a few of days ago, but the tension had been building up between them ever since and now Phoebe knew exactly what she wanted.

And what she needed.

"You have ordered me a very beautiful gown, sir, for which I am truly grateful." Gently she nipped his ear. "But I do not barter anything unless my interest is piqued."

"Your interest is piqued, *now*, Phoebe?" He sounded strangled. "I'm glad to hear it. I'd all but given up hope."

"Either this fine Rhenish has gone to my head, or perhaps we've been leading toward this moment from the start." She slid her body around as she spoke, and sat on his lap, twining her arms behind his neck as she offered an impish grin. Oh, she was in charge and how mightily she was enjoying it.

"I like to think it is the latter."

She closed her eyes as she gently ground her bottom over his growing erection. They would make love, and she would feel safe and enjoy it. The anticipation of what the next few minutes... night...might bring was singing through her veins. Her brain throbbed with excitement, and the heat and moisture between her legs made her lightheaded.

Kissing his ear while he gently ran his hands over her, she acknowledged that she desired this man deeply and sincerely.

She felt his thighs tense and heard his slight exhalation as she pressed her lips to Adam's apple.

Tipping her head and tightening his arms around her, he kissed her long and hard, and excitement fueled her body to fever pitch. She'd never felt like this before.

Yet she had to remain in charge. She could not be the weak vessel, the slave she'd been to Wentworth.

Mr Redding's hand was on her knee now, beneath her skirts, and climbing higher. She'd given him license at last, and he was succumbing to the ecstasy of the moment. She could see it in the lust-fueled glaze of his eye and his smile as he touched her.

Her own excitement was growing, but to remain in charge, she needed distance.

Within seconds, she realized distance was not going to be possible. She was as swept away as he by this moment of mutual desire when she had surely everything to gain by abandonment.

With one practiced hand, Phoebe unbuttoned his trouser flap while she continued to kiss him, then slid her hand into the opening.

"Oh God!" he gasped, jerking as he was taken by surprise, cupping her chin, but ever so gently. Not like Wentworth, though dear Lord this was no time to make comparisons. Not when the men were as different as chalk and cheese, and the reasons for her behaving no better than a whore purely life preserving.

No, that wasn't true. The only time she'd offered her body up to a man's like a whore was when she'd married Ulrick. She'd felt nothing for him. At least with Wentworth in the early days, she'd been listening to her heart.

Rising swiftly and pulling up her skirt, she quickly straddled him, aware that even without stimulation she was highly lubricated as she impaled herself on his straining member.

"Wait, Phoebe!" His voice came through a wall of sensation, for the feel of him inside her was more exciting than she could have believed possible.

"I want this as much as you do," she gasped, for he was about to withdraw and, like the real lover, bring her to climax first, but she needed him inside her more.

Phoebe tightened her knees around him. She had less than two weeks to get with child. It was only a matter of time before the murdering Lady Cavanaugh of Blinley Manor was located and brought before the courts, and justice in this country was harsh and summary. Her noble position in such an instance would carry no weight. Not when she was branded by everyone as a whore with the motive to murder her husband. Only if she carried supposedly noble cargo was there any possibility of a reprieve. Justice was swift in these times. No wonder so many women in prisons sought the offices of the turnkey, or whatever willing man was available to get them with child so they could plead the belly and postpone the noose. Justice did not serve women in her situation kindly. This was her most hopeful solution.

Did it make her a whore? She was desperate, yes, and she'd been trying for a child for five years. Wasn't this the first time she was truly answering the wild beating of her heart?

Grinding her hips against his, she felt his objection die as he was overpowered by his own lust and her determination to see this thing through.

He was large and deep within her, and his breath felt soft and sweet on her cheek, for all he was gasping like a man in the throes of the greatest ecstasy.

Then, to her astonishment, something deep within her began to happen. The very first time Wentworth had seduced her he'd done things to her that had made her feel this way. Never since. And never without direct stimulation.

Each delve and thrust of this man before her—her lover, she hoped, for the next two weeks—sparked something exquisite and tantalizing in the depths of her core; something that grew in tandem with his own excitement.

So when he plunged into her for one final thrust, his gasp of pleasure was echoed by her own as she came in his arms, shuddering at the impact of this unexpected encounter with the first man she thought might be worthy of her affection.

"By God, Phoebe," he gasped, "you are extraordinary."

She sagged against him and tightened her arms about his neck. She didn't want to let him go and was afraid of meeting his eye for the first time.

They were lovers now. What would the future bring?

❧

Yes, they were lovers, each day reinforcing their desire and need for each other. They did not speak of Wentworth or the murder, vengeance or the future, as one week turned into two, and their quiet cottage became an idyll from the outside world. Despite the fact she could see the lights of Blinley Manor far in the distance, Phoebe felt safer than she'd ever felt.

Hugh was a kind and caring protector who seemed as reluctant as she to leave this strange, honeymoon world they'd created.

But of course, change had to come. Although Phoebe knew the end of the lease of the miller's home was approaching, Hugh had insinuated he would take her to London with him. As Phoebe had only once been to London and was unfamiliar with the fashionable set, she'd accepted now that she would never become the lady she once was.

Nor did it matter, for what were fine clothes and servants if the price was being bound to a man who did not care for her, or worse?

As Hugh's mistress, she had an affection and freedom she'd never had as Lady Cavanaugh.

But of course, her happiness could not last forever.

10

Hugh ran his fingers through his curls and tried again, gripping the back of the wooden chair as he prepared to rephrase his explanation in language less calculated to set up Phoebe's bristles. This was not going well.

Angrily, Phoebe faced him across the room. "Let me understand this, sir," she whispered tightly, holding herself up with all the dignity she could clearly muster. "You've just had news your sister is arriving unexpectedly, and now, suddenly I am relegated to the servant's quarters. Yesterday you were very happy to take what I offered, but now, like a discarded toy you've grown weary of, I am to be sent back to where I came from."

He crossed the room in a few strides and gripped her hands.

"Please don't be hurt. You make it sound as if I regard you as a novelty when nothing could be farther from the truth." Kissing her knuckles, he was filled with dismay. He'd never expected this, but then, perhaps she thought this was a precursor to him being rid of her. Perhaps this is how her last protector had let her down. He tried to reassure her. "Phoebe, you've bewitched me and that is the truth! But my sister is a gently-reared young woman who cannot possibly know you. No gentleman would introduce his..."

She raised an eyebrow at his want of the right word. "Doxy?" she supplied.

He shook his head vigorously, and a strange and unexpected sensation filled him from his boots upward. Not lust. Well, not that alone. "Mistress," he whispered. His mouth parted slightly, and he held her back from him. "You're my mistress, Phoebe. Do you know, I've never taken a mistress? Yes, I've had women and liaisons that have entertained me for weeks at a time. But I've never..."

"Kept a woman as you would a wife only without offering her the security of a marriage contract."

He shook his head in frustration. "You really do have ideas above your station, don't you? You know as well as I do that gentlemen do not marry lady's maids." He moved to wrap his arms about her, but she remained stiff.

"How much time do you anticipate I will continue to amuse you, sir?"

He pushed her resisting hands down to her sides and gently sprinkled kisses along her jawline. "I could be honest and say that I forsee a long future of love and happiness before us. Or I can vex you, since you are determined to be vexed, it would appear, and say, who can tell when you constantly surprise me with your sweet charm, Phoebe love." A tentative hand upon her shoulder met with no resistance, and when he closed the distance between them she fell into his arms.

He touched her cheek then, unable to help himself, slid his hand down into her bodice. "You know I will do what is right by you, but also what is right by my sister," he whispered as the mere feel of her, and her awareness of him, began to take possession. He chuckled when she shuddered slightly, in clear anticipation of what might come next. "Ah, but you do still like me, even if I've made you cross."

To his surprise, she kissed him then, with a need for reassurance that instantly fired his senses.

In three backward steps, he had her against the sideboard, and she was making no attempt to stop him as he rucked her skirts up past her thighs. "You could not feign desire like this were you the most accomplished actress on Drury Lane."

"No, I could not," she acknowledged, slackening in his embrace as he played her like a violin and her breathing accelerated. "But we must not do this here for Mrs Withins could enter at any moment."

"Not before I do, sweet Phoebe," he quipped, quickly unbuttoning his trouser flap. God, he wanted her *again*. He'd never experienced the lust and need that fired him so unexpectedly whenever she was near. He was not the kind of man who rutted like a bull, or even had the desire to, like some of his compatriots. Nor was he one to take his fill with lightskirts either. No, he'd enjoyed women of his station with a roving eye who crossed his path from time to time but, as he'd told her, he'd never taken a mistress. Not when he was half on the lookout for a wife. He liked the idea of domesticity and children. He wanted a woman he could love and be proud of. One who loved him back.

"You are wicked, Mr Redding," she gasped into his hair as he slid his hands under her bottom and hitched her up, so she had her back against the wall and her legs wrapped about his waist. "Making an innocent girl like me want to go to the devil for my sins."

"Ah, not to the devil, Phoebe...but to Heaven and back."

"What a honeyed tongue you have, Mr Redding."

"All the better to know you with, my dear Phoebe," he muttered, enjoying her surprised gasp as he drove into her.

"Not expecting that so soon, were you?"

"No...sir."

She was wet and hot and smooth, and Hugh was almost ashamed by his lack of self-control were he not having such an astonishingly good time. Her soft little moans in his ear spurred him on as with each thrust his need ratcheted up.

"Quick, I hear Mrs Withins coming!" Phoebe's horrified whisper drove him to the edge within a second, and then the door was thrust open, and Phoebe slid to the floor before they turned guiltily toward the housekeeper who was bearing down upon them like an avenging bull.

"Sir, yer sister's jest bein' admitted through the front door. I wanted ter warn ye now so's ye could get this...piece out of 'er way." She raked Phoebe with narrowed eyes and curled lip.

"Where am I to go, sir? Downstairs?"

Guilt needled him. If he didn't know better, she could pass for a lady except for the ghastly gown, another belonging to the wife of the miller which had been retrieved from an old trunk. Clearly, it was not even one that she wore any longer, for even he could see the fashion was years out of date. In the two weeks he and Phoebe had been sating themselves in one another's arms, they'd barely left the house.

"Perhaps you should go into the village and find yourself something fitting to wear, Phoebe." He tried to modulate his tone, hoping his words and actions would not inflame either Phoebe or Mrs Withins though he knew that was an impossible task. The housekeeper looked like a trussed-up turkey growing even more purple in the face as Phoebe looked smugly between them.

"How very kind, sir? So I might wear it to take tea with your sister?"

"No!" He'd not meant to sound so panicked. Phoebe clearly didn't take kindly to his tone for, with a toss of her head, she picked up her thick, cumbersome skirts and swept to the door. "I shall go through the kitchen, and of course I must be quick if I'm to avoid embarrassing you, sir. However, I cannot do your bidding on thin air."

Embarrassed, Hugh waved his hand dismissively toward the housekeeper. "That'll be all, Mrs Withins. Please see my sister into the parlor. Phoebe, come with me now."

He led her hurriedly down a short corridor to the room where the miller did his book work, closing the door behind him.

"How much do you want, Phoebe?"

When he glanced up, he was scorched by her fulminating look.

"I am not a...whore!" she hissed.

He blinked.

"Five minutes ago you were taking your pleasure, despite my protests that the timing could be better—"

"I did not force you, Phoebe. And you were more than ready for me."

"And immediately you'd had your pleasure you banished me downstairs because I'm not good enough to see your sister, and then you ask me what payment I require."

"You're being too sensitive, Phoebe—"

She cut him off. "Half a crown will do for the moment to amuse me with bibs and bobs. I shall see what else I need in the way of suitable attire, and then you can arrange payment later."

"Oh, so you're well accustomed to transactions like this, yet you speak to me as if I've insulted you." Hugh wasn't sure if he was more needled by her accusations of insensitivity on his part, or the fact that Phoebe appeared used to having protectors shell out money for her charms.

He'd been going to reassure her before Mrs Withins entered the room of his honorable intentions with regard to setting her up nicely. He wanted her much more than he wanted a wife, and Phoebe, with her looks and prowess in the bedroom department, would be quick to look elsewhere unless Hugh got himself in order. He'd wanted to reassure her that he was madly in love with her, and it would be a while before he even got down to the serious business of finding a wife; that for the foreseeable future, she would be the focus of all his attentions.

Instead, he was silent as he watched her hand close over the money he gave her.

❧

CAST OUT ON THE STREET WAS EXACTLY WHAT IT FELT LIKE AT first. And then the extraordinary sensation of freedom hit Phoebe like a sack of oats. She'd rarely left the confines of Blinley Manor without someone by her side, whether it was her aunt or Barbara, her lady's maid.

Well, there was no one who'd have anything to do with her now, and the pin money she had in her pocket would hardly result in the number of parcels that would require another's help to carry.

Phoebe had only occasionally visited this town that was somewhat larger than her own local village. It had a busy marketplace and quite a substantial high street. In her matronly garments with a hideous lace cap upon her head she'd go unrecognized, and while she might abhor the ugliness of her rig-out, she was soon enjoying the anonymity that plainness of appearance brought. She'd not left the miller's cottage in two weeks.

The sun was high in a cloud-studded sky as she sauntered down the rutted road, her hand closed around the coin in her pocket. Ulrick rarely gave her so much for he insisted on sanctioning every purchase. Her father had negotiated a poor deal for her with regard to pin money when he'd signed the marriage contract on her behalf.

As her pique with Hugh abated, she began to see her surroundings with fresh eyes. Villagers scurried about their business carrying baskets laden with bread and vegetables; wheeled wagons rumbled down the street. Everything was a hive of activity, and no one seemed to give her a second glance.

Such anonymity and freedom were intoxicating.

And this was her first real opportunity for purchasing those necessities that would augment the several gowns she'd need, such as gloves, a decent bonnet, and some shoes. She was a kept woman now. There was no coming back from that fact.

She'd heard Mrs Withins say the new lordship was ensconced while the search for Lady Cavanaugh continued. As Phoebe pored over a selection of kid gloves on a barrow down a narrow laneway, she welcomed the idea of moving to London with Mr Redding. She only had to look over her shoulder to see Blinley Manor perched upon the hill, and a deep chill permeated her bones.

Right now, Mr Redding was in love with her, but she knew how men behaved when they were weary of the women with whom they were saddled. The truth was that she, in turn, was deeply attached to Mr Redding, but her survival required her to think like a man. That meant she must take whatever opportunity she had to put together a few garments that would see her through the near future.

She could not allow sentiment to interfere with what she needed to do simply to prevent herself being shot through the heart by Wentworth—oh, and he'd do it, too!—or dangle from the end of the gallows.

"I 'ear she did a runner with all 'is jewels 'an plate. Don't blame 'is new lordship fer wantin' a piece o' her. I 'eard Lady Cavanaugh were an easy bit o' muslin. Reckon she deserves what's comin' ter 'er. Won't be long now. She can't 'ide forever."

Horrified, Phoebe swiveled her eyes to see who was speaking. A man and woman were inspecting the goods of the secondhand barrow a few feet away, sifting through musty-smelling garments as they spoke first of domestic matters, and now of the on-dit that clearly continued to enthrall the locals.

She was about to turn away when unwittingly she caught the eye of the woman, a shifty-eyed creature with a rattish face and thin greying hair beneath her faded bonnet.

"Oi, ye!"

Phoebe froze with both fear and indignation. No one had ever addressed her in such a manner. Pure terror followed quickly. She surely couldn't have been identified? The last two weeks had transported her into safety's embrace, but now, suddenly, she felt the hard, rough rope of the noose tighten around her neck and thought she would faint.

With a panicked look toward the end of the alleyway, she assessed her options. She could flee, dive under the cart that was lumbering down the cobbled laneway for protection and hope to make her escape that way.

In fact, she was about to do this when the woman inquired

pleasantly, "Where'd ye get that cap? From this barrow? It's right 'andsome, it is. Ain't it, Jonas?"

Phoebe's mouth, if anything, dropped ever lower. She put her hand to her brow and touched the hideous headpiece. Handsome? Was this woman testing her?

Dry-mouthed, she shook her head and muttered something in the way of a denial and thanks before she sidled away. But the words the woman had uttered just before her dubious compliment lingered. Did *everyone* really think she was guilty? That Lady Cavanaugh was the harlot Wentworth portrayed her to be? That she'd driven in the knife that had killed her own husband? Did even her own maid, Barbara, think it? How loyal was *she*, really? Right now, Phoebe's only sanctuary was Hugh.

Despair weighed heavily on her shoulders as she left the barrow without making a purchase. How would she ever clear her name? Well, she would not. She'd already accepted she'd never have a fair trial; that her only chance of survival was to hope she was never discovered; that she'd be condemned to spend the rest of her days as a servant.

She swallowed again. As mistress to Mr Hugh Redding? Was that the best she could hope for?

Phoebe continued her shopping expedition, spending all the money Mr Redding had given her, most of it on a morning dress she'd found at the secondhand shop. It had probably belonged to someone with pretentions to grandeur, for the cut would have been stylish two years previously though the material was not of high quality. Still, it was flattering and the best of a bad lot.

The moment she returned, going through the servants' back entrance to the small room allotted to her now that Ada was here—thank the good Lord she wasn't sharing with Mrs Withins as Mr Withins was away for a night—she slumped down on her pallet bed and put her head in her hands; the dress draped across her lap.

Once, she'd been fired up by the possibilities of clearing her name. She'd been fired up by Mr Redding. Just thinking about him now made her tingle inside, and set in motion a strange roiling feeling in the pit of her stomach.

But for how long would she really be satisfied, knowing he regarded her as no better than a servant, and the real Lady Cavanaugh as a murderer?

For a start, she'd have to accept being banished the moment a 'real' lady in the form of his sister appeared.

Rising with the knowledge she had to make the best of things, Phoebe put on her new dress. Her spirits rose when she ran her hands down its skirts for it fitted her better than she'd expected. And when she'd added the gloves and shawl, she looked more like a poor country cousin than a servant with aspirations to grandeur, which was some consolation. As there was no looking glass in her attic room, she decided to make her way to the parlor but stopped belowstairs to find herself a glass of milk.

Here she learned from the tweeny that Mr Redding and his sister were out on a walk. Phoebe had met little Sally rubbing raw her hands scouring pots on a number of occasions, but the girl was clearly under orders not to associate with her. However, as Mrs Withins was having an afternoon rest, Sally was emboldened to ask her own questions.

"Are ye a servant or friend of Mr Redding's? Mrs Withins says you's more one than the other but she won't say which."

Phoebe drained her glass and put it on the table. "Mr Redding was good enough to take me in when my family became ill. Don't believe the lies Mrs Withins tells you."

Sally, still on her knees, eyed Phoebe with interest. "So it's cos ye're poor ye're not respectable?" She ran the scrubbing brush back and forth on the flagstones, staring at the wet wash thoughtfully. "I'm poor too, so I don't know why Mrs Withins warned me agin you." She glanced up, putting out a hand to touch Phoebe's skirts. "An' ye ain't dressed like them fancy-pieces wot hides in alleyways to lure the menfolk?"

Phoebe's eyes widened.

"Mrs Withins said that's where ye'd end up, an' if I didn't want ter end up there too, then I weren't ter talk ter yer."

Phoebe cleared her throat. "I won't end up there because I'm going to London in a few days," she said, leaving the room and feeling mightily relieved that this was indeed the truth.

For in London she could disappear.

In the parlor, she stood near the center of the room so she could get a better idea of the effect in the reflection of the mirror above the mantelpiece. She'd found a bonnet, quite nicely trimmed, and the shawl was good quality paisley. So even if the dress were coarser cotton than she'd have liked, and the fullness of the skirt not in accordance with this year's fashions, she was pleased enough with the effect. No one would remark upon her, and that was the main thing.

A small gasp, followed by, "Who are you?" made Phoebe swing around.

Standing in the doorway stood a pale but pretty young woman in a jonquil pelisse, a few strands of damp blonde hair curling below her bonnet, and a clearly damp pair of walking boots. Her surprise and curiosity were a welcome contrast to the sly or condemnatory looks with which Phoebe was used to being greeted by the visitors who came to the house to see Mrs Withins.

"I'm your brother's friend, and you must be Miss Redding." Phoebe did not intend to feel ashamed or cowed by any young lady who definitely was no better than she was.

"Hugh's...friend?" The girl was clearly caught by surprise. "I didn't know my brother was the kind...." She turned away, blushing furiously, her gaze going to the window, perhaps for fear of her seeing her brother coming up the path.

The girl's embarrassment fueled Phoebe's own. In a rush she said, moving closer to her, "Actually, your brother saved me from a rather terrible situation several weeks ago when he found me on the road after I'd escaped from Blinley Manor."

"Blinley Manor?" Miss Redding gasped the name as she swung

around. Round-eyed as she untied her bonnet which she tossed onto the sofa, she said, "Wasn't there a murder there?"

Phoebe thought quickly and decided that being truthful, while a risk, was ultimately the safer course. Miss Redding would not mix with those in the area who were looking for the supposedly departed Lady Cavanaugh. Also, the girl had a fresh-faced and rather innocent look about her, despite her brother's despair at her apparent ruin.

Oh my goodness! Phoebe shuddered. This girl and she had more in common than Miss Redding might suppose. To gauge the effect of using his name, Phoebe said cautiously, "His lordship, Mr Wentworth, murdered his cousin in order to inherit and pretended...my mistress did it. I saw what happened, and I ran away before Mr Wentworth murdered me as he tried to do. Your brother picked me up on the road and has been looking after me as I've nowhere else to go. At least, not until I clear my mistress's name by ensuring Mr Wentworth gets justice."

Miss Redding had gone very pale, and was holding the back of the sofa to keep steady it appeared. Her lower lip trembled. "My brother *told* you about Mr Wentworth and...?" She closed her eyes, finishing on a whisper, "He must have, else why would he have taken *this* house so close, and why would you tell me such terrible things when you've only just met me?" She began to cry, crumpling onto the sofa just as the door opened and Mr Redding entered.

His confused, concerned look took in his sister before sliding across to Phoebe, whereupon his eyes darkened. "What have you said to Ada?" He sucked in a breath. "I explicitly said you were not to be in her company." He hurried forward, taking Phoebe's wrist, drawing her away from the weeping girl as he said in a low tone, "See how vulnerable she is? Please leave, Phoebe. Ada, are you all right?" His tone gentled and he sank down onto the sofa, taking his sister's hand and murmuring softly to her.

From the doorway, Phoebe stared at the scene while tears pricked her eyelids. Mr Redding loved and respected his sister, but Phoebe was nothing but a low-born creature in his eyes. She half turned, torn between defending herself and quietly slipping away. She thought Mr Redding was falling in love with her, but now she realized that again, his feelings were fueled by lust and nothing more sincere than that. Why had she deluded herself it was anything else? No man had ever been concerned over her feelings. No man had ever held her hand or crooned words of comfort to her. She'd been alone since the day she'd been born.

Her throat felt swollen, and she rubbed the back of her hand across her eyes. She knew she was jealous. Mr Redding had excited her, sent her pulses racing, made her body feel like it was a temple.

But that's all she was to him: a body, young, and to his liking. Convenient. He didn't care about *her*.

Wishing she had a handkerchief, she left the room. What future did she have if it depended solely on bringing pleasure to the men prepared to pay for it? That had been the truth when she was offered to Ulrick in marriage. At least, then, she'd been protected in part by birth and respectability.

Now she had not even these.

11

Walking in the back garden by the cherry tree later that afternoon, Phoebe was surprised to hear her name called. She'd avoided remaining indoors to escape the dreadful prospect of bumping into Miss Redding and inciting the brother's ire. In fact, Phoebe's ire toward Mr Redding was so great she wasn't sure she'd know how to address him when the time came.

Turning, she saw Miss Redding standing on the garden path that led into the orchard where Phoebe had been whiling away her time. "Hugh says I'm not to speak to you, but it wasn't you who upset me." Miss Redding came immediately to the point as she joined Phoebe. "Shall we walk?" Unsmiling, she indicated the line of trees.

Phoebe shrugged. "If you wish."

"It was your talk of Mr Wentworth." Miss Redding looked proud and haughty as she said his name, though it wasn't long before the mask slipped and she appeared as little more than a diffident schoolgirl. "I'm supposed to avoid even the mention of his name in my brother's company because I've so shamed him, but I think it might be rather a relief to speak to you since you knew Mr Wentworth on account of his visits to Blinley Manor where you worked." She glanced over her shoulder. "Don't worry, I shan't say a word. Hugh says you're in danger because of what happened there but not to bring up the subject. He says I should just let Mr Wentworth's memory fade away until he's not even a shadow in our lives."

"So you're defying your brother just by talking to me? Aren't you afraid he'll look out of the window and see us?"

"Hugh's just ridden into the village, so he won't be back for a while."

Phoebe observed the determined dark eyes that were in such contrast with her trembling mouth. "Mrs Withins will tell him if she sees us," Phoebe warned, walking on a little. "And you know your brother will be very angry." Righteous indignation made her tremble. How could she ever have found her heart engaged by a man who thought so little of her?

"Well, I don't think I've ever associated with a woman like you..." Miss Redding's voice trailed off as she followed Phoebe out of line of sight of the windows, doubling back so they were within the shelter of a large hedge.

Phoebe swung around, one eyebrow raised. "A woman like me?" she repeated. "I thought your association with Mr Wentworth made you a woman just *like* me."

Miss Redding gasped. "How dare my brother confide to you so much about me. You've...beguiled him. You're his mistress, aren't you? That's why I mustn't talk to you." Trembling, she muttered furiously, "I hope his trust is not misplaced, and that you won't reveal anything that might damage my reputation."

Phoebe relented a little in her anger toward Mr Redding when she considered that he *had* trusted her to such an extent. Her ire toward Miss Redding also abated as she considered how young the girl was. Surely she'd have been still in the schoolroom when she'd been so easily led and Phoebe, more than anyone, knew how vulnerable she must have been to Wentworth's charm.

Just as she was about to say something ameliorating, Miss

Redding raised her head. "Our situations couldn't be more different though, so you must understand my brother wanting to protect me from you. I succumbed to the charms of a gentleman because of my foolish heart, whereas you are forced to do so—"

"*Forced* to do so?" Phoebe's sympathy drained away. "Are we talking about Mr Wentworth?"

Miss Redding looked confused for a second before her brow cleared. "I was talking about you and my brother. Yes, I was disgraced through my association with Mr Wentworth because I lost my heart..." she took a breath, adding, "...however, your association with my brother is through pecuniary necessity." She put her hand up to stay Phoebe's protest. "I'm not condemning you, but you can't tell me you love my brother when you've only just met him and it's clear you have nowhere else to go."

Phoebe resisted the urge to slap her. "You are more straight-talking than you look, Miss Redding," she murmured at last.

"I pride myself on speaking the truth as I see it." Miss Redding looked disgustingly virtuous. "I also love my brother very dearly. He's been both father and mother to me since the early death of my parents. But I can see he's lonely, and that you coming into his life in such a manner has made him susceptible to...what you might offer. I'm sure it's a very convenient arrangement and, of course, I quite understand his concerns that I should not associate with you—"

"Except that I might suggest your association with Mr Wentworth has blurred those lines between us which you suggest preclude a certain leveling in our stations," Phoebe said hotly. Who did this young woman think she was, taking the moral high ground like this?

To her astonishment, Miss Redding promptly burst into tears. Again.

Phoebe shook her head as the girl buried her face in her hands, rocking her shoulders while the green feather of her bonnet threatened to snag on the spikes of the hedge.

"Stop behaving like a sniveling infant," Phoebe muttered,

putting out her hand awkwardly and then withdrawing it. "First you accost me, and then you insult me and say you're not supposed to be speaking to me. I think it's time to bid you good day, Miss Redding, before your brother or Mrs Withins sees us and accuses me once again of upsetting you."

Miss Redding looked up at her through reddened eyelids. "Don't go," she pleaded. "I know I was rude even though there's truth in what I say—you surely must admit it. But my situation is so much worse than yours. I have lost everything!"

"Your virtue, which you so foolishly offered?"

Instead of another angry outburst, Miss Redding merely nodded sadly. "My virtue...and then..." she took a deep breath "... that which I cannot speak of. So much worse. And now my will to live." She began to cry again, but this time with such heartrending sobs that Phoebe *was* moved.

Drawing Miss Redding deeper into the garden where there was no chance of being observed, she asked, "There was a child?"

"Yes...no, it must never be spoken of!" Ada heaved in another breath and rested her head against the tree trunk behind her, her eyes closed as tears coursed down her cheeks. "I was not supposed to know it lived, but the wet nurse who was going to take little Emily away became ill and...and there was no one to nurse it but me for three days. I grew attached, realized I couldn't live without my child, that I'd sacrifice *everything*. But Hugh said my reputation would not survive, and that without that, I might as well be dead." She dropped her hands and stared at the sky and Phoebe, who'd tried so desperately for a child for so many years, felt a deep and primal tug for this foolish, deluded schoolgirl who, like her, had thought she was in love with Wentworth.

"Hugh took your child away?"

"He arranged it, yes." Miss Redding stared at her feet, before glancing up. "What could he do but find a good home for her? I am not yet twenty and must find a husband for we are not wealthy, and he is concerned about my future. With a child, that would of course not be possible, and not only would I be socially ostracized, but Emily would be too. But oh, sometimes I wish I were dead."

Phoebe frowned. Ada looked even younger with her face pink and puffed from crying. She did a quick mental calculation. So Ada had been Wentworth's plaything when he'd been playing with his cousin's wife: Phoebe. No doubt he nightly congratulated himself on his prowess in luring the innocent child into his bed—or wherever the deed was done—and then foisting a child on her, believing it wouldn't be long before he'd impregnate Phoebe with the heir who would give him the keys to Blinley Manor. Oh, how she loathed him.

"When was your child born?"

"Eight months and three days ago. Hugh won't tell me where Emily is, except to say that she's with a family who loves her and not in the Foundling Home, which was my greatest fear." The girl slanted a look at Phoebe. "Hugh said you were good at the voice and mannerisms of a lady. That you were Lady Cavanaugh's lady's maid. You'd have seen Mr Wentworth often, then. I wonder if you ever heard him mention me."

"Oh, I barely saw Mr Wentworth," Phoebe said quickly. "I came to work for my mistress only a short while ago. Of course, I heard her speak of him, and I know the ill he did her, but I know nothing about him other than that." No, the last thing Phoebe wanted was to be quizzed, or inadvertently reveal something she ought not to about her own shameful past with the odious creature who had done so much harm to both her and Miss Redding.

Miss Redding looked disappointed. "I loved him, you know," she whispered, plucking a leaf from the tree against which she rested. "I never would have done what I did had he not told me he would marry me as soon as he could extricate himself from a certain difficulty—a woman who had a hold on him, he said, and whom he had to kindly let down since they'd known one another for many years. He said he'd obtain a special licence and we would elope."

Phoebe bridled. Was this the way he spoke about her? She was about to speak when Miss Wentworth said, studying her fingernails, "I thought he was talking about Lady Cavanaugh but..." she hiccupped "...I later learned it was much worse than that, and that's why there's no point in my brother thinking he can force Wentworth to do the honorable thing."

At Phoebe's puzzled look, Miss Redding replied, "Wentworth is married already."

A sudden rushing in Phoebe's ears made her grip an overhanging tree branch to steady herself. "Married?" She shook her head. "You can't be right. I knew nothing... " She corrected herself, quickly. "I'm sure my mistress knew nothing. Why, she hoped to marry him, you know, because it was her dying husband's wish that she keep the estate in safe hands. You know Lord Cavanaugh's heir was an imbecile. Yes, I speak frankly to you for you have spoken so frankly to me. My mistress was at the mercy of her husband's desire for her to..." She floundered. She couldn't say marry when that made no sense, and she could hardly admit the truth of Ulrick's sordid little plan—which Phoebe went along with so willingly she was now ashamed to admit—to this chit of a girl.

Ada took this in with a small frown, but without puzzling it out too much she shook her head. "Mr Wentworth married a woman some years ago, only he's kept it a secret, and he's been paying her to keep silent. I wonder if she'll keep silent now he's inheriting Lord Cavanaugh's estate and title. What woman wouldn't want to be a duchess and live on an estate attended by hundreds of servants?"

Phoebe could think of one, but instead she asked, "Are you sure Mr Wentworth is married?" She simply couldn't reconcile this piece of news. "With all due respect, my mistress would have known this. You surely can't know for *certain*. He'd never have told you such a thing, especially if he's paying his true wife to keep silent, as you said."

"His manservant took a liking to me. He told me Mr Wentworth was already married, and made me promise I must not ever reveal that he'd told me, or else he'd lose his job and a lot more besides. He was frightened, I see now, but he was a decent man and no doubt he could see that Mr Wentworth had designs on me that could not be honorably followed through." Miss Redding managed a wan smile.

"You knew Collins? Goodness, you must have..."

"Gone often to Mr Wentworth's lodgings? Yes." Miss Redding sighed. "I was still at Miss Wilkins Seminary in Kensington when I met him after I dropped my handkerchief on the pavement, and he seized it up and returned it to me. I remember the look we shared and the admiration on his face before I received a note a few minutes later asking me to meet him."

Phoebe stared. "Why, that must have been years ago."

"Three years ago. He was mad for me, and I was mad for him. He attended an Assembly near where I lived so he could meet my brother but the meeting didn't go well, he said. He told me he'd need more time to win Hugh over before we could be wed. Yes, I was flattered by his attentions—"

"But you were a schoolgirl!"

"But soon I'd be out and looking for a husband. I was a foolish child who thought I'd beat all my schoolmates to the altar. But look what happened to me? I was led like a lamb to my fate. And now I wish I were dead."

"Wouldn't you rather you had your revenge on Mr Wentworth?"

She'd thought that Miss Redding, a girl of such fire and vulnerability, would either return a vigorous *yes* or burst into tears once more. Instead, Ada said, rather listlessly, "If it could be done, I would like to see Mr Wentworth brought down, though once I'd have given my life for him."

"Just as you would happily sacrifice it now for the unhappiness he's caused you."

Miss Redding shrugged again. "It can't be done. Mr Wentworth is too cunning. My brother can't touch him. No one can. He's now Lord Cavanaugh, and he's bent on apprehending Lady Cavanaugh, or should I say, the widowed Lady Cavanaugh who killed her husband, though no doubt he's secretly pleased to have his cousin dead else he'd not be enjoying his title and estate."

It was hard for Phoebe to listen to this. "Lady Cavanaugh was my mistress, and she did not murder her husband," she said hotly. "He forced her hand around the paper knife he then drove into his heart."

Miss Redding sent her a level look. "How do you know this?"

"I saw it."

"And Mr Wentworth observed that you'd seen it?"

"Yes, and that's why he'll kill me if he finds me.

"So you escaped, fearing your life was in danger, and my brother picked you up on the road?"

Phoebe nodded. "That's right. Just as I told you earlier. Now my greatest wish is to see my mistress exonerated, which in turn will mean I am safe in my own right." She looked meaningfully at Miss Redding. "And you wish to see Mr Wentworth exposed. Not for what he did to you as that would be ruinous to you, but to ensure the world knows he's a married man with a wife he chooses not to acknowledge." She shook her head, her mind whirling. All these years Phoebe had been consorting with this man she'd thought loved her, when, in fact, he was married.

"We must find his wife," she said, with rising conviction. "That is the only way. We must find out who she is and where she lives."

All Phoebe's earlier anger, uncertainty, and despair were swept away by this newfound information. At last, she had the means to expose Wentworth for the scoundrel he really was.

For if Wentworth were keeping a wife secret, who knew what other secrets he was guarding at the cost of his newfound position?

12

Hugh was feeling decidedly guilty when he stopped to greet Phoebe under a pear tree, having seen her alone as he'd brought his horse up the road by the bend near the river on his return from the village. She was wearing the new dress she'd just bought. It was simple and becoming, but when he drew closer and could see the signs of wear proclaiming it was so obviously secondhand, he felt a pang of remorse for the cavalier way he'd dismissed her when his sister had arrived earlier than expected.

He glanced about him and was glad to see no sign of Ada. No doubt she was devouring her romance novel by that Jane Austen woman she seemed so infatuated with. If Hugh took Phoebe into the woods, Ada would not miss him if he were gone another twenty minutes.

The need to atone was very strong.

"I'm sorry for this morning, Phoebe," he said when he drew level, leaning down from the saddle and stroking her cheek. "I slighted you and that was wrong." He smiled, indicating the thickening forest on the other side of the hedge with a look. "Come with me?"

She took a step back at his approach, jutted out her chin and ran her hands down her dress. "I suppose you feel that my accompanying you to the woods is the least you deserve in view of your generosity."

His dismounted, taking her hands, feeling the cad he knew he was.

"I was too quick to say the things I did in front of my sister and, it's true, I'm too eager to enjoy your company now that I see you on your own." He hoped his smile conveyed the forgiveness he craved. "You drive me wild with desire, Phoebe."

The look in her eye did not soften. "You were indeed quick to remind me of my inferior station, sir, and you are very quick to reinforce the gratitude you expect from me."

"Phoebe, I truly am sorry." And he was. "I was a boor. I admit it. A thoughtless boor."

"But now you think your honeyed words can make everything all right. I'm not good enough to be in the same room with your sister, but you can have me at will. It's true you've bought me dresses and given me food to eat in return for what I've given you. But...what security do I have?"

He shrugged. "I *will* look after you, I've told you. I'm sorry I offended you. Would you like another new dress? I shall send a message around to the village dressmaker—"

"Stop! I'm not a lightskirt, a Cyprian, or whatever they're called. You cheapen me to say such things, when the truth is that I would never have given myself to you had I not felt a strong desire to enjoy that which you enjoy. Even if my very life depended on it. I am not that sort of woman."

He seized her hands and brought her knuckles up to his lips. "You *really* had feelings that matched mine? I'd never have guessed! Well, that's music to my ears, even if I'm not the first."

"Do you want me to slap you?" She shuddered, and to his astonishment, raised a pair of eyes that shone with tears. "No, you are not the first, but you are the first to whom I've given myself with little in the way of cajoling. There! Perhaps that massages your pride."

She glanced over her shoulder at the house as he took her hand, saying, "Come, Phoebe, walk with me."

"To the woods?"

"To somewhere you and I can be alone. Nothing more."

"I have little choice since you're already marching me there."

He squeezed her hand tighter. He liked her spirit. She was unlike any young woman he'd ever met.

When they were deep amidst the spreading oaks, he suspected a more gentle mood had overtaken her. She was gazing at the spreading branches above their heads, her expression thoughtful. The pale sun that penetrated the dense canopy highlighted the softness of her features. She was beautiful.

"Tell me about yourself, Phoebe," he coaxed. She'd mentioned she came from a harsher part of the country. Her accents were so contrived it was impossible to place her. "We've not spent enough time getting to know who we truly are. I've thought long and hard about that this morning after I realized how unbecoming my conduct was toward you."

Her hand in his did not stiffen as she walked, but her tone remained distant. "I come from by the sea where the cliffs plunge into the waters, and smugglers ply a healthy trade. This is a gentler part of the world," she remarked.

"Yet it has not been so kind to you, has it?"

She stopped and turned. "It has not."

"I will protect you, Phoebe," he promised, drawing her into his arms and meaning what he said. "I've been many things I should not have been, but one thing I do promise you is my protection."

"You do?"

He drew back to look at her, offended by the skepticism in her tone. "Have I not promised it from the moment I rescued you? And I have followed through. You will accompany me to London, as we agreed when we spoke of it. I thought you were excited at—"

"The prospect of being your mistress?"

"Better that than the maidservant in danger, surely?"

She shrugged. "You think I'm giving up nothing to be your...paramour?"

He considered this. "You've told me you have no family. You fear discovery. I thought you considered my proposition with no misgivings. Particularly since you gave me reason to think you cared for me."

He couldn't make out the look she sent him and then realization struck. "You've been disappointed before, haven't you? That's why you don't trust that my word is good?"

She gave a small nod. "It's true; I have been disappointed before, but I do trust your word."

"Who was this man who let you down, Phoebe? You've never said his name. This protector of yours...he promised to protect you and then didn't?"

"He promised a great many things." She shook her head, then raised her arms and twined them around his neck, wordlessly resting her head against his chest.

He stroked her hair, the comfort he felt suddenly making him realize how ill at ease he'd felt until now. Having her forgiveness meant more to him than he'd believed. "You can feel safe with me, Phoebe."

The ground beneath them was soft, and he drew her down beside him, sitting with his back against the trunk and one arm around her shoulders. Gently he kissed her brow. Her eyes were closed, but when she smiled, a great spreading happiness seemed to infect his veins. He turned a little, and she opened her eyes, her lips parting so that instinctively he drew closer and kissed her.

Her mouth flowered beneath his, and he deepened the kiss, stroking her cheek with one hand while his other slipped beneath her bodice to cup her breast. He expected her to open her eyes in outrage and push his hand away, but instead, she yielded to him, her body shifting to accommodate him in the soft hollow of earth beneath them while her mouth grew hungrier.

The lust he'd felt earlier raised its nagging head, and he

checked himself once more, not wanting to proceed if there were any hesitation on her part, but she seemed under the same spell. She didn't protest when he took the hem of her dress and slowly raised it, watching her carefully to gauge her reaction.

Above them, the sky winked blue, glimpsed beneath the dense canopy of the forest.

Hugh broke contact to shrug off his coat. He laid it down, drawing Phoebe up and onto her knees. "You don't want to spoil your new dress," he whispered. "Perhaps you'd better take it off."

Her eyes widened. "But then I'd be..."

"All but naked," he supplied. "That is, unless we remove your petticoats and chemise and corset." Just saying it made him as hard as a rock. The idea was as intoxicating as it was novel. Imagine! He would see her naked. In the daylight. He'd never seen a woman in all her glory quite like that, but now he wanted Phoebe 'just like that' more than he'd wanted anything before.

"I'll help you." He was already shimmying the garment up over her body by the time her smile popped out, her eyes shining at the wickedness of it all. That was good. He didn't like to think she might not be an equally willing partner when it came to pushing the boundaries quite so far.

"And what of you, my Lord?" she whispered with an impish look at his nether regions.

"Oh, my pleasure will be seeing you revealed, layer by layer, like some tasty morsel. My *ultimate* pleasure can wait."

The undergarments she wore were not the fine linen of a lady. Somehow the utilitarian petticoat, gleaned from the miller's wife's trunk, rough and coarse, struck him with guilt.

"I shall buy you the finery you deserve, Phoebe. Without the expense of a wife, you shall be clothed as you'd wish."

"And when you take a wife I'll go naked?"

He laughed. She was smiling, teasing him for she knew how it was. "I'll always want you, Phoebe."

"Always?"

"And how do you know that?" she asked. But when he pulled

her final layer over her head—her chemise, having just unlaced her corset—he could not speak. She was exquisite. Her soft, pert breasts were revealed for the first time, unbound and in all their glory, their small pink buds an invitation for him to swoop and take into his mouth. But equally in evidence was the gentle undulation of her belly, which tapered into a pair of creamy thighs at whose juncture a thatch of dark hair hid a world of hidden delights.

"Because I'll never get enough of this, my darling," he murmured at last, sliding down to take her right nipple into his mouth while his other hand contoured her belly before sliding between her legs.

She was already wet but she gasped when he touched her, and he could hear the smile in her voice as she stroked his head. "Music to my ears, of course, Mr Redding, but that is what gentlemen say when they want a lady, is it not?" She shivered as he got to work pleasuring her, adding, "You've not had too much of a struggle to get me where you want me, so you needn't say things you don't mean."

"I should be hurt, Phoebe." He chuckled as he sucked at her nipple, rolling it over his tongue, loving her small, involuntary gasps and jerks as he found just the place to tease her. "You seem to think I don't mean what I say. It's clear that you more than just like me. If you hadn't said it so plainly, I don't need any more evidence than this."

He rose above her for a moment to meet her eye while he unbuttoned himself. "Tell me again. I want to hear you say that you want me as much as I want you."

"Only if you keep doing to me what you were doing before," she groaned, relaxing back against the tree and closing her eyes.

"There, see what you do to me." Hugh kissed her mouth as she positioned his long body against her curves, guiding her hand to his member. He gasped again, then growled, "I'm ready to explode...but only when you've had your pleasure. I want you to want more, Phoebe. I want *you*!"

It was pure delight. A wicked, sensual, carnal encounter spontaneously taken beneath the trees, and into which she entered with as much enthusiasm as he, despite the morning's poor start.

Carnal delights with Phoebe were greater than any pleasure he'd ever experienced.

13

Smoothing down the skirts of her dress, which Hugh had helped her into just a moment before, Phoebe watched Hugh ride into the distance. She was deeply unsettled. This was not supposed to happen. Not this fusing of the heart, as if he'd invaded her very being. He was a man, and men had only used her in the past to further their ends, while she'd been forced to compromise her heart and body to retain a tenuous security.

What's more, he'd belittled her this morning. Was it the start of something more insidious? Experience with men had taught her that any initial hope or pleasure would soon be snuffed out. That would inevitably happen with Mr Redding. They'd go to London, and soon he'd be squiring his sister to balls and assemblies where he'd meet the kind of woman he'd marry.

She didn't doubt that he believed her exquisite. Men were like that. They said what they needed to say to get what they wanted. As soon as Mr Redding felt the pressure to take a wife, Phoebe would be discarded.

She closed her eyes and clenched her hands into fists as she strove for the strength she'd one day need to summon.

Before that time, though, she'd need to shore up her position so that when Mr Redding left, she'd not be entirely destitute.

Unfortunately, she was doing what she knew she should not. Her heart was not just warming to him, but regularly throughout the day her mind would thrill at the memory of the wild and wanton sensations he evoked in her.

She knew it was time to leave this place, and hoped she'd feel safer living in some small cottage in London where no one would know her.

She'd thought long and hard about Miss Redding's revelation regarding Wentworth's secret marriage, and had decided it was not something she intended to bring up with Mr Redding. They'd not spoken of Wentworth in days. In fact, Phoebe intended never speaking of him again. Ada Redding's words had struck a chord. It would be better never to mention Wentworth's name in the hope he would eventually fade from memory. Phoebe's ideas of bringing him to justice could never be realized without sacrificing herself, now that it had been made so clear there was not a single person who would vouch for her if she were caught and faced trial.

Raising her eyes to the blue she glimpsed beneath the canopy, she ran her hand down her belly and felt a shiver of apprehension.

She could never be Lady Cavanaugh and continue to enjoy her freedom. She could never be a *lady* again.

But she could be happy. At least for now, and that was better than nothing.

If life had taught her anything, it was that its few moments of happiness were fleeting.

She started to walk back to the house, deep in thought, her body still humming with the pleasurable sensations her new lover had unleashed in her while her mind ran over the probabilities.

She would have to live as a lower-class woman with no reputation, when she was used to privilege. When Mr Redding tired of her or took a wife, she'd be discarded.

That meant she had to make the most of what generosity he was prepared to extend her. She needed to ensure a measure of future security before she could give sway to her heart, which was proving as foolishly susceptible as it had when Wentworth had wooed her in such a calculating fashion.

She was barely into the house when Ada's loud whisper in the gloomy corridor took her by surprise.

"Phoebe, come here! Quickly, before my brother sees us!"

Startled, Phoebe was pulled into the storeroom, Miss Redding closing the door behind them.

"I've had an idea," she said, then, in more disappointed tones when Phoebe didn't reply, "Our conversation this morning has given me a brainstorm. Listen to me, Phoebe. You want to see Mr Wentworth brought low on account of your mistress, just as I want the same thing. I'm determined to do it, but I can't do it alone."

Phoebe could see where this was going and shook her head. "Despite what I said this morning, I've changed my mind. I can't help you with regard to Wentworth, Miss Redding," she said firmly. "Your brother is right. You must forget about Mr Wentworth. I'm very sorry about what he did to you—"

"But, for the sake of my *child*—"

"Your child would have no future branded as a bastard."

Miss Redding gasped, but Phoebe went on quickly. "Your brother was doing the only thing he could by the two of you: ensuring you both had a future. You must not think of Mr Wentworth or your child again. You are not yet twenty, and you have your life ahead of you. It's full of possibilities as long as you can put the past behind you."

Phoebe's hand strayed to her belly, and fear gripped her by the throat. *Please, dear Lord, don't let me be with child*, she thought. *I don't think I could bear to lose a babe like poor Ada, and I do not have the wherewithal to see justice done by Wentworth.*

In the ribbon of light that sliced across the small utility room, Phoebe saw the pain in her eyes yet Miss Redding was not going to let it go.

"You must help me find out who the woman is to whom Mr Wentworth is legally married. Don't you see, if it were made public, he'd be forced to live with the common creature and at least that would be some consolation. Please, find out who she is and entice her to come forward. If he has treated her as badly as he has treated me and your mistress, then she'll be only too pleased to inform the world of the kind of man he is. It's not full justice he'd be served, but at least it's something."

"A fine plan, Miss Redding, but how do you suppose *I* can learn the whereabouts of his wife? I'm—"

"An ignorant servant, but Phoebe, my brother was speaking about you earlier, and he is full of admiration for your ability to mimic your betters. Why, he declared you could fool a duke! Therefore, if you can as easily deport yourself with the aristocracy as you can with the serving classes, then you can be a spy. Search out Wentworth's contacts. I can help you! I know names, Phoebe, but *I* can't do it. I've my reputation to think of, and I cannot go places alone as you can. I'd be recognized in some quarters—certainly as an unmarried woman in need of a chaperone."

"And so would I!" Phoebe shook her head. She was not entertaining any of it. Her mind was made up. There would be no fair trial for her if she fell into Wentworth's clutches, and word from Mrs Withins was that he'd offered a handsome reward for anyone whose information led to Lady Cavanaugh's arrest.

Thank the good Lord Mr Redding would be taking her to London before the end of the week.

"Wentworth and his staff wouldn't recognize you either as a servant or a lady. You said it yourself! Why, you were only in your mistress's employ for a month, and you say you met him but a couple of times."

Phoebe bit her lip. "I can't do it. He would recognize me. I'm sure of it."

Ada looked fierce. "That's not what you told my brother. You're just saying it because you're afraid."

"I *am* afraid, Ada. Mr Wentworth is a horrible man. I saw what he did to my mistress. No, I'm not going anywhere near him."

"I'm not suggesting you consort with him. Just that you quiz his circle: friends or his aide de compte. I know where to find Collins. He served Mr Wentworth during the war and for five years after that. He was kind to me, and I think he feared Mr Wentworth, but he would do it for me—he'd tell me where to find Wentworth's wife. And then I'd tell you, and you could seek her out."

When Miss Redding gripped Phoebe's hand and begged her once more, Phoebe knew it really was time to leave. Agreeing to Miss Redding's request that she move in more aristocratic circles would be like signing her death warrant.

"HUGH, I'VE BEEN ORDERING MY THOUGHTS SINCE I came here."

Hugh glanced up from the writing desk in the parlor, surprised to see that his sister's usual vacant look was replaced by an almost mutinous expression. Ada, before her tragedy, had been neither vacant nor fiery. Just a sweet, pliable girl with an occasional tendency to speak her mind to her brother.

He blinked a couple of times, trying to reconcile for a moment just who this new young woman before him actually was.

"Ordering your thoughts, have you?" he repeated.

Ordering his thoughts was just what he'd been trying to do, but the book in front of him was still at the same page as it had been an hour before, and Hugh was as far advanced in deciding what to do as he had been when...

When his life had been turned upside down. He blinked again. Good Lord, he couldn't work himself out.

"Hugh, are you listening to me?"

He nodded.

"When I first got here, I thought some mad impulse had taken possession of you to lease a house like this. Why, there's nothing here for miles around."

He thought he wouldn't push the point that Wentworth lived

only one hour's walk north. Not when Ada seemed more in possession of her faculties than she had in a very long time.

No, he'd not bring up Wentworth ever again, for the more time passed, the more he realized that pursuing Wentworth was not going to achieve satisfaction for his sister.

Right now, she looked exactly as any unspoiled young woman of his acquaintance might look, and he was certain she could get away with her sins and make a fine marriage were it not for Ada's own insistence that she never intended looking at another man again.

For the hundredth time, Hugh wished he'd not sought the counsel of their Aunt Belcher who, while taking matters in hand, and looking after Ada before and after the unfortunate business, considered Ada a disgrace and never lost an opportunity to tell the girl her thoughts.

"I've been talking to Phoebe—"

"Why?"

She raised her chin. "I know what she is to you, Hugh. Don't pretend I'm the pristine innocent I was before..." her eyes flashed before she continued, "...I met Mr Wentworth."

"Don't speak of him, Ada."

And don't speak of Phoebe like that either, he thought angrily as his sister's words rang in his ears: *"what she is to you..."* What *was* she to Hugh? A sweet, immoral creature whose freely offered charms were a marvelous diversion?

No, she was more than that. For the past hour, he'd been staring at the blank pages of a book, trying to come up with some practical reason to extend his tenure in this house where he could be free to follow his heart. In London, he'd have to squire his sister around; pay calls on various notables. In short, he'd have less time to spend with Phoebe, and right now, that's all he wanted to do.

Their lovemaking still had that illicit edge to it. He'd taken her in joyous impulsiveness in the still room, the parlor, and finally beneath the spreading branches of a beech forest. The only place they'd not consummated their passion was in a proper bed. God, he wanted a whole night with her. He wanted to wake up with her beside him and know she'd be there when he turned in for the night. Like a properly sanctioned union.

Sanctioned? That was not a desire to articulate when it could never be. He shook his head to clear the nonsense from it. Phoebe might be clever at pretending to be a lady, but he must always remember that she wasn't.

"Like you said, Hugh, Phoebe is an utterly marvelous actress. Why, were it not for her dress, I could have imagined she really was a fine lady. So my idea is this, Hugh. Are you listening?"

Hugh focused his attention on Ada once more. Her talk was extraordinary. Well-brought-up young girls like his sister should know nothing about women like Phoebe.

"What is your idea, Ada?"

"If you stop sounding so condescending, I might tell you."

He resisted the impulse to reprove her for speaking to her brother in such a fashion, for it was pleasing she was finally breaking free of the shame and sorrow that had made her a shadow of the girl she'd been.

"Wentworth was married before I knew him. Yes, you have every reason to look shocked. I was when I learned it." Ada sent him a look of triumph as she put her hands on the desk and leaned close to him. "Mr Wentworth is married, and now he is Lord Cavanaugh. I imagine he's doing all he can to keep his first marriage secret since clearly it's one he wishes dissolved."

"Good Lord, Ada, why didn't you tell me this before?"

"If you remember, Hugh, I couldn't talk to you about *anything*, much less Mr Wentworth after what he did to me." She took a deep breath. "Yes, I know you felt partly responsible. After all, you've tried to teach me right from wrong after Mama and Papa died, but when it came to Mr Wentworth, I lost sight of all common sense. He was so utterly charming and believable. I truly thought we would be married. But then I learned to my horror he was married already, only it was too late, and I couldn't tell you. But now I know it's important to find out who his wife is so she can announce it to the world. She's probably some low-class woman he wishes to keep in ignorance of his new status. He probably abandoned her years ago, though she could be dead, of course."

"But what has Phoebe to do with all this?"

Ada smiled. It was the first time Hugh had seen the glow that transformed her from a rather wan little creature into an extremely pretty young woman. If she'd glowed like this for Mr Wentworth, Hugh could well imagine the effect she'd have had on him. He clenched his fists into tight balls.

"Hugh, Phoebe is a marvelous actress and clearly able to convince anyone she's a lady. As a servant, she'd be able to question Mr Wentworth's staff on their level. But she'd also be able to deport herself in good company. I feel sure she's the best person to discover who it was Mr Wentworth married all those years ago. Please, Hugh?"

"I don't know what you're pleading for me to do, Ada, when you've just said Phoebe is in the best position to find out about Wentworth's wife, though you know I don't approve of you having anything to do with her." He felt a traitor, but it was the truth.

"You need to give Phoebe some money and some clothes, so she can do what she needs to do to discover Wentworth's wife and then expose her to the world. Phoebe only has two dresses."

"And one of them cost me a pretty penny."

"You had to give her something in return, though," he sister said reasonably and without a blush. "I'm well aware that everything in this world is a trade. And now I'm trading with you: do as I ask and I'll meekly return to Aunt Belcher's and let you live your life as you choose."

Hugh shook his head, not in the least liking to hear his sister talk like this. "I don't think Phoebe will be too enamored of the idea. She's afraid."

Ada sighed. "I know. She didn't want to do it when I asked her, but I thought you'd be able to persuade her. Offer her something.

Dresses, money. A woman like that would never say no to such enticements."

"I'll thank you not to speak of her in that manner, Ada," Hugh said grimly, not liking to hear his own uncharitable reflections articulated by his sister. "Regardless of what you might think of me, Ada, I am trying to do what's best for Phoebe, just as I once did for you. She has no family or friends and no funds since she fled Blinley Manor. I can understand she'd be afraid of having anything to do with the household after witnessing what she did."

"You mean the terrible murder Lady Cavanaugh committed? I've heard it's not the first time Lady Cavanaugh tried to kill her husband. I know Phoebe is full of loyal vengeance, but the duchess sounds like a terrible woman. The worst kind! She was immoral and devious, and she had numerous lovers behind her husband's back. Not just Wentworth. Don't look at me like that. I overheard the servants talking about it. She will hang when they find her, won't she?"

Hugh felt uncomfortable in the face of his sister's blind acceptance of Lady Cavanaugh's guilt, considering Phoebe's insistence that her mistress had been wronged.

But then, Phoebe's faithfulness was one of the reasons he loved her.

He hoped she'd be as faithful a mistress to him as she had been a faithful servant to Lady Cavanaugh.

"So you'll offer Phoebe something to do as you ask?" Ada was like a dog with a bone. "Tell her you'll buy her a necklace. She won't be able to resist that. Women like that need to take what they can get, when they can, so they have some security for their future, since she knows she can't marry you."

"Stop!" Hugh put up his hand and strove for forbearance.

Surprised, Ada looked at him.

Hugh closed his eyes and drew in a breath. "You've just said Phoebe is faithful. It's true. She's a good woman, and I don't like to hear you speak in this manner. You should not!"

"It's only the truth."

"Phoebe does not need to shore up her future for I have promised to protect her, look after her. We are going to London at the end of the week, and you are going to Aunt Belcher's." He sent her a warning look when it looked like she might interrupt. "After that, I don't want you ever to mention Phoebe again."

"You're getting rid of her?"

"Lord, no!" He was surprised at what a jolt his sister's question occasioned. "To the contrary, I'm very much looking forward to the future we will fashion together in the anonymity of London, but she is not someone you are to mention, ever again, for you should know nothing about Phoebe and women like her."

"Goodness, Hugh, you do sound fierce. Does she feel as strongly about you in return?"

Hugh wished he could have responded with greater alacrity. He certainly wished he'd not hesitated so long that his sister eyed him with skeptical satisfaction.

The truth was, he'd not yet won Phoebe's heart. It shouldn't matter. But it did.

14

So now she had a walking gown, full dress for evening entertainments, and a promenade gown. She had a shawl, a pelisse, a pair of boots, dancing slippers, and an assortment of feathers and pins to dress her hair. It wasn't nearly enough, but with imagination, she could probably equip herself for most events a lady or a servant might attend.

Phoebe stared through the window of her attic room at the patchwork of fields disappearing into the distance, and tried to feel hopeful for the future.

Instead, a pall of gloom had settled on her shoulders.

Hugh had been away for several days. He'd taken Ada to see some people. It was all rather mysterious, and she wondered if it had something to do with the child Ada had so reluctantly been parted from, though surely Hugh would not sanction his sister visiting her illegitimate child.

The truth was, Phoebe was starting to feel vulnerable. She had come to enjoy feeling safe with a man who made her come alive, even if the surroundings were not ideal, but now she feared the awful wrench that would inevitably occur when Hugh decided to part with her, or Phoebe had no choice but to leave.

Sighing, her mind filled again with the image of Hugh; of his smile, his humor, his adherence to a strict moral code.

He'd been assiduous in not having relations with Phoebe under the same roof while Ada was here. *Clearly, he regarded Ada as a paragon of virtue, despite his sister's fall from grace which was interesting,* Phoebe thought, with a touch of irony.

He'd been assiduous in following through with his promise to equip Phoebe with a decent wardrobe in the week since Ada had arrived and this, she knew, was in preparation to set her up in a townhouse in St John's Wood, or some vicinity in easy proximity to his townhouse when he returned to London.

A few months ago, the idea would have been laughable, shocking, untenable.

But that was before she was branded a murderess with no means of a fair trial.

No, in London Phoebe would start a new life as a fully-fledged fallen woman, but the strange fact was that she didn't mind the idea of sharing her life with a man she felt strongly about and who'd pledged to look after her. Who'd have thought her damaged heart was capable of such feeling...still?

The unfortunate fact was, though, that Phoebe would much prefer to be his wife. Yes, she'd once been Lady Cavanaugh and mistress of several estates, but she'd be far happier as the wife of a man of more moderate means who simply loved her.

Always, though, was that lurking doubt. Would he still love her if he knew the truth about her? That she was, in fact, the murderous, adulterous, Lady Cavanaugh?

Listlessly, Phoebe trailed to the window and wondered when Hugh would return. He'd been vague, saying there were matters concerning Ada to attend to, and he really couldn't say. He'd kissed her affectionately, holding her tightly against him in a parting farewell that spoke volumes about the state of his feeling for her. And hers for him. His eyes had been filled with genuine regard and genuine regret at having to be parted from her.

Now, as she saw a carriage crest the hill coming in their direction, she felt a surge of hope and quickly dashed to the chest at the foot of her bed to change her dress.

Hugh was back, and she wanted to look as charming and desirable for him as was possible. Quickly she combed her hair, pinning it into an ensemble her own maid had perfected with her quick and nimble hands. She wondered where Barbara was now, and whether her maid believed her mistress Lady Cavanaugh guilty of murdering Ulrick. Barbara had been a dour retainer, and there'd never been much intimacy between them during the eight months the woman had been in her employ though Barbara had always seemed loyal. Phoebe suspected her husband had ordered their housekeeper, Mrs Fenton, to inform the servants that no conversation beyond the necessary was to be entered into with their mistress. It was one of his many ways of keeping Phoebe restrained beneath his roof.

It didn't take Phoebe long before she was satisfied by her appearance. The lack of fear, and the increasing joy with which she received Hugh had erased the fine lines of worry around her eyes of which she'd become so conscious.

Pushing the ivory comb into her hair to properly secure it, she went to the window, her heart beating with excitement as she threw wide the casement, eagerly anticipating greeting Hugh as he stepped from the carriage.

Instead, it was Sir Roderick's carriage below, and there was Sir Roderick stepping out, leaning heavily on his silver-topped cane but glancing up at the house and catching sight of Phoebe.

She ducked her head back in and ran to her iron cot against the wall, alarm making her weak-legged. She'd been in full view for less than a second. She had to believe he'd not recognized her.

The casement was still open as she heard him rapping on the door before Mrs Withins opened it.

Phoebe dare not be caught out, but she had to hear what had brought him to the house and be ready to flee, if she had to. With quiet stealth, she returned to the window where she stood just out of sight while the sounds of the visitor conversing with the housekeeper filtered up to her.

It was as dire as she had feared. A warrant was out for Lady Cavanaugh's arrest, and a recent sighting confirmed the belief she was still in the area. Thereafter followed a description of the "dangerous murderess" as she was referred to. A description that was frighteningly similar to that of Phoebe when she was dressed according to her station.

But would Mrs Withins draw any parallels? She wasn't particularly intelligent or observant as far as Phoebe could see. No, she'd never think of low-born, immoral, lazy Phoebe in the same way as highborn Lady Cavanaugh. Would she?

She heard Mrs Withins tutting and then her wheezing voice. "Ah, but it ain't surprisin', Sir Roderick, fer we've long 'eard the stories of Lady Cavanaugh. She's a wicked, wanton creature an' all us servants are shocked with the tales of 'er doins'. No, I ain't seen 'er, but I'd be the first ter tell yer so's I could see 'er face justice. What's the world comin' to if a 'usband can't be safe in 'is own bed?"

Phoebe could hardly bear to hear any more, though she waited until she heard the sound of the carriage departing. With a sigh of relief she collapsed on her bed, but in less than half an hour the crunch of wheels on gravel had her again dashing in terror to the window, prepared to flee with just the clothes on her back. Had someone come to apprehend her?

However, it was Hugh and her heart surged with joy to see him. Not caring what Mrs Withins might think, she ran down the stairs and out into the garden where she threw herself into his arms the moment he issued from his carriage.

"Good Lord, Phoebe, what's this?" he asked in some alarm, but she stopped his questions with a kiss.

"I don't care what anyone thinks. I've missed you so much!" she cried when he broke away, staring down at her with some bemusement.

A slow, spreading smile transformed his face. "Did you really, Phoebe?"

"Yes, really. And not because you've bought me a new wardrobe, but because you do something to me here." She tapped her heart and took his arm, happily allowing him to lead her into the house. What did she care for appearances? Right now, her heart was filled with the simple pleasure of being once again in the company of the man who made her feel safe and loved. She wasn't going to dwell on her recent fright, and nor was she going to worry about what she must do for her own survival.

Hugh felt for her as she'd always wanted a man to feel for her. She could see it in his smile and the gentle way he cupped her cheek while he dipped his head to kiss her once more on the lips, this time gently but with great feeling, before they disappeared indoors.

Soon he would take her away from here, to the anonymity of the city where she'd be safe. One day, when the time was right, she'd reveal who she really was.

And then, *possibly*, he might make her his wife. It's what she wanted above all.

In the parlor, she looked inquiringly at him. "And where is your sister?"

A shadow crossed his face, and he took her hand. "Ada should not have come here. She ran away from her aunt's without a word, though I didn't know it."

"You've taken her back?"

"I'd never force her to remain with Aunt Belcher when she was so unhappy there." He smiled and put his finger to Phoebe's lips, tracing the curve with a look of bemusement. "By God but you're beautiful, Phoebe," he murmured. "There's another reason I was so eager to be rid of my sister, beloved though she is to me."

"And what might that be, sir?" Phoebe asked archly, though she knew the reason well enough, and her body was already melting at the thought of being in Hugh's arms and feeling his warm, naked body against hers.

And then she remembered the risks of bringing a bastard into the world, and her breath froze in her throat.

"What is it, Phoebe?"

She was surprised he was so observant. She tossed her head. "Nothing of any account. I think I heard Mrs Withins, that's all."

"You certainly don't like the woman, do you?"

"Not as much as she dislikes me."

"You'd like to be away from this place I take it."

"I would indeed! Far, far away! I can't wait to get to London."

"You know I'll look after you." He grasped her hands and brought her knuckles up to his lips. "You know you're safe with me. I shan't let anything happen to you, my love. Upon my honor, I swear it with my last breath."

She was astonished at his sudden fervor. No man had ever spoken to her of love and of putting her wellbeing to any amount of inconvenience.

"Will you, sir?"

"Hugh. Please call me Hugh. We're...lovers, Phoebe. Do you know what that means? You're mine, and I'm yours. I've never taken a mistress; I've never taken a lover. Never wanted to before I met you. I promise you that if you're not happy with the house I lease for you, I'll find you another. I want you to be happy, Phoebe."

He was leading her into the corridor as he spoke but now, instead of parting at the stairs, she to return to her servant's attic and him to his own quarters, he kept hold of her hand as he drew her toward his own chamber.

"No need to look so concerned." He grinned, loosening his cravat and unbuttoning his waistcoat as he put his hand on the doorknob. "The servants are two levels below us. Besides, they're very well aware of the state of affairs between us, and in a week, what will it matter to anyone but ourselves? We'll be in London, and you'll be ensconced in your own lover's bower. Why, look what you've done to me at the mere thought?"

The door was already closed behind them, and Hugh's breeches were off, his rampant manhood springing proudly free before them.

She looked from him, now almost naked, to the bed, and her body throbbed with desire. But acting on desire was a dire risk. No, she couldn't afford to conceive now. Her future was too uncertain.

"Yes, a real bed, my sweeting," he growled, sweeping her into his arms and depositing her on the mattress. "How's that for comfort?" His face was inches from hers as he caged her with his body. She could smell the fresh sweat from his recent ride overlaying the faint smell of sandalwood and leather.

Slowly, she raised her hand and traced the lines of his sinewy arms, trailing down his chest with her forefinger. He closed his eyes and gritted his teeth, but she could tell he was enjoying it.

"Do I please you?" he whispered.

"You please me," she responded softly, "but I am afraid..." She wasn't sure how to phrase this. A married woman was only good for producing children, so voicing concerns that regarded procreation hardly had its place.

His eyes kindled with a softness she'd not seen before. She could almost believe he cared for her concerns, and maybe he did. What did she know of men, after all? This wild romp with Hugh transcended the boundaries of her experience. She'd played the whore, and now suddenly she'd changed her mind. How could she put that into words? Yet the way he was looking at her now suggested he might care.

She cleared her throat. "I know we've been very...abandoned," she began. "And this has all taken me quite by surprise. I fled in fear, and I was rescued." She ran her forefinger the length of his finely chiseled nose while her heart flooded with gratitude and some other emotion she couldn't define. It couldn't be love. What did that feel like anyway?

"But I'm afraid of bearing a child and facing those consequences on my own." She squeezed shut her eyes, not sure what she'd see when she opened them. To her surprise: understanding and tenderness.

"You won't be alone, Phoebe. I promise you that. I love you too much. But you're right; it would not be fair either to you or a resulting child. I should know that, of course, in view of what Ada has gone through."

"Then what can be done?" she cried despairingly. "I must leave you—"

"Good Lord, there's everything to be done. Has no one ever spoken to you about such matters?" He frowned. "To be honest, I thought you had that side well under control, knowing I'm not your first."

Phoebe twisted her head to look at the wall and sighed. "I don't know a thing about it," she admitted miserably. "Just that I've never conceived. Perhaps I'm barren. But perhaps not, for contrary to what you might think, I'm not in the habit of throwing myself at men. My experience, I assure you, is limited. It's just...I would not bring a child into the world to bear such shame if we were not married."

"That's a conversation for another time. If I find you as sweet in a year as you are to me right now, perhaps a child would not be such a tragedy. Our royal family has dozens of bastards happily romping around, and no one seems to think any worse of them."

"What if you found a wife?"

A shadow of discomfort crossed his face. "I'm not looking for a wife, Phoebe. I've got you."

Very unsatisfactory. But not so his gentle stroking of her breasts.

"No need to look so concerned, my precious. I hear what you say, and I know what I need to do. Now, does that satisfy you?"

She was dubious. "I'm sure whatever it is, it won't satisfy *you*, sir."

"Ah, there are plenty of other ways you can satisfy me, although I'd like to add that seeing you take your own pleasure is immensely satisfying to me."

He rolled onto his back and pulled her on top of him so he could suckle her nipples. He was hard beneath her, and she wriggled down and without warning took him deeply into her mouth while gently playing with his balls.

"Oh my Lord, where did you learn that, Phoebe?"

She was hardly about to tell him: Wentworth. Wentworth was debauched. She'd not try half the things Wentworth would have her do to him—or that he liked to do to her. Then she shuddered with fear at the thought of what he might do to her now if he got the chance. It wouldn't be nice.

Mistaking her response for anticipation, Hugh gently rolled her over once more.

"I'm so close, but I'm desperate to taste all your charms, Phoebe dearest, before I bury myself in you."

Burrowing deeper into the bed, he parted her legs and gently touched his lips to her most intimate parts. "Like it?" he whispered before he ran his tongue the length of her cleft.

She gripped the sheets and tensed. "Oh, I didn't know..." She could feel the tension within her building with an intensity she'd never experienced. "Stop, Hugh. Stop!"

But he didn't. He kept kissing her, until she could bear it no longer, and with a great thrashing and moaning, she took her pleasure before she could stop him.

"So you did like that?" he asked with a wicked leer as he climbed back on top of her, entering her swiftly with a grunt of unadulterated pleasure.

Phoebe merely smiled her satisfaction. She might be sated, but not for long, as Hugh clearly was transported by his own heady pleasures as he thrust into her in smooth, rapidly increasing strokes.

Phoebe rode the storm, loving his total abandon, loving the pressure within her grow once again until he came with a great cry of triumph, true to his word as he withdrew just in time.

"Oh my sweet lord, Phoebe, but that was marvelous!" he

gasped. "I daresay the servants heard it all the way down in the basement. Well, it's time I took you away from this place where you feel the censure, and I can see you're so unhappy." He grinned, and Phoebe's heart contracted at the guileless look on his face. Wentworth was always so dismissive and self-satisfied after acts like this, declaring that if there wasn't an heir to be had after "that," then he didn't know what Phoebe's problem was.

She tensed at the thought of him. Sir Roderick was sniffing around the neighborhood; a bounty was on her head. She needed to leave.

"Let us go soon," she begged, and he nodded as he pulled on his breeches. Slanting a look at her, he said, "Why not tomorrow? You can wear that fetching new carriage dress you ordered, and we shall exit this part of the world as if you were my wife. Wouldn't that be novel?"

Alarmed, Phoebe sat up clutching the sheet to her chest. "No Hugh, I shan't leave dressed as a lady and nor with you. I won't be branded a whore to the entire district, but worse is the danger of being recognized."

"Come, Phoebe, you are my chosen," he said cajolingly. "Aren't you proud of the fact? It means you'll never have to curtsey to a demanding employer again. Wouldn't you love to see the expression on Mrs Withins's face?"

"But I *am* fallen. The very dirt beneath the feet of people like Mrs Withins. And when you tire of me, I shall be even lower than a servant. Destined for Hell, no less."

"Don't cry, Phoebe!" His light-heartedness was replaced by concern as he went to her and gathered her in his arms. "I'd never treat you so shabbily. You won't starve, whatever happens."

"Meaning, if you take a wife or tire of me."

"Please don't talk like that! I can be as loyal as the Duke of Clarence who has lived with his mistress and ten children for two decades or more." He started to button his waistcoat, warming to his theme. "And if you don't wish to travel in my carriage, then you can follow by post. See how willing I am to humor you?" Now fully dressed, he knelt by the bed and cupped her face, smiling. "Your happiness is paramount, Phoebe." For a moment, they stared at each other.

Then his kissed her on the forehead and was gone.

15

Phoebe stared down at the soft brown curls of her sleeping lover beside her, and her heart filled with love. And fear.

The little bower he'd leased for her on the outskirts of the metropolis was as charming as she could have wished. Hugh was certainly delighted by the arrangement. His desire for her seemed insatiable, and she responded with just as much ardor. Her heart had never been more engaged. Yes, she knew she'd never be redeemed, but what did that matter when the alternative was the noose. If she didn't think about her soul and the afterlife, she could take what happiness was offered. She'd had little enough of it in her lifetime.

She was astonished by the size of London. She'd never had a proper come-out. Her father had arranged her marriage with Ulrick when she was barely seventeen, delighted to avoid the cost of the wardrobe she'd have needed to find a husband, no doubt. And Ulrick had never taken her to town. He'd never taken her anywhere. Of course, she'd hated being so confined at the time, but now she was relieved to know she'd go unrecognized.

In the leafy suburb of St John's Wood, she had a comfortable house with a park across the road. She had a cook, a general maid, and her very own lady's maid. Hugh had been generous indeed, as well he might for he all but lived here himself. Initially, he'd indicated he might make his visits an irregular three or four days a week, but he'd rather established himself as part of the furniture, returning to stay the night, in between going to his club and attending to his other business.

Phoebe had no complaints. She was madly in love, and their increasing intimacy through such habitation gave her the greatest happiness.

All that was missing was a ring on her finger and a contract, sanctioned by the church, which would give her security should Hugh's interest wane. In every other respect, she was completely satisfied. She didn't need the title or status that went with her old life. In fact, she didn't even need to be acquitted. She was much happier living a more lowly existence with a kind man.

Hugh stirred and opened one sleepy eye, his grin broadening when he realized Phoebe was awake and watching him.

"Come here, wench," he mumbled fondly, drawing her down beside him so he could fondle her breasts. "Ah, you are missing me," he added as he drew his forefinger between her legs and felt the wetness. Immediately she felt his manhood pushing into her stomach, and a great surge of awareness flowed through her.

"You're insatiable," she chuckled, snuggling next to him and hooking a leg over his flanks. "And you seem to think I'm just here for the taking, Hugh Redding."

"Well, aren't you? That's why I've set you up so handsomely. I need to keep my beloved satisfied in all ways so your pretty blue eyes don't stray."

"And where would they stray, dearest? To the boot boy? Or the man who delivers the coal? It's not as if I'm surrounded by temptation."

Hugh cocked his head. "Do I interpret a desire for some more lively company?" Hugh rolled on top of her and put his forehead to hers, his expression concerned. "Are you lonely, Phoebe?"

"How could I be when we've been together like we have? I was just funning, Hugh!"

He seemed relieved. "That's good, for I do worry that when I'm gone — for I hate to tell you that I have to go away for a week very soon — you will be champing at the bit for diversion." Grinning, he pinched her bottom. "You're such a lively piece I have my work cut out to keep you occupied. Talking of which, where were we?" he asked, diving beneath the covers before his muffled voice emerged with, "Ah yes, between your legs."

And indeed, Phoebe would have admitted that in that moment, she'd never been happier or more content with her lot.

Four days later, though, with Hugh having been gone for two, she was as he'd suggested in his equine comparison, "champing at the bit," so that when her maid handed her a message, her heart raced with anticipation at the thought that it was from Hugh and he was returning early.

To her surprise, she discovered it was from Ada with a request to meet her in the little park opposite as soon as possible.

Quickly changing her dress and putting on a bonnet she'd happily dressed with floral blooms in the drawing room the previous week while Hugh had read the newspaper, the pair of them the picture of domestic bliss, Phoebe arrived at the entrance of the little, gated park wondering what on earth Ada wanted with her.

She smiled to see the young girl heavily veiled and asked, "Are you in disguise, Ada, because you don't wish to be seen with me?"

"Well, of course I can't be seen with my brother's....you know what I mean," she added slightly defensively. "And now I'm living with a friend of my mother's who is even more exacting than Aunt Belcher, I need to be even more careful of my reputation."

"Well, I'm sorry you think being seen with me will besmirch it." Phoebe felt a stab of pique before acknowledging the truth of Ada's words. As Lady Cavanaugh, she was naturally Ada's superior. She brushed the thought aside. "Now, tell me what this is about?"

She tried to inject a kindly curiosity into her tone to make up for her prickly defensiveness.

"It's about Mr Wentworth, of course, and what I've discovered."

"Oh." Phoebe felt a stab of fear. She'd seen a snippet in the paper Hugh had been reading regarding Mr Wentworth's stated declaration to find Lady Cavanaugh and bring the husband-killer to justice. Hugh had thought she'd stabbed herself with her embroidery needle the way she'd gasped involuntarily.

Phoebe knew her safest course was anonymity. With no friends among the servants or even the local community where she'd lived for five years with Ulrick, the truth would never prevail. No, she would be safest here with Hugh.

"You see, I've learned where his wife is."

"But Hugh told you to give it up. As did I." Phoebe stopped walking, put her hand to her chest, then forced herself to continue her measured footsteps. "There's nothing to be gained from all this, Ada. Just leave it be."

Ada ignored her. "She's a regular at Mrs Plumb's Salon in Soho."

Phoebe stopped and looked at her. The name meant nothing.

"It's a salon where I've learned ladies and gentlemen meet for music and dancing, though it's not for respectable people like me or Aunt Siddons who I'm living with now." Ada looked appealingly at Phoebe. "That's why I'm asking you to go."

Phoebe shook her head. "I can't, Ada."

Ada put her head on one side. "Not even for me?"

"Not for you, not for my mistress, and I'll tell you why not? Because your brother wants nothing more to do with the man," Phoebe said with some energy. In fact, Hugh had not mentioned Wentworth's name in two weeks, but Phoebe needed to make it as clear as she could that Ada must not meddle in matters pertaining to Wentworth. It was too dangerous.

Ada raised her veil and sent Phoebe a level stare. "Mr Wentworth's wife is a dancer at Madame Plumb's. Is it fair to *her* that she remain in ignorance of the fact her husband has inherited a dukedom?"

"No, it probably is not," Phoebe said with forced restraint.

"And is it so difficult to wear a veil, visit a house filled with other people wearing veils, and simply mention to the unfortunate woman the fact that her errant husband is now a duke?"

Phoebe made no answer, and Ada stamped her foot. "Then I'll go. Yes, *I'll* go, and Hugh will be terribly angry with me, but I'll tell him I had no choice because you refused."

❧

PHOEBE NIBBLED THE END OF HER PEN, THEN TESTED THE NIB, then stared at the blank sheet in front of her. She'd had writing implements brought to her in order to scratch a note to Hugh informing him of what she was doing. Ada had suggested Phoebe say nothing about her visit to Mrs Plumb's, but Phoebe had been adamant she was not going to keep secrets.

Now she was in two minds. Hugh had been away three days, and she wished heartily she might have discussed the matter with him, but Ada's pleas had prevailed, and now that Phoebe had had time to digest the possible ramifications of speaking to him as opposed to not speaking to him, she was highly undecided.

If news got back to him that she'd gone to Mrs Plumb's Salon, he might think her underhanded and seeking diversion, and she'd hate that.

On the other hand, Ada had said she'd ascertained that Thursday was the one day of the week the mysterious Mrs Wentworth made her appearance at Mrs Plumb's and today was Thursday, while Hugh would not be home for another three days.

No, she really had to tell him. She dipped her pen into the ink and began, "*My dearest Hugh, I hope you will not be angry with me but....*"

Then she scratched it out. That was not a good start. If she were his wife, he'd have every cause to be angry with her for not seeking his permission. Sadly, that was a wife's lot, but she was not his wife, and one of the few advantages was that as Ulrick's widow and Hugh's kept woman, she was mistress of her own decisions. This would have to be a practice draft, she decided, making another attempt with: "*Dear Hugh, though I do not wish to displease you, I have decided....*"

With a sigh of frustration, she crumpled the paper and tossed it into the grate. A letter wasn't necessary. She'd make a clandestine visit, in disguise, to Mrs Plumb's and Hugh would be none the wiser. Then she'd report her findings to Ada and they could decide how to proceed. All she was going to do was go to Mrs. Plumb's house—whoever Mrs Plumb was—which was in a respectable area, and speak to Wentworth's wife. No doubt Mrs Wentworth would be as eager as any of them to find a way to make Mr Wentworth accountable for his actions. Obviously he'd abandoned her. It was quite possible he'd forced her to live on a paltry allowance for years, simply to get her out of the way while he lived the life he chose. No doubt she was an innkeeper's daughter or someone of lowly rank whom Wentworth had either been forced to marry through honor, or with whom he'd rashly eloped as a very young man.

Whatever the case, clearly he deeply regretted this marriage, but fact was that his wife was entitled to share in the spoils resulting from his elevation in status.

Pulling on her gloves and tying the ribbons of her bonnet, Phoebe went down the stairs and into the darkened street. She'd told her maid she was going out and not to wait up for her. Hugh had taken the carriage, so Phoebe hailed a hackney, and pulling down her veil when she was inside, prepared for an evening that, even if she felt somewhat guilty about, promised to be a good deal more interesting than spending another evening at home, alone.

Despite persuading herself she was doing no wrong, her heart beat rapidly as she paid the hackney then watched it disappear around the corner, leaving her standing on the pavement by the iron railing of a somewhat ordinary four-square house. The blinds were drawn, but she could see the glow of lamplight behind as she was forced to step aside for two ladies elegantly attired but veiled, and then two gentlemen in evening dress. If this was the right address, it looked benign and ordinary.

A little maid greeted her at the door with far more confidence than the usual menial given the girl's tender years. "Welcome, ma'am, if ye'd like ter follow me to the refreshments' room. Ye've not bin here afore."

Phoebe did so and soon found herself in an elegantly furnished room with a table heaped with jellies, blancmanges, thinly sliced ham, tarts and plover's eggs, around which milled more than a dozen ladies and gentlemen. The sound of a fine alto sung by a woman with a deep, clear voice issued from beyond, and Phoebe wondered why Ada had said her aunt would not deign to step over the threshold. It all looked perfectly respectable to her.

Nevertheless, she felt dreadfully exposed being on her own though her veiling gave her confidence. Some ladies had pushed theirs back, but Phoebe noticed others wore masques or were entirely shrouded.

"Good evening, are you looking for someone?" The fact that the question was asked by a kindly looking matron was comforting, especially when the woman introduced herself as Mrs Plumb.

Phoebe nodded, and Mrs Plumb patted her on the shoulder. The woman was stout and grey-haired with no veiling or masque to add mystery or concealment. She was neither plain nor handsome. "No cause to look so anxious, my dear; discretion is what we pride ourselves on. Just tell me what kind of gentleman pleases you, or point him out if he's here, and I shall effect a proper introduction."

Phoebe drew in her breath, startled at what she interpreted as a great vulgarity and affront to good breeding before remembering to what she'd been reduced. "I'm not interested in any gentleman, but rather a woman," she said quickly.

"Ah." Mrs Plumb nodded sagely, running her hands the length of her cerulean sarcenet skirts. "You want a woman. Well, there are plenty of lovely ladies here who also have no interest in the gentlemen, and I'm certain I can introduce you to just the right soul mate, if that is your heart's desire." She smiled. "Mrs Plumb's Salon is where wishes are granted, and no dream is too strange to come true."

Emphatically, Phoebe shook her head. "I'm looking for one lady in particular. I was told she came here on a Thursday." She paused and lowered her voice. "I don't know what name she might go by other than Mrs Wentworth for I was told only that Mr Wentworth's wife works here."

A flash of surprise registered in the depths of Mrs Plumb's expression. "Who would like to know? I keep a safe house, my dear."

"So she is here? There is a woman known by that name?"

Mrs Plumb hesitated. "Possibly."

"Please, I do need to speak to her. It's about her husband."

Mrs Plumb jerked back her head, her eyes widening. She glanced about her quickly, before whispering, "He's not dead, is he?"

Phoebe bit her lip. "He's not, but I think Mrs Wentworth should be given the chance to decide whether she wants to talk to me or not."

Mrs Plumb inclined her head. "Wait here," she ordered, turning on her heel and disappearing through a curtained doorway.

Phoebe stared at the food while she slanted a surreptitious glance at the odd assembly. She noticed a slender, elegantly-attired young woman in an elaborate, feathered masque take the arm of a gentleman and disappear through a doorway behind a tapestry she'd not noticed before. Could half these people be prostitutes? she suddenly wondered, shocked. Surely innocent Ada would not have sent her to such a place like.

"Would madam like to view the paintings in the blue room?"

A rather distinguished gentleman, somewhat older and with gray peppering his hair, proffered his arm but Phoebe stepped away. "Thank you but I'm meeting someone," she said quickly, and with a nod he slipped into the crowd.

More couples disappeared into chambers hidden behind paintings or plinths. Phoebe heard a smattering of clapping as the singer finished her song, and then was loudly congratulated by an admirer. “Madame Zirelli, our songstress of the evening, has now concluded her art. Please show your appreciation once more, ladies and gentlemen.”

Peeping past the curtains, Phoebe observed a tall, handsome woman of middle years dressed in a slightly shabby gown of cerulean blue. She’d heard the name before, and remembered that Madame Zirelli had been a singer of some renown who’d passed through the towns of the north when she’d been a child.

“Would Madame like some refreshment? I’m told you are looking for someone, and I am here to lead you to satisfaction.”

Phoebe glanced around and found herself looking into the eyes of a beautiful young woman dressed in diaphanous robes with an impish smile. Her long, golden hair was unbound though held in place with a circlet of flowers, and her gaze was the purest blue Phoebe had ever seen.

The young woman smiled again and held out her hand. “I’m Ariane. Come with me.”

Unresistingly, Phoebe followed the girl down a passage and into a darkened room filled with a strange scent of musk, and the soft singing of four similarly dressed maidens who swayed in time to their lovely chant.

The door closed behind them, plunging them into semidarkness, but rather than feel fear, Phoebe was mesmerized, unthinkingly bringing the goblet that was placed in her hands to her lips. Its contents tasted like mead, the honey and strange herbs astringent but pleasant against the back of her throat. Smoke scented with the same herbs drifted into her nostrils, stinging the back of her throat, but the sight of the four young girls on a dais surrounded by candles in the center of the dim, smoke-filled room, swaying and softly chanting, was too transfixing for her to step away.

Ariane put her arm around Phoebe’s shoulders and drew her to a velvet throne in the corner of the room. "Would you like to watch?"

Phoebe blinked a few times. The smoke and odd scent were making it difficult to concentrate. "I'm looking for Mrs Wentworth," she whispered. "You said you'd take me to her."

Had she asked for Mrs Wentworth earlier? she wondered, but before she could recall, the young woman smiled, tracing the curve of Phoebe's lips with her forefinger. "I am Mrs Wentworth," she said softly.

Phoebe jerked out of her caress and blinked stupidly.

Ariane laughed gently while behind her the vestal virgins swayed, heads together, eyes closed, expressions rapturous.

"You are Mrs Wentworth? But..."

"But I do not live with my husband? No, that is correct." Ariane looked amused as she bade Phoebe be seated, then lowered herself into the velvet banquette beside her. "I worked here before I met him, and now I am back here where Mrs Plumb takes care of me and I am surrounded by kindness. I have no complaints." She stroked Phoebe's hair. "But I am curious. How do you know my husband, or perhaps I should not delve too deeply into that question? I suspect he knows many women, not all of whom are happy to have known him." She raised an eyebrow.

Bitterness and fear rose up in Phoebe's throat. "How do I know him? I wish I didn't. I..." she floundered, wishing also that she'd not drunk the mead so quickly for she was aware of less clarity in the workings of her brain than she would like. "Let me assure you, Mrs Wentworth," she whispered, "I do not judge you for having left your husband."

"He was not good to you?" Mrs Wentworth's smile did not lose its sweetness. "Oh, that does not surprise me at all. I am sure you have many questions, otherwise you would not have sought me out, my dear, but first I would like to know your name."

"Phoebe." Her Christian name only. That would suffice. She was fortunately clear-headed enough to know how to protect herself.

"Phoebe. Well, I hope I can help you. As you can see," she waved a hand about her, "I have safety and freedom and a measure of security and happiness. I would not live the life of a conventional married woman again, let me tell you."

"Mrs Plumb looks after you?"

"And I dance for her clients in return." Ariane looked satisfied as she added, "It is perfectly respectable. Mrs Plumb has a legion of vigilant servants to ensure any unwanted overtures are summarily dealt with. Now, what else would you like to know?" She reached across the table laden with grapes and other fruits and refilled her goblet from a flask which she handed to Phoebe. "Let me start from the beginning, shall I? Perhaps recount my miserable childhood as the seventh daughter of an innkeeper, and my equally unhappy marriage to the fine gentleman, Mr Wentworth, who used to break his journey at our inn at regular intervals. We both soon regretted our impulsiveness."

"And then you went your separate ways? Oh, but I can see why!" Phoebe put down her now empty goblet and clasped her hands. "He's a cruel man. But he's also a very wealthy one now. I am sure you cannot know that else you'd not be content to remain here, in all but poverty, when he could be furnishing you with all that to which a lady like you is entitled."

"A lady like me?" Ariane smiled. "I am as much a lady as Mr Wentworth is a gentleman."

"But a lady is what you are. A titled one on account of Mr Wentworth having inherited the estate of Lord Cavanaugh, his second cousin, following the unexpected deaths of his two brothers." Phoebe knew she was growing too excited without perhaps explaining matters properly since Ariane did not appear to be either believing her, or overjoyed at her new lot in life.

"Well, that's hardly going to benefit me if it means I have to live with the man." She shrugged. "I'd rather forgo all the riches in the world."

"Oh, I can well imagine it," Phoebe declared warmly. "But if it's revenge you're after, then I know exactly how to achieve it. We suspected Mr Wentworth had married but was keeping it secret so he could make another more advantageous marriage."

Ariane raised an eyebrow, and Phoebe went on; her tongue unleashed as if she could not have maintained discretion for all the world. "To me, in fact. He wished to marry me once my husband was dead. I can't give you all the reasons, but I will tell you this: Mr Wentworth is not only a brutal man to any innocent female with whom he has any dealings, but he is also a murderer!"

"A murderer!"

Phoebe wiped her brow. The exertion of her strong declarations was making her feel weak and addleheaded. At least she had Ariane's attention. "I know how to expose him, or if not expose him, then make him acknowledge you so that he receives the justice he is due."

"Expose him?" Ariane shifted closer to Phoebe on the seat. She seemed confused.

"First, though, you'll need to produce evidence to show you both are legally married." Phoebe wiped her sweating brow once more, gratefully accepting another glass Ariane poured for her. The closeness of the room was almost unbearable. Though the lamps cast only the dimmest light in order to show the dancers in their pale, sheer clothing to best advantage, the glow still seemed too bright.

Ariane looked skeptical. "And how would that profit me? Would Wentworth not wish me harm if he knew I was doing this?"

Suddenly, it seemed of the utmost importance to convince her. "It could be done in secret," said Phoebe. "If you provided me with evidence, we—or rather you—could go to the authorities. Wentworth would then be forced to acknowledge you as his wife."

Phoebe swayed, her head suddenly feeling too heavy for its stem. Mrs Wentworth was still looking skeptical.

"Perhaps the wife of such a brutal fiend would prefer to remain hidden. Or not wish to be acknowledged as such in view of the fact her husband was apparently a murderer."

Phoebe tried to raise her head from where she'd rested it on

Ariane's shoulder, but for some reason couldn't. She wished she'd thought better how to address such reasonable fears. "I'd help you," she said, finding it difficult to articulate her words. "You needn't come out of hiding. I have another friend who also has had experience of Mr Wentworth. It was she who suggested the idea. Wentworth said he'd marry her, and then she realized he was already married. He needs to be exposed."

Phoebe felt Ariane stiffen. "Who else knows my secret?" She sounded fearful for the first time, and Phoebe almost confessed the reason for her own hatred of Wentworth except that her anonymity was as important to her as Ariane's seemed to be to herself.

In a moment of clarity, she thought that perhaps she should leave now. She'd explain to Ada that Ariane didn't want it made public she was Wentworth's wife because it put her entirely back into his power. No doubt she'd kept her location secret all these years, and was so terrified at the prospect of finding herself in Wentworth's clutches again, that not all the trappings his new position afforded were worth the danger.

Phoebe rubbed her eyes and tried to focus on Ariane's face as she answered Ariane's question. "My friend, Ada, asked me to come here and find you. She was badly used by Mr Wentworth too."

"Ada?"

"I won't reveal her full name, but she was concerned for you."

"Just as I am concerned about you, Phoebe." Ariane patted Phoebe's shoulder and pushed a pillow under her neck as she rose and went to the bell pull. A young servant answered quickly, curtseying after she'd received Ariane's instructions.

"Now, let us take refreshment," Ariane said with forced brightness, indicating the other dancers who appeared oblivious to them. Phoebe stared, wondering how they could appear so vacantly happy all this time. She rubbed her eyes again. The room really was swimming. "Please, may I have some water?" she asked. The back of her throat was burning.

Ariane bent to pour her a glass from the other decanter on the table before stepping away and beginning to pace. "I really cannot understand how my whereabouts were discovered," she mused. "I was so careful."

"Please don't be concerned, Mrs Wentworth. Neither Ada nor I would dream of revealing your whereabouts if it were against your wishes. We'd simply thought you needed to know. And that we could help you." Phoebe stopped, closing her eyes, and Ariane said quickly, her voice warm in her ear, "Goodness, you don't look at all well, Phoebe. Perhaps you should go. This is not the kind of place I think you are familiar with. The strange vapors are affecting you."

Phoebe tried to rise but couldn't. She mumbled, "You must expose him, though if you do not wish to be found by Wentworth, I can arrange that."

"Can you indeed?"

A moment before, Phoebe had been half asleep. Now the familiar honeyed tones jerked her into terrified awareness. The voice came from the doorway which had just opened to admit a tall gentleman in evening clothes who was now rising from his elaborate bow, a familiar leer marring his handsome features.

"My, my Lady Cavanaugh, this is an unexpected surprise," he purred. "I am sure you have no idea how hard I've been searching for you. The last place I expected to stumble upon you was here."

He took a few steps toward Phoebe, staring between her and his wife. The scantily-clad vestal virgin stood like a vision of purity hiding her betrayal—for wasn't that was it was?—in the center of the room gazing at Phoebe with a curious expression, while a dull fear lodged in the pit of Phoebe's stomach. With the greatest effort, she forced herself to remain calm as she straightened.

Wentworth was here and Wentworth intended to see her dead.

Slowly, her mind became clearer. She had to get out of here. All the self preserving tactics she'd adopted screeched to the forefront of her mind. If she didn't leave in the next few moments she had no chance of doing so. Ever.

Wentworth was blocking the doorway. She sucked in a deep breath. If he would only take a couple more steps into the room, she'd seize her chance and run. Despite the mind-numbing drug she realized she'd been given, her body suddenly pulsed with life. She shifted forward, her limbs feeling sluggish but her mind racing.

"Oh, I know you've been looking for me," she said. "I heard the gossip, all of which branded me a murderess when it was your hand which drove in the knife that killed my husband."

He chuckled. "You must admit, it's a fine thing to commit the act but to have a legitimate scapegoat. *Your* hand was around the handle of the paper knife, my dear. I just elicited a little more force to drive it home."

"Drive it home? I was nowhere near Ulrick when you seized me and used all your strength to make me the unwilling instrument of the murder *you* committed." She turned toward Ariane, expecting to see shock.

Ariane appeared unmoved.

"Do you know what kind of a man your husband is?" Phoebe demanded. She was trying without success to put some pressure onto her legs in order to stand. "You've not lived with him for some years, I gather. I didn't want to reveal the extent of his... depravity, but now I have no choice. You're better off knowing the truth. I presume you left because he was as cruel to you as he has been to me...and to Ada who sent me here."

"Ada?" Wentworth raised an eyebrow and took a step forward, though Phoebe was disappointed to see he still blocked her only means of escape. It was hard to breathe evenly, and she was doing her best to remain calm.

"Miss Ada Redding?" He gave a surprised laugh. "*Ada* sent you here? Why, that silly goose hasn't the gumption to say boo to anyone much less discover what I've gone to such pains to keep hidden."

"Perhaps she's had to change since you ruined her," Phoebe said bitterly. "She lost her reputation, her baby, and her will to live. No wonder she was at such pains to find your weak spot. Obviously, now that you've inherited my husband's title—that is, the title of the man you murdered—you don't want to be saddled with an innkeeper's daughter when you could have a lady with a vast dowry to help you with those gambling debts of yours." She swung around to face Ariane, saying defiantly, "I was Wentworth's mistress, you know. I didn't want to wound your sensibilities when I thought you were an injured party, and I wanted to protect you from the truth, but you need to know it. My husband wished for an heir, and it certainly didn't seem likely that Wentworth would inherit, so he was more than happy to woo me and then make me his mistress." She spat out the words, as disgusted with herself as she was with the couple before her, for Ariane had now moved to her husband's side, and he'd placed an arm casually about her shoulders.

Phoebe stared, barely able to comprehend the truth. "Who *are* you?" she whispered, staring at Ariane. The woman looked like something between a water sprite and a witch, with her translucent gown clinging to her curves with such indecency and her piercing eyes, more virulent green than celestial blue as Phoebe had first thought, boring into her.

"I am the wife Wentworth can't live with but can't live without." She gave a mirthless laugh. "Wentworth would be nothing without me."

Phoebe was familiar with Wentworth's overbearing pride and arrogance. No woman could speak to him like that. She fully expected to witness Ariane receive an ear-boxing for having been so boldly insulting in front of him. To her astonishment, Wentworth's mouth split into a slow grin. "My wife speaks the truth. I'm a gentleman fond of the cards, but as you quite rightly point out, a gentleman does not consort with an innkeeper's daughter, though an innkeeper's daughter who works as a hostess in gambling dens and is a dab hand at keeping a sharp eye out in the interests of her husband, can further a fortune to a surprising degree. I'd go so far as to suggest an innkeeper's daughter with such a talent is a far better financial proposition than, say, a lady of impeccable breeding with three thousand a year."

Ariane inclined her head in appreciation of the compliment. She raised her hand to stroke her husband's cheek. "When Wentworth is sufficiently plump in the pocket, I shall sweep into his life suitably kitted out as the foreign lady of fashion he's waited for his whole life."

Phoebe stared aghast. "But he...he's no husband if he follows his roving eye as he does, let me assure you."

"What's good for the goose is good for the gander, my dear Phoebe, or Lady Cavanaugh, I ought to say." Ariane indicated the decanter upon the table. "Another glass before my husband takes you away? You may find a lack of such concern for your comfort in the next place you visit."

Phoebe didn't answer. So this was how it would end. She stared at her feet. What a credulous fool she'd been.

"I'm afraid you have little choice." Wentworth's tone was regretful as he barred her progress to the door. Striding swiftly forward, he took Phoebe's arm and jerked her to her feet. "What do you think, Ariane, my love?" he asked, cupping Phoebe's chin painfully. "She's a charming piece. Shall we share her before we surrender her to her miserable fate?"

Ariane's expression was assessing, her mouth trembling with what suddenly seemed like anticipation. "Oh, Wentworth that would be a treat," she murmured. "She's a tasty morsel to be sure."

"No!" Phoebe's piercing shriek rent the air, shattering the calm and causing Ariane to step back in sudden alarm. Then Wentworth's mouth was on Phoebe's, and the scream was truncated by the disgusting repossession of the man she feared above all others.

Self-preservation was stronger than it had ever been. She brought her knee up sharply, ducking out of his grasp and making for the door with a sudden surge of speed that had not seemed possible minutes ago when the lethargy was heavy upon her.

"No!" she screamed again as she fumbled with the door handle and flew into the passage, nearly bowling over a woman veiled and dressed in black.

Wentworth was right behind her, his hand gripping her shoulder, swinging her back to him as the woman asked haltingly, "Is…is everything all right?"

"Please help me!" Phoebe sobbed. "Don't let him take me away."

"A touch of hysteria. Pay no mind," Wentworth said smoothly although Phoebe heard the waver in his voice. It clearly didn't convince the woman who said more firmly now, "I think you should drop your hand, sir. The woman appears…frightened."

"The poor creature came seeking pleasure, just like yourself, ma'am." Ariane was now between Phoebe and the disguised woman. To Phoebe's astonishment, Ariane put her hand on the woman's sleeve. "But the pleasure was not to her liking, after all. She certainly didn't enjoy it as you did, my lady."

The sudden stillness—no doubt from shock and embarrassment—rendered the other woman immobile for a moment. Then she shook off Ariane's hand and stepped back against the wall.

"Help me!" Phoebe sobbed again when it appeared she was going to continue along the passage. "I'm being taken against my will. You have to help me."

"I shall call someone!" the woman said with unexpected strength, glancing at her companion who'd just brought up the rear, a diffident-looking young man some years her junior.

"Perhaps the bailiffs," Ariane suggested smoothly. "Do you realize who this is? A murderer. That's right. This is Lady Cavanaugh who has stolen the newspaper headlines for the past weeks, the murderer of her own husband whom the authorities have been seeking, and now we are taking her to the magistrate."

"How can you be sure?" The woman's hand went to the ruby pendant at her throat.

"Oh, I know her well. But to reassure you, ma'am, I shall bring one of the servants along for the ride," Wentworth suggested smoothly. "You, boy! I'll give you sixpence if you stand sponsor for the safe conduct of this woman to the magistrate. I shall accompany you both."

The woman stared at Phoebe, her companion standing awkwardly to the side. Phoebe clutched at her sleeve.

"This man is the villain. I won't go with him. If I do I'll..."

"Die?" Ariane insinuated herself between the veiled woman and Phoebe. With her hands on her hips and her eyes flashing, she looked more like a Valkyrie than a vestal virgin. "Yes, and only because justice will be served at last!" she addressed Phoebe directly. "You'll be dangling at the end of a noose, which is where you belong for driving a knife into the heart of your poor defenseless husband."

Phoebe made to run, but Wentworth's arm shot out, and he dragged her back. She tried to struggle, but it was no use. So she screamed instead. "After *this man* forced my hand so he could claim I was the murderer and therefore claim my husband's inheritance."

"She's rambling, of course, but you see she *does* admit she's the lady who's been sought the length and breadth of the country, and furthermore, that she held the murder weapon as it went in." Wentworth looked with satisfaction between them all. "So, Lady Cavanaugh, now that you have declared yourself, it's time for the judicial process to take over." With an ironic bow to the veiled woman and her companion, he caged Phoebe's hand on his arm, indicated to the lad to escort her on the other side, and swept her down the corridor and into the street.

16

Hugh had never been so anxious to return home.

"Phoebe, dear heart, I'm back! God, I've missed you! Where are you?" Fired up with excited expectation, he burst into the drawing room, tossing his low-crowned beaver onto the ottoman as he looked about him. He was surprised not to have been greeted by the maid, but more so that his beloved had not made a hasty appearance.

"Oh, sir, ye're back! Thank the good Lord!" cried the girl as she flew into the room, her eyes wide. "I thought ye'd never come. The mistress 'as been gone these two days, an' ye also. Who was ter pay me wages? I feared ye both dead."

"Your mistress is not here, Mary? Two days, you say?" Alarmed, Hugh swung around as if he might be furnished with the very clues the young maid had missed. The elegantly furnished room looked just as it had done when he left. "Why has no one reported the matter?"

"There were no one to report it ter, sir—"

"A note? Surely she's written—"

"Nothin', sir, beyond a couple of drafts tossed in the grate," said Mary, scrabbling among a pile of correspondence in the rolltop desk before handing him a couple of crumpled, soiled sheets. "She jest dressed 'erself all in black with a veil over 'er face an' then she went into the night, and that were the last I seen," Mary was saying as he scanned the few unhelpful lines.

A painful throbbing of his heart was competing with a growing thundering in his brain as he tried to reconcile Mary's explanation with the cryptic words Phoebe had written him...two days before?

"Where did she go, Mary?" he asked, crumpling the paper into a ball and advancing upon Mary, who stepped back in alarm. "I'm not going to hurt you." He tried to master his emotions and the urgency in his voice. "I just need you to tell me all she said to you!"

"Oh sir, she told me nothin', I swear, else I'd 'ave found a way ter stop 'er. I dunno what's she's done or who she's met or what she planned. On me honor, I don't."

Hugh strode to the window and stared out into the street as if that might throw some light on what had happened.

"Her clothes, Mary...did she take any of her clothes?" He swallowed. "Or come back for them?" he added as the terrible thought intruded that she might have planned to run away the moment he was gone for any length of time. Surely not! She loved him madly. She'd declared it in as many words, just as he'd pledged his own affection. He'd not stinted when it came to making it very clear the strength of his feelings.

"What possible reason could she have had for disguising herself and slipping away in the dead of night, never to return?"

"I dunno, sir. I dunno anythin', sir!"

"Go, Mary! Ask anyone you can think of. The neighbors. If you hear anything, you must tell me, obviously. Just go!"

He thought he'd break down any moment now. The devastation at the thought that Phoebe might have left to seek new diversions, just as she'd left Blinley Manor the night she entered his life, was too much to bear.

She'd spoken of boredom when he was away. Could she have gone out seeking fresh entertainment? No, she'd have come back to him. She'd not planned to desert him. Surely he could be confident of that, at least? But what if she'd gone out pleasure-seeking, intending to come back, yet something had happened to her?

He thrust his knuckles into his eye sockets and breathed heavily. Where had she gone? God, he loved her, but could he forgive her if she wanted to return?

No, he mustn't think like that. Something inexplicable had happened. He must not be so quick to think ill of her. And yet, she'd left the house unaccompanied and on some clandestine mission.

And she'd not returned.

Breathing heavily, he began his weary progress to the door. How would he ever find her if she chose not to see him again? Should he even try?

"Sir! A note's jest come from yer sister." Mary was back upon the threshold brandishing a piece of parchment.

Hugh groaned when he read it. The last thing he needed right now was to meet Ada, who apparently would be waiting in the park opposite just as soon as he indicated he was back home. Why she didn't just come to the house, he didn't know.

But he was ever the loyal brother. Just as he'd considered himself a loyal lover.

Ada hailed him, raising her gloved hand from the far end of the park as she advanced with her lady's maid at her side.

Her dimples popped out when she saw him, and she tilted her face to receive his kiss. "I've missed you, brother," she said. "I have such exciting news to tell you, too, and you were gone a whole day longer than you said."

"Well, what is it, Ada?" he asked. "I hope it is important as I've only just returned from a long and tiring journey."

"My, but you are grumpy today. Perhaps I shan't tell you, after all."

Hugh rolled his eyes. "Don't play games, Ada. I'm not in the mood."

His sister let out her breath in a sigh. "You've taken away all my excitement when I've been waiting two days to tell you my news," she pouted. "And for so long you've been telling me I must open my heart up to the opportunity of meeting a nice gentleman."

"My goodness, that is news," he remarked drily.

"Yes, indeed, I have met a very nice gentleman, though perhaps you don't consider that as noteworthy as the fact that Lady Cavanaugh has been apprehended, and Mr Wentworth will be testifying as a witness to her murderous actions in doing away with her husband. I'm sure that's hardly news to you."

Hugh sighed. "It's all I've been reading about for the past two days." He stopped suddenly. "Why, Ada, you said his name without...."

"Yes, without weeping and wailing. That's because I have a plan, Hugh."

"You can't possibly do anything at such a public juncture that might bring attention to yourself, Ada—"

She cut him off. "Or shame on the family. Of course I know that. No, I have a plan as regards my new young gentleman that'll help me recover and get on with my life. I don't intend ever mentioning Mr Wentworth's name again. There! That's the last time I'll say it out loud. I've practised putting it in a coffin, like my baby, and throwing away the key. They're dead to me, Hugh. Aunt Alexa has been counseling me well. I thought she was worse than Aunt Belcher, but in truth, she's been good for me. I can be strong, and I can have a life. I intend Mr Xavier to consider me a good prospect, Hugh. Because I am. I will not be branded beneath contempt when Mr...you know who I mean, should suffer equally for the crimes we both committed. I just hope Phoebe didn't do anything foolish after I asked her to seek out Mrs Wentworth. She assured me she'd be careful though she didn't want to go, and for that I feel a trifle guilty."

"What?"

"A few days ago, I begged Phoebe to go to a certain not quite respectable salon I'd discovered Mrs Wentworth was known to frequent. *You* wouldn't do it for me, Hugh, but Phoebe is so much more accommodating than you are at times, so I asked her. She can go anywhere, being the kind of woman she is."

"Don't speak like that, Ada," Hugh warned. "That was unnecessary and beneath you. I happen to love her." He ran his hand distractedly through his hair. "But she's gone." He looked away, embarrassed.

"What do you mean, she's *gone*? Not *gone* gone, surely? She'll come back. She loves you."

"Mary told me that three days ago she put on her black cloak over her finest dress, topped it with a veiled bonnet, and disappeared into the night. She has not returned."

"Three days ago?" Ada put her hand to her mouth and stopped in her tracks. "Oh Hugh, three days ago was when I asked Phoebe to go to Mrs Plumb's Salon."

Hugh grew cold. "That was just about the time Lady Cavanaugh was apprehended. Surely Phoebe would not testify on behalf of her mistress, would she? Not if she were so convinced of the threat Wentworth posed." He knew he was talking aloud about matters Ada would not know about, but he had to tease out every possibility. "Phoebe is loyal but not that loyal that she'd risk her neck—and not without consulting me?"

Ada looked surprised. "You really trust her so much that you'd attribute her disappearance to something noble, rather than the fact she might have grown bored and sought diversion elsewhere?" She gripped his arm and put up her hand to prevent him from interrupting. "You forget that I know just how deeply one can be sucked into the maelstrom of intense feelings for someone. Why, I thought Mr Wentworth as worthy of my regard as you seem to of Phoebe. I don't wish to be unkind, Hugh, but Phoebe is a lightskirt. She was never prepared to work or soil her hands like a common servant, though she was no better. No, she wanted a new wardrobe so she could flaunt her handsome looks, and you gave her one. No doubt she's moved on to find bigger fish to fry. Someone with a title and a fine fortune."

Hugh felt himself gaping just like that supposedly bigger fish

Ada claimed his darling Phoebe was out trying to lure. Angrily, he shook his head. "You do her a grave injustice. Besides, she took no jewelry and nothing else of any value. No, she went out empty-handed to do *your* bidding, Ada. She went out seeking information upon your request, and something happened. That's what I believe."

"Well, I hope you're right. I certainly thought she was very fond of you," Ada conceded.

"Fond of me! She was more than that, I can tell you!" Hugh removed Ada's hand. There was nothing to be gained from losing his temper. The truth was he was angry with himself, not Ada. He was responsible for Phoebe, and he'd promised to keep her safe. "It's getting late, and you must call your maid and return to Aunt Alexa's," he muttered.

"Yes, so I can dress and attend a dinner where several MPs, including my charming Mr Xavier, will be in attendance," Ada simpered. "Aunt Alexa introduced us three days ago."

"Ah yes, so that's my cue to quiz you on your beau." Hugh tried to sound interested, but his mood was fearful and heavy. "My apologies for allowing myself to be distracted."

"Don't be churlish, Hugh. Phoebe will come back if she loves you as she says she does. And please be glad for me. Since you asked—or rather, didn't in so many words—Mr Xavier is a widower with no children and no title but an adequate fortune and a fine Mayfair address, and Aunt Alexa says I'd struggle to do better. Fortunately, I find myself rather intrigued by Mr Xavier. He is very kind."

"Very kind? And doddery? Oh Ada, don't sell yourself short. You don't need to settle for an old man."

"I don't plan to settle for anyone I don't choose to ally myself to for the remainder of my days. Mr Xavier is fifteen years older, interesting, and well-connected."

"Are you brave enough to risk—"

"Do you mean have I covered my tracks well enough to confidently entertain Mr Xavier's attentions without fear of discovery of the fact that I'm no better than your Phoebe?"

"No need to bristle like a hedgehog, my dear Ada." Hugh shook his head. "My, but you are not the meek and mild little sister I once knew."

"That's because I've seen Mr Wentworth win a fine estate and profit despite the crimes he's committed against me. I will trouble myself no more with him, but if I cannot get my revenge in seeing him reduced in status and fortune, then my revenge will be in prospering in my own life. I will not be an unpaid companion to a crotchety aunt for the remainder of my days because of Mr Wentworth. I shall be the wife and hostess of a man of politics. I shall not be afraid, Hugh, for nothing can be as bad as that which I've endured already."

"Fighting words, indeed," Hugh said admiringly. "I wish you great success in your endeavors toward such ends. Meanwhile, I must return and decide what to do about Phoebe."

"You can do nothing until she decides to return."

Hugh looked at her sadly. "You truly believe she has left me?"

Ada smiled. "I also believe she will return to you, Hugh, when she grows tired of her pleasure-seeking and realizes no kinder, sweeter man existed. And you will take her back because you love her. It will end happily; I've no doubt. Now go to your club and stop mooning about like a lovestruck calf."

17

It was just after midnight that Phoebe was roughly pushed into the withdrawing chamber of the receiving lackey on duty, who raised his grizzled head and looked at them blearily. He'd obviously been asleep in a chair before the grate.

In the disconcerting silence, she heard the time burst forth from the far-too-cheerful street caller just below the window, and shivered as the door opened to a stooped gentleman punctiliously adjusting his bagwig, his expression sonorous. His displeasure at seeing them was in contrast to Wentworth's transparent satisfaction. He looked as if he'd been recalled from far more pleasurable pursuits.

"Lord Mayberry, I'd like to present Lady Cavanaugh, the woman who murdered her husband and my cousin. The woman all England has been looking for this past two months."

Lord Mayberry wiped rheumy eyes with a handkerchief and peered at Phoebe, his gaze traveling critically from the dirt-encrusted hem of one of the secondhand gowns she'd acquired, and which was partly concealed beneath her faded black bombazine cloak. She was not dressed like a lady, she knew. Nor like a servant either.

Lord Mayberry squinted at her, and with horror, she realized she'd seen him earlier that night at Madame Plumb's.

"She does not look like Lady Cavanaugh," he muttered, no doubt confused by her appearance as he signaled over his shoulder to a hovering maid to pour them all a brandy.

"For Lady Cavanaugh, too," he added. "She'll need it."

They sat down and the maid brought over the drinks, whispering something in her employer's ear which he waved away with a flicker of irritation. "Reassure Margaret that all is well," he told her. "And that I've been at home all evening, but that my sleep has been disturbed by an apprehended murderess. That'll have her down in a trice, wanting to know this and that, never satisfied," he muttered, though Phoebe was sure they were not intended to hear what he just said, just as she knew Lord Mayberry had *not* been in his own bed all night.

Fear had locked up her throat, but now she managed tightly, "I did not murder my husband."

His lordship looked at her sharply. "Oh, so you admit you are Lady Cavanaugh then. That's a pity. I'd thought to release you with a warning for solicitation and leave it at that." He glared from her to Wentworth, then sighed, waving his empty glass in the air for his maid to collect. "Well then, we'd better get on with it, hadn't we?"

❧

IN THE DIM CHAMBER OF ELONGATED SHADOWS, NAMES AND titles, alleged crimes and statements, were recorded by a tall, lanky young man with a prematurely-aged face and small pointed ears, who'd been summoned for the task. Then they were all on their feet again, and Wentworth was pressing himself close to Phoebe while Lord Mayberry and his secretary, heads bent close, discussed proceedings in a low murmur at the far end of the room.

Wentworth's eyes glittered in his self-satisfied face.

"You thought you could best me, Lady Cavanaugh, but you

were wrong." His breath was sour; his voice thick with gloating. How well she remembered it. How could she ever have felt a spark of anything for the man? How could she not have been repulsed and riddled with mistrust and contempt? The thought that he'd savored her body like her darling Hugh had done—and that she'd given herself to each with equal abandon—sent the bile surging into her gullet.

Then she reminded herself that she'd only given herself to Wentworth because her husband had demanded it. No. She'd done it to save her own skin; she had to admit that. If Ulrick had died without an heir, she'd have been at the mercy of her husband's half-witted brother who'd formed a very definitely expressed disgust of her, though she'd never understood why.

With no other resources to fall back on, her life would have been intolerable.

She shivered and turned her head away, addressing Wentworth coldly. "You used me as it pleased you, and then you discarded me when I could no longer be of use."

When he pushed his leering face into her line of vision, she was tempted to scratch his eyes out—if only it would have served its purpose.

No, she was doomed, and not even her darling Hugh had the power to save her, if he even knew where she was. Her heart clenched at the thought of him. If she could send him a message...

Lord Mayberry was in brief consultation with his secretary, bent over by the light. Wentworth took her shoulder and drew her attention away. "Ah, but I am clever, my dear Phoebe. Much cleverer than you would allow. You plotted and planned your own future comfort on the basis of the child you desired from me, just so that you could remain dowager Lady Cavanaugh in your poor dead husband's fine house. Admit it! You're no better than I am when all is said and done. It'll all come out in court, and as your reputation is already worse than an opera dancer's or a fair Cyprian's plying her trade behind the Red Door, I'd say you had little chance of winning over even the most tenderhearted magistrate."

"Why do you hate me so much?" She turned back to face his malice. "What have I ever done to you that you would actually see me die—and by your own hand for that's the truth of it."

She glanced at the door, half inclined to make a dash for it, but Wentworth's fingers bit painfully into her wrist, and already Lord Mayberry was clearing his throat and shuffling back to them.

Wentworth chuckled. "Because you thought you were too clever, but it's my wife who's the clever one. Ariane saw the danger you posed, and she's not about to give up what we've waited so long for."

Phoebe put her hand to her throat, nearly felled by the image she conjured up of the angelic creature for whom she'd searched on Ada's behalf. She'd imagined her a lost soul, frightened for her life and miserably discarded by an abusive husband. But Ariane was just waiting for Phoebe to be deposed so that she could emerge when the time was right as the new Lady Cavanaugh. Once again, Phoebe had been duped. She really wasn't a very good judge of character; clearly.

Lord Mayberry indicated for them all to stand, and a stab of fear made Phoebe cry out, "Please don't leave me here, Wentworth!" despite the fact she wanted never to see him again. Yet he was all that was familiar, and only he had the power to change her fate. Yes, she would die if he'd not vouch for her.

And admit culpability himself? Of course he'd never do that.

"Please…I want to send a message."

The three men turned. Lord Mayberry's expression was ameliorating, but immediately Wentworth blew the suggestion into the realms of the preposterous.

"To her lover, no doubt, and then there'll be no end of trouble as he beats upon your door in the early hours of the morning to interfere with the law. No, Lady Cavanaugh, you are a criminal and must be treated as one."

"Just one message," she pleaded, her voice cracking, all other defense dying in her throat, for all she wanted was the kindness and reassurance of her darling Hugh. "Why should he not be allowed to help me? I am not guilty until proven so."

"You are a self-confessed murderess. You admitted so in your own words in this chamber." Wentworth appealed to the two other men, both of whom looked momentarily undecided before Wentworth said, "And now who shall convey her to prison to languish with the other criminals?"

Phoebe clutched the froth of black lace at her throat and stared in horror between Wentworth and Lord Mayberry. The extent of Wentworth's loathing should not have come as such a shock.

Lord Mayberry put up his hand for calm. And although his directive brought some comfort, there was scathing in his tone as he went to pull the bell rope.

"Lady Cavanaugh's character may be a matter of lively debate, but she is nevertheless the wife of a peer and will be tried as such. In the meantime, I shall house her here until she be removed to a place more suitable, after which she shall be tried as befits one of her station." He cleared his throat then looked at Wentworth. "Lady Cavanaugh is innocent until proven guilty and is entitled to those items of her wardrobe and otherwise in her possession which set her apart from the lower echelons of society to which she has chosen to align herself while on the run." He sent a critical look at her clothing. "That is, if she so wishes."

❧

HUGH HAD NEVER BEEN MORE AT HIS WITS' END. IT WAS ONE thing for Phoebe to have vanished with not a word, but the fact she'd taken no objects of value when she'd been so determined to have a wardrobe befitting her aspirations suggested foul play. While the thought was horrifying, it lessened the likelihood of her simply having waltzed off with the first decent offer no sooner had Hugh departed.

Ada obviously thought this the case. "Hugh, darling; I know

your heart is bleeding, but it will mend," she soothed him on his fourth evening home. She'd dropped her tatting onto the sofa and moved to kneel on the floor by his chair, resting her hand on his arm just as she'd done when she'd been a child. The words resonated for they were the very ones he'd used when Ada was about to be banished from all she knew and held dear after her terrible transgression with the evil, manipulative, Wentworth.

Hugh stroked his sister's fair hair. "I'm sorry I didn't bring Wentworth to justice," he murmured. "A good brother would have chased him to the ends of the earth as a matter of honor. I set off to do what I could but—"

She cut him off. "There was nothing you *could* do without dragging my good name into the muck. Remember, it's only thanks to you I can still hold my head up and *pretend* to be as good as all the other misses who parade themselves around the dance floor in the hopes of a good marriage."

"And you have an admirer, Ada." Hugh ignored the implication that she wasn't, in fact, as good as her competitors. In his eyes, she was as pure as she always had been. It was Wentworth who had used trickery and cajolery to make her rebel against the careful manner in which she'd been brought up. "And a good man at that. I'm delighted!" Hugh tried to shift his mood. For the first time these past few days, Ada had been in joyful spirits. She'd introduced Hugh to her new admirer, and Hugh had been impressed. Mr Xavier seemed an upstanding chap with a genuine regard for his sister.

"And," Ada continued, "you rescued Phoebe from goodness knows what terrible situation. I know she's gone again," she added quickly, "but it proves that you still have a heart capable of tenderness when I was afraid you were never going to fall in love again." She stood, smiling fiercely. "And if I can fall in love again, so can you."

But he wasn't sure he really could. Every breath was painful. It was as if Phoebe's loss had dragged the spirit from him. And yet he must retain his fortitude. He had to find out what had happened to her, even if it were only to prove her the venal creature Ada was happy to paint her, and that he feared she may be.

"You will, of course, attend the trial of Lady Cavanaugh, won't you?" Ada clarified suddenly. "If there's anywhere you're likely to find Phoebe, it'll be there. You saw how fiercely she defended her mistress every time it was suggested Lady Cavanaugh was guilty of anything."

Hugh shook his head. He'd contemplated it, but he had business that clashed with the court hearing, though the truth was he didn't want to encourage Ada while his mind was still churning over what to do. He tapped his fingers on the chair arm. "Phoebe was too afraid to see the magistrate or Wentworth. I doubt she'd have the courage to show her face in a place where she might be recognized."

"Oh, but you must go!" Ada cried. "It's all anyone is talking about. I mean, a duchess murdering her own husband! She'll be tried in the Lords, but I hear she has few friends of any importance who are likely to be sympathetic." Ada sat down in a chair opposite and picked up her tatting. "Aren't you interested just to see what Lady Cavanaugh looks like, knowing what kind of woman she is? *I* am. Beautiful and calculating, they say, and prepared to do anything to make a man bend to her will. She cuckolded her husband for years with an endless number of lovers. Will she play the injured wife whose hand was forced, or appear with more defiant countenance?"

Hugh sent his sister a shocked look. He was about to ask what she knew of such matters but thought better of it. Ada was far more worldly than she ought to be, but they themselves had a charade to maintain in order to preserve the pretense that she really was the unblemished virgin she must present to the world in order to marry well. Before he had a chance to interject, Ada sighed and said, "Of course, I wouldn't have dreamed of showing my face where *you know who* would be strutting about, but without my even bringing up the subject, Mr Xavier said he believes it would not be a delicate thing for any lady to hear the particulars in view of the dastardliness of Lady Cavanaugh's crime, and that he presumes I'd not even think of attending. Those were his words, more or less." She dimpled. "If he's afraid for my delicate sensibilities, then I'm not about to prove that they're not very delicate at all." She giggled. "You see how I'm made bold and able to talk about Mr Wentworth—there! I said his name—because I now have Mr Xavier."

She sent her brother a look of entreaty. "Please go, Hugh. I'm dying to hear all the details."

Hugh knew he'd have gone anyway. Anything that might possibly yield Phoebe was a chance he'd chase, but Ada's insistence had him nodding his head, while his heart beat wildly at the thought of ever seeing Phoebe again.

18

So that's how he found himself at a special court session on a chilly afternoon, shivering in his caped coat, though the temperature was rising rapidly with so many heated bodies packed in to see England's most sensational female criminal show her face.

Not that Hugh was especially interested in Lady Cavanaugh. The gossip surrounding her suggested a vain and self-centered woman who traded on her beauty to achieve her venal ends. Such women held no interest for Hugh. The possibility that Phoebe, however, might have slipped into the courtroom, disguised, to observe her beloved mistress, was his inducement for cancelling his other engagement; one of considerable potential importance too, since it involved discussion about a sinecure which, if awarded to him as had been hinted, he hoped would establish him on the political scene.

Yet he was not going to throw away his best chance of locating Phoebe; darling Phoebe whom he'd fondly accused of being venal in her attempts to cajole him into providing her with the clothing and other accounterments she required to better herself. But she had loved him. Certainly, she had for a while. It was impossible that she could have feigned such physical reactions toward him.

Hugh bowed his head. Why had she left him? Her timing could not have been more unexpected, though she had hinted at the possibility, telling him she would accept no man as her master.

He might not have liked what she'd said, but at least Phoebe was transparent, open, and honest. Unlike her mistress. Hugh could not imagine the horrors of being wed to a conniving, unfaithful wife like Lady Cavanaugh, who deceived and plotted murder.

A small group entered the courtroom, and surreptitiously, Hugh scanned each face. Both women were veiled, but the way they carried themselves was enough for Hugh to dismiss them in an instant. Phoebe had such a regal carriage.

The benches had quickly filled for the most notorious court case in years, and when no more people were allowed through the door, Hugh settled back in disappointment. Phoebe did not appear to be here, after all.

A sea of wigs belonging to the older gentlemen, and a sprinkling of bonnets on all sides of him; people chattering; all made him feel very alone, reinforcing how much he missed Phoebe's bright and lively chatter.

And then a hush fell upon the assembly as the magistrate entered the courtroom, taking his seat and banging his gavel loudly for quiet before calling for the prisoner.

The woman on his right whispered loudly that she'd never seen a real live murderess before. It didn't strike Hugh as odd that Lady Cavanaugh had already been convicted in the court of public opinion. All he'd ever heard of the woman were vile insinuations about the lovers she'd had behind her husband's back. That was something the common folk did not forgive.

He wondered if Lady Cavanaugh's cold, defiant gaze raking the spectators would flare with recognition if she happened to catch sight of Phoebe. He hoped so. Sadly, though, it seemed that Phoebe was the duchess's only supporter.

Footsteps echoed in the silence. Everyone in the courtroom turned, Hugh included, as a woman in a black cloak was led from a holding room. She clasped her hands together and her head was bowed, but her carriage was straight and proud as a court official led her to the stand.

Not until the defendant actually appeared before the courtroom assembly, her large blue eyes staring out at the crowd with a mixture of defiance and apprehension, her demure manner of dress so at odds with her reputation, did Hugh convulse with shock at the light of recognition that tore through him.

Dear Lord, my eyes are deceiving me. He blinked, but when he refocused his gaze, he was close enough to the front to see her clearly. Every last fine line about her eyes, the curve of her lips, the graceful sweep of her throat, the purity of her gaze, were images he'd carried with him since she'd disappeared. Seeing her in the flesh sent a shudder through him of the greatest ecstasy mixed with the deepest dread, the utmost dismay. Here was the notorious Lady Cavanaugh, whom everyone was convinced had murdered her ailing husband to secure her comfort. And Lady Cavanaugh was none other than his own darling Phoebe.

Except that he wasn't sure if he could call her that any longer. Darling was a term of endearment reserved for someone who was forthcoming in their dealings, honest and true. Not someone who claimed to be an ill-used underling dependent on her rescuer's mercy, while all the while pulling the wool over her latest protector's eyes.

He continued to stare at her, willing her to meet his gaze. Her face was without expression, staring stonily into the judgmental crowd. She hadn't picked Hugh out in the sea of faces. Her line of vision was somewhere over the tops of people's heads, and only the tapping of her right forefinger upon her forearm as she hugged herself gave any indication of her agitation.

The magistrate identified her, and she nodded her head as she accepted that she was indeed Lady Cavanaugh, Duchess of Blinley.

A list of charges against her was then read out. Hugh could not drag his devastated gaze from her face, white and frightened, but still the beautiful compilation of features he'd contoured during the lazy, sensual sessions which had bound them together.

The crackle of alertness in the room seemed to pulse around all but him. His was the only interest that was not prurient. None of these people had ever met Lady Cavanaugh, but for a small section of the courtroom set aside for the aristocrats. Hugh was not one of them. Though he could claim lineage on both sides to the aristocracy, he was merely third in line to a baronetcy; a gentleman but not a noble. Not like Lady Cavanaugh, though he wondered briefly at her status prior to her marriage, and then realized with a stab of shame that, in truth, he knew nothing about her. Nothing about the woman to whom he'd lost his heart, and whom he'd wooed with a roughness and lack of respect that now horrified him. As horrifying was that he'd taken her at her word, not questioning her when she'd declared herself Lady Cavanaugh's servant, and consequently regarding her airs and graces with amusement, if not mild contempt.

Yet shouldn't he be more horrified that she was to all those in the room today, a sensational murderess?

Could she truly be guilty of a crime so foul and premeditated as the one of which she was charged? It went against the grain of everything he knew her to be.

He gave himself a mental shake. Phoebe had lied to him from the start. Everything she'd ever told him *must* have been a lie. The fact she'd not trusted him with the truth lay heavy and bitter on him now. She'd disappeared, obviously because she'd been apprehended, but she'd not even spirited a message to him. Because she didn't believe he could help her? Because he could no longer be of use to her?

His disordered feelings were not soothed when the night he'd first met Phoebe became the focus of questioning.

The late Lord Cavanaugh's manservant was called as a witness and asked about the series of events leading up to the murder.

"Mr Wentworth—I mean, the new Lord Cavanaugh as he are

now—were payin' 'is fortnightly visit an' after the dinner plates was cleared away, he an' Lady Cavanaugh left me master ter do what they usually did."

"And what was that?" the magistrate asked.

The manservant cleared his throat. He looked embarrassed. "They went to me lady's bedchamber, sir."

A titter ran through the courtroom, and Hugh fixed his stony gaze on Phoebe. Dear God, she and *Wentworth*? But of course, that was all he'd ever heard about Lady Cavanaugh. That she'd despised her husband whom she'd cuckolded with the odious Wentworth, the seducer of Hugh's own sister. And she went willingly with him every *fortnight*?

His eyes bored into her as he tried to see in her the sweet, ingenuous creature he'd once believed her to be; as he willed her to see him. But her expression remained implacable through every damning statement, as if her perfect features were carved out of alabaster.

Let her deny it, he found himself wishing urgently.

But when the magistrate asked her if everything the manservant claimed was true, she merely nodded.

"And was there any indication of impropriety, Mr Duckworth?" The magistrate asked. "The implication merely in visiting a lady's bedchamber suggests there is, but do you have any evidence? We cannot rely on hearsay or merely your *belief* that my lady was cuckolding her husband."

"There were always a lot of noise when them two were at it." The coarse-featured retainer looked embarrassed, but when his audience laughed, he straightened in his chair with a grin and elaborated further, warming to the details which were encouraged by his interrogator.

"And how long do you estimate this affair between Lady Cavanaugh and Lord Wentworth had been going on?"

"'Bout six months, m'lord," Duckworth replied. "Lady Cavanaugh used ter wait at the drawin' room window each fortnight fer sign of 'is carriage an' then she'd meet 'im on the portico.

No, she showed little such affection fer 'er 'usband," he answered when quizzed.

A fornicating, cuckolding, husband-hating woman charged with the murder of a respected peer of the realm. Long-familiar with the description he'd heard from around the village and in the local tavern, Hugh had accepted her guilt, almost as unquestioningly as the rest of them. He'd been mildly impressed that Phoebe had defended Lady Cavanaugh with such loyalty.

Now hearing the description as if with fresh ears, Hugh could not reconcile the Phoebe he knew as the one described by Duckworth, and later by a string of other servants; and finally by Sir Roderick and his mealy-mouthed daughter who all testified against her. The Phoebe Hugh knew was honest and direct, not a conniving liar with clearly murderous tendencies. Yes, in the space of half an hour, he'd at least made that turnaround.

Despairingly, he wondered what would happen to her. Not a single person was prepared to offer a different version of the woman he'd loved. As the evidence of her poor character mounted, and no one spoke in her defense, he realized she was going to die. She admitted she was a faithless wife who disliked her husband; admitted to everything that gave her a motive for killing the late Lord Cavanaugh.

More damning than all else, though, was the account of the maids who ran into the drawing room at the sounds of screaming, to find her holding the paper knife, wet with blood, that she'd just plunged into her husband's heart.

Hugh remembered the night she'd thrown herself from Wentworth's carriage and fled from him into the woods. She'd been covered in blood. Terrified by the shocking events that had just occurred. She'd told him she was Lady Cavanaugh's maid; that the crime was wrongly attributed to Lady Cavanaugh. Could there be another explanation? One that, despite her having every desire to wish her husband dead—with her lover waiting in the wings—exonerated her?

Now it was her turn to speak about the events of that particular night. The courtroom became hushed following riotous comments following the unflattering testimony of one of the chambermaids who went into even greater detail than Duckworth about her mistress's bedroom exploits as she "were the one wot 'ad to clean up after them an' they did like a good romp."

"Where were you when you heard about the death of your husband's heir, Lady Cavanaugh?" asked the magistrate.

"In my bedchamber." She held her head regally, no doubt in anticipation of the inevitable rejoinder.

"With your father's cousin, Lord Wentworth?"

She gave a small nod, and Hugh's lip curled in disgust. She'd claimed to be so many things he knew she was not—but he never would have believed she was capable of murder, or of consorting with men for financial gain. Not just any man, but *Wentworth*.

A series of fleeting memories of the two of them, Hugh and Phoebe, entwined as they enjoyed each other's bodies, now took on a far less rosy hue.

Finally came the questions regarding the murder itself. At this point, Lady Cavanaugh became far more vociferous in her responses, declaring that she had neither murder nor intent to harm in her mind when the knife was plunged into her husband's heart.

"But you admit that it was your hand which held the weapon that was the cause of death?"

For a moment she looked helpless, and Hugh prayed that in the final moment she would declare that to be a fabrication, just as she'd declared—when he thought her as sweet Phoebe—that Lady Cavanaugh *was innocent*.

But she did not. Raising her voice and looking at Wentworth who sat nearby, she said clearly, "I have served you well, haven't I, Wentworth? You used *your* superior strength to plunge the paper knife, such an innocent implement in my hands but so lethal when controlled by you, to do what you would not, could not, do yourself." Her voice wavered a moment before gaining strength. "The moment you heard that *both* of your two brothers who stood between you and my husband's estate, which you'd never thought you'd inherit, had died, you had to find a way to eliminate the only other obstacle in your way after Wentworth—me!"

The court erupted into uproar, and when calm had been established, the magistrate scoffed into the vacuum of silence, "Come now, Lady Cavanaugh, that's going too far. He did not eliminate you. Why, you eliminated your husband."

"Mr Wentworth had good reason to fear me standing in the way of his inheriting."

"Pray what motive could he have? You were only his cousin's wife."

Hugh was aware of every movement and twitch of Phoebe's expression. He'd grown to know her better than he'd realized as he watched her inner thoughts flit across her face like a chart only he could read. He knew something momentous was coming, and he was not wrong.

"He had every reason to fear my ability to stand in his way, since I was carrying—and still carry—my husband's child."

A gasp rustled through the assembled room. Hugh's was added to it as his mouth dropped open. Could it be true? He thought rapidly. He'd given it no thought, but he could not remember when she'd last bled.

With an angry roar, Wentworth leaped to his feet. "Liar!" he spat. And then over the top of the din, "The lady is a liar!"

"You cannot disprove what will inevitably come to pass: the birth of my husband's child and, if it is born a boy, then you will no longer have claim to my husband's estate and assets for which you murdered." She spoke with passion, but not unseemly hysteria. Hugh had to admire her for that.

"If you are with child, then it will not be your husband's!" screamed Wentworth. "Everyone knows that!"

Phoebe looked at him calmly. "*How* can you prove that, Mr Wentworth?"

SHAKING, PHOEBE LEFT THE COURTROOM FOR AN ADJOURNMENT, refusing the assistance of the turnkeys who flanked her. She had a sudden urge to be ill, but knew she could not give into weakness now. She'd succeeded in knocking the wind from Wentworth's sails, and that was a small victory that would have to sustain her for now.

As a lady, she had not been housed with the common prisoners as Wentworth had been so insistent should happen. Small mercy, indeed. Instead, she occupied her own pleasant chamber by the turnkey's cottage where the turnkey's wife waited upon her with an air of quiet outrage, and to where she was now led.

"Ye're enough to fill an old woman with horror at what ye done," the woman hissed, as she thrust a plate of food in front of her prisoner before she left Phoebe to the silence she'd become used to.

But it was Phoebe who felt the horror in its full force when a gentle tap upon the door did not herald the arrival of her evening meal but instead, Hugh.

Her first reaction was to hurl her arms about his neck and give into a cathartic bout of weeping, but his stiff stance did not encourage this. Nor had she expected their possible reunion would be sweetness and exoneration. He'd have heard every damning piece of evidence against her.

"You were in the courtroom?" There was no need to ask, but still, her mind raced over all the defamatory statements about her that he'd be digesting right now.

He nodded, his eyes bleak as he looked past her. "May I come in?"

"Of course." She indicated a chair by the fire, but he shook his head. "I won't stay long. I just wanted to satisfy myself that you were well and..." he frowned, unable it seemed to continue.

"To ask why I lied to you?" she supplied.

"Why did you?"

"Oh Hugh...." Phoebe sucked in a breath, "...I cannot expect you to understand why I made any of the decisions I did. I cannot expect you to begin to know what it was like living with Ulrick—"

"Many women live with violent husbands, but that's no excuse to—"

Horrified she cut him off. "*You*, too, believe I killed Ulrick? That it was *planned*?" She put her hands to her face then said more calmly, "Well, you have your answer. You are like all the rest: judging that which you can't possibly know. That's why I did not reveal to you who I really was."

"And who are you really, Phoebe?" Hugh's face contorted as he gripped her arm. "The girl I knew was honest and brazen and fearless. A maidservant with a fierce loyalty to her mistress accused of murder. I admired the fact she would risk so much to raise her voice and testify to her belief that her mistress was innocent."

Phoebe said nothing.

"Now I find that you're that mistress. Mistress to maidservant Phoebe who doesn't exist, and mistress to the evil Wentworth who seduced my sister. And every fortnight you went with him *willingly*?"

Phoebe dropped her eyes before giving him a searching look. "Did your sister not go willingly too? Ask your Ada if Wentworth was not compelling? That he had the charm to woo with honeyed words a vulnerable female." She swallowed. "I was vulnerable because I needed to provide Ulrick with an heir. Not an easy matter when he was impotent. Wentworth had been laying on the charm thickly for years, but finally it was Ulrick who directed me to lie with his cousin in order that Wentworth's eldest feeble-minded brother would not inherit."

Hugh stared at her. "You and Wentworth acted as one in your attempts to beget Ulrick's heir. What about Ulrick's murder? You claim your hand was forced. Yet the two of you had been united in everything else."

"Now do you see why I did not wish to be caught?" It was hard to swallow. "You cared for me enough to make me your mistress, you came to know me better than anyone, yet you consider me guilty. Just like everyone else." She managed a breath though panic tore at her. "And now I'm going to die for a crime that was brilliantly executed by Wentworth. How clever he is," she added bitterly.

"Are you really carrying Wentworth's child?" She saw the effort his question cost him and managed a smile.

"Definitely *not* Wentworth's. How terrified I was that I might be when I fled the manor. After news had been delivered that Wentworth's older brothers were dead, and he was now heir, it was my taunt that, in fact, I was with child—meaning he'd not inherit after all—that tipped Wentworth over the edge. He lunged at me when I said that, clasped my hand around the handle of the paper knife, and forced it into Ulrick's chest." She started to shake, recalling the horror of her helplessness. "And then he tried to murder me. That's why I fled with nothing but the chemise I was wearing."

"But you were Wentworth's...paramour. Why taunt him?"

"I couldn't bear being his whore, but Ulrick forced me. I thought if I told him I was pregnant he'd leave me alone."

"So you *are*...with child?"

"Not Wentworth's, if that's what you're asking."

He put his head on one side, his confusion heartbreaking to witness. "What are you saying, Phoebe? *You* seduced *me*, Phoebe. I remember it clearly. Was there a reason other than my charm?"

She wanted to hold him and reassure him, but of course she couldn't. He'd leave thinking the worst, and she'd die without ever having a final piece of comfort of the man she loved.

"I'll be honest. When I realized I wasn't carrying Wentworth's child, I was afraid. Then it occurred to me that if I *were* with child, I could delay the noose, and perhaps win the time needed to find witnesses to speak in my defense or evidence to exonerate me."

Hugh's expression narrowed. "So when you seduced me, I was nothing more than a means to an end. Of course, later you thought otherwise hence the need for precautions."

"I realized it wasn't fair to trick you like that: not fair to you, or the child that might result."

Calculating the months, he asked again, "Are you with child?"

"I'd rather not answer that."

He blanched but instead of pressing her, said, "Tomorrow, sentence will be handed down. It may not go well for you."

She bowed her head. "I fully anticipate it will not." Hugging herself, she turned toward the center of the room. "I've had some days of silence and the energies of a confessor to prepare myself." Turning back, she smiled. "I would have hoped to have retained your regard, though, Hugh. I thought, perhaps, you might understand my helplessness, my friendlessness. That would have meant a lot to me. You have been my only friend, and that sustains me."

His voice was low. "If there *were* anything I could do to help you, I would. You haven't lost my support, Phoebe, though I still don't understand how you could have associated yourself so completely with Wentworth. But..." she heard the pain in his tone, "...if you are with child, your sentence will be stayed until after its birth."

She flung open her arms, frustrated. "And then in nine months, a preordained orphan will enter the world. One who will have to bear the stain of its mother's crimes, and its bastardy, for the rest of its life. No, Hugh. Much as I have craved your comfort, I am not so cruel that I would visit that on my own flesh and blood."

He looked shocked. "It would give you a stay of execution at the very least."

"If that is the best I have to look forward to, then I would decline." She waved him to the door. "Thank you for visiting me, Hugh. And thank you for all your kindness in the past. You were loving and generous in every sense. I've never known a man as generous. Ulrick, who never loved me, took pleasure in making my life a misery, and Wentworth traded on his charm to make a fool of me, then worked me to his own ends. You were the one bright spot in my short and, until recently, unremarkable history."

She steeled herself to resist him when he would embrace her, pushing him away before retreating. “No, Hugh. It’s not fair to either of us. I lied to you and pretended things I’m not. That’s why I couldn’t write to you when I was detained here. I might not be guilty of intent to murder, but my vanity and foolishness made me as culpable as if I were. Please go, Hugh.”

But he did not.

19

Instead he put his hand on her shoulder to stay her and whereas a moment before she'd longed for his touch, now she wasn't ready for any chink in his mistrusting demeanor. He'd made clear that he believed that, if not guilty of murder, she was clearly capable of it. Her lies had paved the way for his loss of love, and what he'd seen in court today was too raw. She understood that.

She didn't need his pity. "Just go. There's nothing you can do for me now."

"I can't. Not like this, Phoebe. Whatever happens tomorrow, you don't deserve to die." His voice cracked.

"Even though you think I'm guilty?"

He shook his head, unable to speak.

"But you don't believe me entirely innocent?"

"You committed adultery with Wentworth."

Phoebe shook her head slowly at the pain in his eyes. He pressed his lips together. "While your husband was dying, you were...making love to another man. To Wentworth."

"I'd hardly call it 'making love' though I'm happy to accept a charge of adultery. Not murder."

"Why, Phoebe? Why *Wentworth*?"

"Don't think about it if it troubles you so much," she muttered, turning her back on him and moving into the center of the small sitting room.

He stepped in front of her.

"What would induce a good woman to go against all her principles of honor? Even after everything I heard today, I can't help loving you. And now you're going to die for your sins, though I don't believe you killed your husband."

"Oh, but that really cheers me. You can leave right now, Hugh. Or have you decided it might be a suitable time to execute your moral duty and try to impregnate me in the faint hope that pleading the belly might extend my life a further painful nine months?"

"Don't be coarse."

"Don't be bigoted and narrow-minded. If you were a powerless woman married to a tyrant who forced you to lie with his cousin to beget an heir, I'd like to see you try and resist."

He took her hands and shook his head. "I can't bear to lose you."

"You made it clear you didn't like the woman you discovered I really was."

"You take that too far, Phoebe. It was your willingness to consort with Wentworth that turned my stomach. Everything I've just heard...I'll reconcile it with what I know you to be in time, but right now—"

She stepped back. "Say no more, Hugh. I loved you as much for the fact you are the most honorable man I've met, as that you believed I was worthy of your love. Now that I see you think I'm not worthy of the feelings you once had, I don't want to drag out this painful interview. We know what tomorrow's verdict will be, and I'm reconciled. Please spare us both. Just leave."

It had been three hours since Hugh had torn himself away from Phoebe's side, but he'd not returned to his bed to sleep. Sleep would elude him, and right now he wanted to try and make sense of the nightmare he'd just lived through.

The moon was high in the sky as he trod the gravel path that wound among the rhododendrons in the back garden of his cottage in Hampstead. He'd been unable to bear returning to St John's Wood where he'd spent his two happiest weeks.

Phoebe had accepted her fate with dignity and stoicism. She was brave. She'd not wept pitifully or begged forgiveness for a crime she did not commit.

He'd condemned her for her lies, attributed all manner of underhand behavior to her, but she was prepared to accept her fate.

He twisted his head around and stared into the branches of a fir tree at the hoot of an owl. Two black eyes regarded him dispassionately. They reminded Hugh of the magistrate's. Lord Coulson had exhibited little compassion toward Phoebe, giving the impression he already considered her guilty when she took the stand.

Justice would be swift. It was possible, though not likely, she'd be sent across the seas for the term of her natural life. The clamoring for her to receive a death sentence was too vociferous. A husband should be safe in his own bed. Women, as much as men, were outraged.

Tomorrow, when sentence was handed down, Phoebe would know to the last minute the number of hours left to her. As Hugh had kissed her farewell, she'd said softly, "Just know that of all men, I've loved you best."

He turned to find the source of the eerie whirring above him and saw the flock of bats, before his sister's face at the casement came into view. She waved to him, and in a few minutes, he greeted her in the library where a small fire warmed the room.

"You look shocking, brother dearest," Ada told him, wrapping her shawl around her, her expression fierce. "All this gaming and whoring isn't good for the complexion, you know. Are you only just back? "

Hugh ran his hand through his hair before taking a seat in front of the warmth. "I haven't been out. Well, not since being in the courtroom for Lady Cavanaugh's trial, then visiting Phoebe afterward."

She raised her eyebrows, looked about to say something, then muttered in an undertone, "As I said, whoring. So you found Phoebe? I'm so glad. I was beginning to feel quite guilty."

"Phoebe is Lady Cavanaugh." Hugh watched the information register, and wasn't surprised at the horror that dawned on his sister's face. "I saw her in court and will go again tomorrow."

Ada gasped and brought her hand up to her mouth. "What did you say?"

"My Phoebe is, in fact, Lady Cavanaugh, who was, it appears, detained while visiting a shady establishment called Mrs Plumb's Salon of Sin in search of Mr Wentworth's wife."

"*Phoebe* is Lady Cavanaugh...who murdered her husband?"

"She claims Wentworth forced her hand—literally—making her powerless when he used her as his instrument to drive a paper knife through her dying husband's chest."

"Does the magistrate accept her defense?"

Wearily, Hugh shook his head. "Sentence will be passed in the morning. There is little doubt she will hang."

"For a crime that Mr *Wentworth* committed?" Ada gripped the back of the chair then began to pace. "He is the new heir, the new duke, the new Lord Cavanaugh," she muttered, frowning as she digested the news and its implications with new horror. "Let me think, Hugh. What do I know of the case, for I've followed it slavishly in view of Wentworth being involved." She chewed her lip as she moved back and forth before the fire. "Wentworth learned news of the death of his two brothers the very day the late Lord Cavanaugh was murdered." She looked up suddenly. "How very convenient that Phoebe—I mean Lady Cavanaugh—was on hand so that he could simply encase her hand around the paper knife and drive it into her husband's chest. How just like Wentworth to come up with such a plan, though I'm sure it was conceived on the spot. He would snatch any opportunity to use to his advantage."

Hugh was glad that Ada was defending Phoebe, but he had to put her outrage into perspective. He loved Phoebe, but the truth behind that night was almost more than he could bear.

"Ada, she was...caught *in flagrante* with Mr Wentworth by the servant delivering news of the deaths of Mr Wentworth's brothers." He squeezed shut his eyes as he tried to eradicate the image. "She'd been cuckolding her husband for nearly half a year before he died. She had every reason to wish him dead."

Ada looked up, confused. "But you said she *didn't* kill him."

"*Her* hand was around the paper knife. That's what Phoebe admitted, in court. That's what will convict her."

"Yes, but he forced her." Ada looked angry. "You clearly do not know Mr Wentworth as I do. He could persuade anyone of anything, though in this case, I've no doubt he used brute force. He is a master of manipulation, a bully." Her voice was rising now, and Hugh put an arm about her to hush her distress, but she pulled away and went to stand before the fire. "I know how dangerous he is, and I thought you did too." Her expression was both pitying and angry. "Oh, Hugh, how dare you insinuate that there is a particle of blame to be attached to poor Phoebe."

"She lied, Ada. She lied to her husband; she lied to me, and she lied to you."

Ada put her hands on her hips, her expression combative. "Do you think I didn't lie to you when I had my secret assignations with Wentworth? Do you think we're all as holy as you are, Hugh? Who have never had to utter a lie in your life because you've always been so safe and protected? Partly because you're a man, and everything has turned out well for you, so that you only have to play the knight in shining armor and you'll always look so much better than everyone else?"

"I don't believe she should die for it if that's what you mean," he answered hotly.

"Well, that's good! I don't either, and the fact that it was due to *my* request that she even got caught and is where she is now is... intolerable!" Ada was breathing fast now. After a long silence, she said, "So what are you going to do about it, Hugh?"

He stared. "Do about it? What *can* I do about it? She'll learn her fate tomorrow, though God knows I'd do anything to spare her life."

"Because you love her, or because you don't think she deserves to die...despite the fact that she lied to you, and you can't bear the idea of thinking that the same woman who gave herself to Wentworth could give herself to you?" Ada let out a strangled cry of frustration. "You men are all the same. You have no idea that a woman is completely dependent upon the goodness of the men who surround them. You're exactly the same, Hugh. You have this unrealistic notion of what 'good' is all about. The only reason I met Wentworth secretly was because you prevented me from seeing him! You were so terrified I'd be *enticed* after I hinted at my feelings for him after you met him at the Assembly. Perhaps I'd not have been so intent on defying you if had you not been so determined to protect your innocent sister."

"Good Lord, Ada!"

She shrugged. "The folly of youth. What have been your follies? Just because I'm a woman, I'm allowed so little latitude, and sometimes we women chafe at the restrictions imposed by the men on whom they are dependent—even when those men have only the very best of intentions. But now I'm straying from the subject."

"Indeed you are." Hugh felt uncomfortable.

"You agree with the magistrate that Phoebe should be punished for 'lying' though you think a death sentence is a little harsh? Well, Hugh, if you are sincere about enforcing good, then you just need to get Phoebe out of there. Rescue her," she added when he looked at her blankly.

"How on earth am I to do that?" Hugh watched Ada's bent head and furrowed brow and felt his desperation rise.

He moved forward to put his hands on Ada's shoulders and tipped her face up to his. "Ada, do you think I'd really scorn Phoebe like that?" He shook his head. "I've had to confront so much about myself and the way I treated her since Phoebe went missing. At first, I assumed she'd left me, having little regard for anything other than feathering her nest as best she could and having had a better offer. I forced myself to be angry with her as it lessened the pain."

Ada stroked his shoulder. "I know, Hugh," she said softly. "And I'm sorry if I wasn't as sympathetic as I should have been. I thought the same as you."

"And then when I learned that Phoebe had been pretending to be someone else the whole time she'd been with me, that was hard enough. When I saw her as notorious Lady Cavanaugh, and that not a soul stood up to defend her, I could only wonder why she'd never told me the truth at least. What else had she to hide? I assumed she was at least in part guilty, and I felt anger; I admit it."

"But you were persuaded otherwise? I hope so, Hugh, because I can assure you that if Wentworth had any hand in it—as, of course, he does—then Phoebe was the blameless victim. Wentworth gains his power through manipulating others."

Hugh dropped his hands and leaned against the mantelpiece. "How on earth am I to help her, Ada?"

Ada shrugged. "How on earth do I know?" She sighed and rubbed her eyes. "There's nothing anyone can do. Tomorrow, Wentworth will say his piece, and that'll put the final nail in her coffin."

"Wentworth!" Hugh started at the name, glancing up in sudden excitement. "That's it, Ada! Yes, we know Phoebe was framed or manipulated by Wentworth. *And* when she went to this house of... introduction you mentioned in order to find evidence to help your case he was there, and she was caught. But what other secrets might be learned here at this....?"

"Madam Plumb's Salon of Sin," Ada supplied as her lips curved into a smile. "You're right, Hugh. I have no idea if you'll find anything, but at least it's something you can do. Wentworth's wife is there. She may be able to help you. Testify against her husband, perhaps."

He sighed. "I don't know about that but I know I certainly won't sleep. Not now that at least I'm offered this kernel of hope." He shook himself out of his lethargy and said with renewed energy, "You're right, Ada. It's the best I can try: to find Mrs Wentworth and make her talk." He strode toward the door. "I must change."

"And you must go in disguise, Hugh. That's what everyone does, I believe. And I'll whisper the address. Even saying the name makes me blush with shame."

THERE WAS NOTHING OUT OF THE ORDINARY ABOUT THE HOUSE. It stood four-square and respectable by a neat square park surrounded by wrought iron railings. For ten minutes, Hugh sat in his carriage and watched the front door. Some arrivals came with loud, confident companions while others, wearing masks and veils, were more furtive.

He pulled his mask down over his eyes and squared his shoulders. What had seemed a bold and daring mission now seemed fraught with disappointment.

The truth was, what could he possibly learn that would help Phoebe? Wentworth's story was not just plausible, it had not been contested, and not a single person had stepped up to defend the woman he loved. Every member of the late Lord Cavanaugh's household and all of Wentworth's retainers had vouched for their respective masters, declaring it easy to believe the worst of Phoebe.

After gaining admittance and being ushered down a narrow hallway to a suite of reception rooms, Hugh had already decided his greatest chance lay in speaking to Wentworth's wife. She was a dancer, a vestal virgin, he now knew, called Ariane, though he was sure that a woman working in this establishment did not restrict her repertoire to simply dancing.

Over the refreshments table, he learned where to find the six famous vestal virgins. A peephole enabled one secret access, but for a considerable sum, he could himself be involved in the sensual dance. The inference wasn't lost on him, though he recoiled.

"Come and look, and then you can decide which lady you'd like to...invite for further refreshments." The woman who spoke to him was, he noticed, one of the few not wearing a veil. She smiled a coy little smile which sat ill with her advancing years. "This is your first time here?"

He inclined his head.

"I hope you will find the entertainment on offer sufficient to entice you to return to my little establishment. Here, there is no discernment between the highest in the land and the humblest among us. All that is required is the facility for pleasure."

"You are Mrs Plumb?"

"I am indeed. And now if you'd like to follow me, I shall take you to see the vestal virgins."

Obediently, Hugh followed the stout little woman along a series of dimly-lit corridors. To the right of where they stopped was a red-painted door flanked by two large potted palms.

"Take your place between these and put your eye to the peephole. You will be all but hidden from the public so can enjoy yourself as you see fit." She smiled knowingly. "For some that is sufficient; however, if you find your desires are only further inflamed, then you may pass a note through the grille stating your pleasure, and the girls themselves will decide whether or not they have a mind to grant it."

Hugh raised his eyebrows, and Mrs Plumb laughed and tapped him on the shoulder with her fan. "This is not a brothel, my good sir, and the women behind these doors make their own decisions as to how far they're prepared to indulge their appetites. Ariane, for example, likes tall, dark men. I doubt she would take up an offer from you. Helena enjoys a challenge and considers every offer on merit. Minna, now, only ever performs her sensuous dance for peers of the realm who request it. She will consider no offers under five hundred pounds."

"Good Lord, she must be good!" Hugh couldn't help remarking, and Mrs Plumb raised one eyebrow. "She's never been tested. Certainly, not in my establishment, but there is one who has offered that amount and who will take his pleasure tomorrow, so unless you choose to raise the amount, I suggest you confine your interest to one of the others."

Mrs Plumb left him shaking his head, though not for long, for once his eye was at the peephole, he was entirely transfixed. Of course, spying was not a pastime for gentlemen, and Hugh did indeed feel keenly the irony. He was not a man who paid for transient pleasures. Taking Phoebe as his mistress was the first time he'd exchanged money for the keeping of a woman.

Fear for what tomorrow would bring threatened to overwhelm him; there was no pleasure in the erotic sight before him.

The women, all of similar height, one with golden tresses, another dark as a raven's wing, one red-haired, and one with brown tresses past her waist, were swaying in time to a rhythmic chant. A strange mist swirled through the gloom, sending an unidentified, invisible perfume curling under the door.

It was not hard to identify Ariane with her golden tresses and her striking confidence. No doubt the most dangerous in view of what had happened to Phoebe. Her knowing look as she glanced in his direction suggested she was very well aware that she was under observation, and that she enjoyed playing to her audience. *Had* she betrayed Phoebe? Certainly, if she were Wentworth's wife and yet happily consorted with her husband in these premises on occasion, the inference was that she was not the cowering abused wife Phoebe had no doubt believed she was going to meet.

The women clasped each other around the waist, their eyes vacant as their lips found each other's briefly. Breaking into pairs, they delicately contoured faces, traced lips with long fingers, and gently nuzzled throats and breasts. There was something other-worldly about the scene. Hugh felt as if he'd stepped into a world where sin was not a crime. These women looked so serene, and he longed for the gentle touch of a woman. Not of these women, but of his Phoebe.

Phoebe, who came here only a few days ago, and whose liberty ended here. He had to discover a means to discredit Wentworth or Phoebe would die.

Hastily he scribbled a note on the paper provided and slid it through the grille. Ariane was too dangerous, he'd decided. Too knowing and too calculating to confront directly. The young woman with the light brown hair and the innocent face may be less guarded. She consorted with Ariane on a regular basis. It might just be that she'd know something, anything, that would be a start.

The young woman of his choice met him in an antechamber. He'd taken a seat on the comfortable red velvet upholstered banquette with its turned arms that faced a small dais, where presumably Minna would do her little dance for the pleasure of her clients.

To his surprise, she slipped through the door and gracefully crossed the room to stand in front of him, her expression expectant.

"What news?" she asked, her voice breathless. "Where should I go? Is it tonight? Oh please say you'll get me out of here tonight, for I fear if he should come early, then what could I do? I'd rather *die*."

Hugh, who'd risen to his feet, was unsure how to respond to this little speech. The young woman, unaware of his confusion, began to pace. "I never thought I'd win such a reprieve. Oh, dear Lord, I shan't waste it. Shall we go now?" She turned suddenly, and Hugh had to admit at this point that he was really terribly sorry, but he had no idea what she was talking about.

She stared at him a moment, her face a mask of devastation. Then she gave a little gasp. "You are not Sir Gawain?"

He shook his head. "I've never heard the name."

"Oh, a made-up one, I'm sure." Her mouth trembled, and she

stared at him. "So you *really* came to watch me dance?" she asked miserably. "Not to save me from my dreadful fate that will take place tomorrow when I am to be bought like a —" She couldn't go on, bowing her head as her delicate frame was wracked by silent sobs.

Hugh was afraid to reach out to touch her, even in sympathy but then she raised her head and said in a rush, "So, you didn't come to save me. All I can hope is that a stranger who will identify himself as Sir Gawain will make himself known and rescue me before I am forced to commit a sin that will guarantee my place in Hell, though to be sure it's probably already waiting for me." She sniffed, and her sweet rosebud lips trembled. "I had just held out the tiniest little bit of hope that...*you*...might be my last chance." Collecting herself, she added on another faint sob, "But if you're not Sir Gawain, you can't help me." Her shoulders slumped. Then she seemed to snap into a different state, more with the present and businesslike. "I daresay you came here to watch me dance, then."

Hugh hesitated. "Actually, I came for information...which I'm quite willing to pay for," he added quickly, indicating the seat beside him.

"Information?" She looked frightened as she sent a look at the door then back to his face. "No sir, I won't betray any of the girls. And if you are planning to lock up all of us who operate out of here, then perhaps I'll just scream now."

Hugh rose and gripped her arm, immediately dropping his hands when he saw her tense. "I'm sorry, but let me assure you there's no need to get so agitated. I have no intention of doing any harm. I merely hope to gain some information that might save the life of a dear friend of mine who was apprehended in this house last week by a certain Mr Wentworth, before being placed in custody and who is now awaiting His Majesty's Pleasure. I'm hoping to find information that might save her from the hangman's noose."

"Ariane's husband?" Minna put her hand to her mouth. "You

didn't hear it from me," she said quickly as she turned away, clearly conflicted.

"No, I didn't. He's well known to me, and not at all in a way that casts honor on him, for all that he's your friend's husband."

"Well, he's no friend of mine," Minna muttered, "but I'd never betray Ariane.

"It's nice to know some loyalty exists in the world and you dancers—"

"Oh no, believe me, she'd kill me or rather have it done discreetly." Minna looked bleak. "I've been here two years, and I know her methods. She is beautiful but deadly. But..." she hesitated, "...the truth is she's a good friend, as long as one doesn't cross her."

"So you know her story, and that she's wife-in-waiting to a man who now has a title, and is situating himself to take advantage of what has fallen lately and unexpectedly into his lap."

"I know it," Minna said warily.

"But what you don't know perhaps is that it is at the cost of the life of the woman I love."

Minna's mouth dropped open. "I...I can't know what you mean, sir. Wentworth is a strong and powerful man with a great deal of persuasive energy. I've seen it, and I've felt it. But he would never commit murder."

Hugh looked furtively at the door, and then patted the seat beside him in the hopes she would sit there so he could lower his voice. There was little time to say what he must in order to persuade Minna to help him. If she even could. But if she were no friend of Wentworth's, and if she knew something that could be brought against him, then Hugh needed to discover it now.

"I have no choice but to trust you in the hopes you might help me save the life of the woman I love," he said urgently. "Tomorrow, sentence will be passed on Lady Cavanaugh, who is accused of murdering her husband."

Minna's eyes widened. "My Lord, what are you saying?" She looked terrified. "Wentworth is Lord Cavanaugh. He inherited the title only weeks ago upon the death of his cousin and two brothers occurring the same night. Of course I know the story. The papers can print nothing else." Agitated, she hugged herself. "Are you telling me you believe a different version?"

"I believe Lady Cavanaugh when she says Wentworth, who visited her and her husband frequently, forced her hand around the paper knife that killed her husband and made him heir. He forced her hand to commit the murder he desired and then condemned her for it. Tomorrow Lord Coulson will pass sentence on her. Her fate is already sealed for Wentworth has made a compelling case."

"Lady Cavanaugh was his mistress," Minna murmured, staring at her feet.

Hugh bridled. "I'm sure your friend Ariane was very put out and has turned you all against Lady Cavanaugh. Lord knows, she has few friends who will testify to the fact that she has been used as a pawn."

"Oh, Ariane orchestrated the union of Wentworth and Lady Cavanaugh." Minna looked at Hugh, her expression not altering at Hugh's shock. She nodded. "Shortly after I started dancing here, I remember the story well. Ariane and Wentworth had been wed several years but had done so before Wentworth's majority, and they knew he'd be disinherited if the marriage were discovered. Wentworth had two older brothers—one dimwitted, the other an out-of-control drunkard—so as he saw no chance of becoming Lord Cavanaugh, the plan was that he..." she blushed, "...sire Lord Cavanaugh's heir. It was Ariane who conceived the plan that she should make Lady Cavanaugh her husband's mistress and, with collusion from Lord Cavanaugh himself, who was...unable to sire an heir." She looked at the floor. "Poor Lady Cavanaugh. I felt sorry for her, even though I didn't know her. When Ariane gets an idea, no one escapes from her plan."

Hugh winced. He'd felt dead inside when he'd first learned the litany of sins that littered Phoebe's past. He'd believed she was easily coerced, and that she'd done it for gain. Minna painted a different story.

"Then you understand that Lady Cavanaugh is entirely innocent of the charge leveled against her." He gripped Minna's hands. "And I see that there is no love lost between you and Ariane and Wentworth. Please help me find something—anything—against Wentworth that I might use at trial tomorrow, and I'll do what I can to help you."

Minna smiled sadly. "There is nothing you can do to help me. I was a poor vicar's daughter before I was enticed to London to be the mistress of the man I thought would marry me, and now I am a dancer and for the first time have accepted an offer that will both damn me in the eyes of God forever, but will secure the happiness of my little sister who believes me dead. If Sir Gawain does not come to save me, I have *another* plan even if it places my sister's future in jeopardy, though I *will* find another way to protect her—just not through the sacrifice of what last bit of integrity I have left." She slumped as she finished her speech. "I would do whatever I could to help you, but I've told you all I know." She rose, took a step towards the door, hesitated then turned. "All I can add is that Lord Coulson, the magistrate I think you mentioned, is a regular visitor to Mrs Plumb's, and that he is here in one of these rooms now." She rose and held out her hand. "In case it is in the interests of justice, I could take you to the peephole. He's probably had it closed, but there is a possibility you might see something that could be used to...persuade him that condemning Lady Cavanaugh to death is rather extreme when his proclivities invite the death penalty too."

20

Hugh followed Minna a little way down a corridor where she stopped, pointing to the end of a passage at right angles. From the room to the right, he could hear faint singing punctuated with breathless sighs. Several patrons sagging against each other as they traversed the passage brushed past and disappeared through a nearby door, not closing it before shrieks of laughter issued into the corridor.

"Go to the last room," she whispered. "I must return to my antechamber in case Sir Gawain does come for me."

Hugh nodded. "Thank you, Miss Minna, for your great help," he said. "I hope your own story will end happily."

She shrugged. "It will end in some fashion, but whether that is happily, I would not begin to speculate upon. My fate is not in my hands." She turned, saying softly over her shoulder, "I wish you good luck in your endeavors, sir, and will read the papers with great interest."

Consumed by the hope of what he might soon discover, Hugh made his way stealthily toward the room she'd indicated. Like the previous one, its door was flanked by luxuriant potted palms, the perfect cover for putting one's eye to a peephole. He ran his hand over the green-papered walls and felt the slight indent. But the hole was covered.

His spirits fell, and he stood uncertainly by the wall, wondering what he should do. The room was at the end of a long corridor, and his position there was very obvious. He decided to return to the reception rooms, and was a few feet into his return journey when a slight, fair-haired gentleman in evening clothes, wearing a mask and heading in his direction, stopped him.

"Where are you going, my dear?" he asked, looking Hugh up and down with raw appraisal, his hands on his hips, his expression arch. "I haven't missed out on all the fun, have I?"

Hugh glanced over his shoulder and saw that it must be apparent to the young man that he was returning from the very room upon whose occupants he'd hoped to spy.

His uncertainty in what to say was misconstrued, for the gentleman tipped his head to one side and said, "Lost your way, have you? Told all the fun you were looking for was in Room 404?" He giggled suddenly, and to Hugh's incredulity, took his hand. "Well, don't be shy; Reggie will look after you. There's lots of fun to be had in Room 404 if you come with me."

Hugh pulled back. "No, really, that wasn't at all..." he floundered.

Reggie dropped his hand and gave Hugh a considering look. "You just want to watch? Never done this sort of thing? Got a wife at home, eh? Maybe this is your first time?" He began to gently run his hand up and down Hugh's coat sleeve, his smile colluding. "That's all right," he whispered. "You can just watch. We'll find you some nice comfy cushions for you to lie back on and be comfortable while you see how it's done." He flashed Hugh a wicked smile and added, "As soon as you feel ready, you can join in."

With trepidation, Hugh allowed himself to be led along the passage before he was pushed into a dimly-lit room. He stopped abruptly, his eyes acclimatizing to the dimness. Lord, what den of iniquity had he landed in? he wondered as he was gently pushed into a pit of cushions. A faint whiff of scented smoke permeated the air, and when his eyes readjusted, he saw lying on a large embroidered cushion a small, large-bellied man, completely naked, playing with himself.

Hugh forced himself not to gasp with shock. Without his clothes, Lord Coulson looked like a gleaming white walrus with shaggy gray facial hair, his domed forehead topping a pear-shaped body. He started when he heard Reggie and sat up, peering through the gloom. Hugh was glad he still wore his clothes, including his mask, but then he'd no more divest his clothes in a place like this than...give up on Phoebe.

"You've brought a friend, Reggie?" The magistrate's voice was slightly slurred and Hugh, tense with terror, was relieved that Lord Coulson seemed happy about this.

He raked Hugh with an appraising look. "Very nice," he said approvingly. "But perhaps this is your first time." He smacked his lips. "Don't worry; we'll make sure you enjoy your initiation, won't we, Reggie?"

Reggie gave a high-pitched squeal of excitement as he quickly divested himself of his clothes. Throwing his arms wide in theatrical fashion, he threw himself onto Lord Coulson then, in the midst of his embrace with the magistrate, beckoned to Hugh. "Oh, do join us! Don't be coy."

"I...I'd rather watch first time," Hugh said unsteadily. "I... "

"Feel guilty? Don't think about it. It's the way of the world," Reggie assured him, looking up from nibbling Lord Coulson's nipple. "Whoopsy and I are more than happy to give you a little taste of what's in store for you, lucky boy." Reggie rose onto his knees and gripped Lord Coulson's engorged member, flashing another wicked smile at Hugh over the tip.

Hugh turned his head away, his mind reeling as Reggie whooped, "Your turn next, handsome stranger," before he proceeded to pleasure the magistrate with great enthusiasm and thoroughness.

Soon the men were entirely caught up in their own pleasure.

Hugh rose to his feet and quietly made his way to the door. He felt ill, but exulted too.

He mightn't have found Wentworth to squeeze the truth out of but he'd discovered the next best thing.

"TAKE THE PRISONER AWAY!"

Phoebe stared at the two flunkeys who moved forward at the magistrate's direction. She'd survived the last two hours by pretending she was in another sphere, looking down upon herself. Now, with the howls of derision and feet banging, and so many angry faces glaring at her, she had to accept the truth. She had failed to convince the magistrate of her innocence. Not that she'd been given a great deal of opportunity. Wentworth's version was brilliantly compelling, and it all came down to the same two factors. Phoebe had been in bed with Wentworth when news arrived of his brother's deaths, and Phoebe's hand had gripped the paper knife used to kill Ulrick.

So she would die.

Judgment was to be passed before the afternoon was out.

In her cell in the tower, she stared at the gray sky and remembered what it felt like to be in Hugh's arms. How sweet and treasured those memories were to her now.

Closing her eyes, her mind ran over the soft, sensual touch of his hands upon her limbs, soothing, caressing. She smiled reluctantly. What worth had her life ever really had? She'd not been born into a position of power or influence. She'd been a pawn for her father to use to better his family's social and financial position. As Ulrick had married her for convenience, not love, she'd never had any power over him.

Wentworth had professed to love her, but how ironic was that?

As for Hugh, well, he had realised his love was based on a lie.

A waxing moon hung heavily in the sky, and she stared at it. Wondering how many moons she'd ever stare at again.

THE COURT CASE HAD BEEN A FARCE FROM THE START. HUGH could scarcely believe the smoothness with which Wentworth's bald-faced lies tripped off his tongue. He knew Phoebe was none of the things Wentworth had called her. Not that he even wanted to think about what had been said by others. Men and women no doubt in the pocket of Wentworth.

It was even probable that Lord Coulson was in some measure in collusion with Phoebe's vile and undeserving relative by marriage. Hugh would not allude to the fact she'd been his former mistress. That was so irrelevant now.

He'd tried every trick he could manage to speak a few words to the magistrate before the two-faced man of the law had donned his wig and taken the stand, but Lord Coulson had waved him away each time.

Desperate now, Hugh bowed before the rotund gentleman during a rare moment he was alone. In his robes he looked very regal, standing amid a room of fawning acolytes. His word was law. He was the keeper of the rule of law, the minister of justice, arbiter of all that was right.

"My Lord, a quick moment if you please." Hugh spoke rapidly, assessing the crowd, realizing his time was short. "I've come to beg clemency for the prisoner," he responded when the magistrate inclined his head.

Lord Coulson let out an unregal guffaw. "In an hour, justice will be done and your pleas will be answered."

"But my Lord, she is innocent."

"And if she is, judgment will reflect that."

"I don't believe judgment will do justice to the truth."

Lord Coulson stiffened. "You insult me, sir!"

"Hear me out just one moment, my Lord, for we have met before." He spoke hurriedly, watching the hand that snaked upward to beckon for assistance to usher Hugh away. "Yes, under very unusual circumstances. Do you not remember it?"

Lord Coulson's eyes slid upward to Hugh's face, assessing him, clearly trying to place him.

"You are mistaken. We have not met." His tone was suspicious. "Do you not think I know all the tricks there are? My word is law, and I cannot be bought. I could have you thrown in jail."

"You must do what you know is right. Lord Cavanaugh—Mr Wentworth who was—is not being honest in his account of what happened the night his cousin was murdered."

Lord Coulson sighed. "We have endured two long sitting days to ensure that there can be no conjecture on that score. Now you've had your time. Leave."

"Don't you wish to know who I am?"

Lord Coulson stiffened and he turned, his nose raised to the air. Hugh shot out a hand to grip his arm, and instantly Lord Coulson swatted it away; face mottled with indignation.

"In the cushions at Mrs Plumb's last night. I was the man invited in to observe your antics." Hugh spoke rapidly, pausing to watch the magistrate turn the color of thin gruel. Triumphantly, he went on, "Your *illegal* antics, my Lord, and I have witnesses who were at the peephole."

"The hole was shuttered." Lord Coulson spoke quickly and without thinking, for no sooner were the words out than he realized his error.

"The hole which I slid open as I left." Hugh was fabricating this last though there was no proof either way. Lord Coulson would have to decide whether to take him at his word. He certainly was taking a moment to decide his next move.

Cornered, he began to walk away. Hugh was confused until he realized Lord Coulson was moving to somewhere they could speak in private.

"What do you want?" the older man hissed, careful to keep his features under control as he pretended to consult a paper in his hand.

"The prisoner's freedom."

"That's not possible."

"She's not guilty. You know that."

Snake eyes stared out from beneath Lord Coulson's wig. "There's nothing I can do." His words sounded dead.

"All London shall know in the morning what you are guilty of, sir." Hugh nearly spat the words. "Then we shall see what justice is really about."

"I can't do it else Lord Cavanaugh will exact his own pound of flesh. I'm in an impossible situation. It flies in the face of every bit of testimony heard to exonerate the prisoner."

"You should have thought of that before you played in your cushiony dell with such inappropriate bedfellows."

Lord Coulson tapped his fingers on the document he was holding. Finally, he said, "There is but one concession I can make."

Hugh stilled. He put his head closer to Lord Coulson's and did not draw back from his foetid breath. For though unpalatable, what he offered was better than Phoebe's assured death.

❧

RAVENS WERE COMMON ENOUGH, BUT THE RAVENS AT THE TOWER were huge. After days of being unable to eat, Phoebe's stomach seemed to have folded in on itself. She wondered if she would make a tasty morsel for the flesh-eating birds if she were allowed to wander the battlements or gardens.

No point in such foolishness, she thought as she was led onto the waiting barge.

For a moment, Phoebe just stood on the deck, staring out across the mud and silt and the detritus left by the tide; wondering how soon before she would hear carpenters making the gallows.

"Reckon me old lady'd be right impressed wiv the week's sport. A feeble woman killin' a man. An' then gettin' her jest desserts." One of the prison guards laughed loudly as he scratched at a sore on his cheek before picking up his oars. "The beautiful assassin they calls yer." He winked at his friend. "Reckon no one would know if we 'ad us a piece of the beautiful assassin afore she's an assassin an' beautiful no more, if yer gets me meanin'."

Again they both guffawed, and Phoebe put her head over the side of the barge, fearing she was about to be sick.

"Wait! One minute before you push off!"

They turned at the shout of a young man dressed in the robes of a court official. He strode down the embankment and pushed a document into the hands of the closest of the two prison guards, stabbing at a signature and a wax seal.

"You're to surrender the prisoner into my care. I shall accompany her on her final journey downstream."

The guards exchanged looks of surprise, but made no objection as the man put his hand on Phoebe's shoulder after he'd stepped into the boat. "Sir Gawain at your service, my Lady."

Phoebe stared, confused, asking, "And what service do you render me? I am to die, by order of the king."

"I am to ensure that justice is done."

His voice was without emotion, but for some reason, Phoebe felt a stab of hope as the vessel was navigated into the middle of the current. Softly, she repeated, "Sir Gawain? Of the Round Table?" Then she giggled, shocked at the hysteria she heard in the sound. Narrowing her eyes, she tried to focus into the gloom of the bridge underpass that was coming up.

He stooped a little, and she glanced up to see his lips close to her ear. "Whisking hapless maidens from the very depths of despair is my job. You are not the only one but you must trust me if I am to help me."

A shiver ran through her. "Is that what you're doing now? Helping me?"

The temperature had dropped several degrees now that they were beneath the bridge. The sluggish river lapped at the embankment against which the ferry now abutted as it drew into a landing stage. An official in red and black was waiting to hand her onshore, and Phoebe leaped nimbly onto the quay to avoid her shoes getting wet, slipping a little so that the man hurried forward to grip her elbow, holding it a moment longer than was seemly, and whispering, "Saving hapless females from danger is not only Sir Gawain's job today."

"Hugh!" Phoebe gasped, but he shook his head, indicating the prison guards.

"Nearly came a cropper, m'lady," he said loudly, "but never fear, I've got you safe now."

Phoebe glanced from Sir Gawain, now conducting an official handover of his prisoner to Hugh, before turning back towards the road while the unquestioning guards returned to their ferry and pushed back into the current.

In the grey light, Phoebe stared at Hugh, unable to believe her eyes. They were alone at last.

And she was free? A strange feeling, half disbelief, half hysteria, clawed its way up her throat, releasing itself in a great sigh of relief.

Behind Hugh, the riverbank sloped downwards, to meet the landing stage and fast-flowing water. Dozens of vessels bobbed upon the river. It would be so easy to slip away and disappear into the seething metropolis on either bank. She had nothing to lose, after all.

But what about Hugh? He'd come to save her but she couldn't let him risk or even sacrifice his future for her.

Tears stung her eyelids as he stepped towards her, his arms outstretched, joy lighting up his face. When he registered her retreat, the hurt in his eyes cut her to the quick.

"You saved my life, Hugh, but I must leave you, now," she said, brokenly. "Please...you know there is no future happiness for us together if my only guarantee of safety is to live in exile. I would not ask that of you."

He dropped his arms. "You've asked nothing of me, Phoebe—beyond a new gown... Do not presume to tell me what I should or shouldn't sacrifice. Do you love me?"

"You know it very well." She exhaled on a sob. "Too much to let you sacrifice your ambitions."

"And I love you too much to let you go."

Phoebe brushed away a tear. The wind off the river was cold and she shivered. "You protected me when I needed protection. I used you and I abused your trust. Surely you see I am not a woman who should be trusted? If you don't think it now, the time will one day come when you will. And I can't bear that!"

She took a step backward up the incline. No, this would be her moment of sacrifice when she'd show Hugh how much he really meant to her. He might not thank her now, but he would.

"Phoebe! Please!" he entreated.

She shook her head, opening her mouth to deliver the terms that would sever them; she, by leaving and he by offering her the final proof of his love: the means to begin a modestly independent life somewhere on the Continent.

But instead of dry, emotionless business matters issuing forth, she exhaled upon a shrill scream. Danger! She'd been primed for it all these long weeks she'd been poised to flee for her life. Now, the coiled up energy she'd stored found expression in a swift lunge forward.

Behind Hugh, stepping out of the boat that had just drawn up at the landing, was the man she loathed and feared above all others: the murderer Wentworth. How could she not have noticed him approaching? But she had not amidst the general traffic on the river.

He was straightening up, one foot still in his boat, the other upon the landing, and Hugh, with his back still to him, registered only confusion as Phoebe leapt forward, pushing him out of the way just as Wentworth extended his arm to curl around Hugh's neck.

Such was the force of Phoebe's battering ram action that even her slight body had enough momentum to knock Wentworth off balance so that his legs parted and before he could right himself, either in the boat or on dry land, he came crashing down.

❧

HUGH SWUNG ROUND, ARM OUTSTRETCHED, BUT NOT WITHIN range to catch either of them before they plunged into the water with a shared scream of terror and rage.

"Phoebe!" he cried, so loudly it hurt his lungs, as he ran to the water's edge.

They were wedged between the boat and the landing but Wentworth had the advantage. With one hand clinging to an iron spike, his other held Phoebe's head below the surface of the water. As he watched Hugh loom above him, his lips curled up into a rictus of a snarl.

With a choke of laughter he hauled Phoebe up by a hank of hair to taunt, "You thought I loved you once and by God it was amusing to see you beg for crumbs of my regard when you were nothing to me! And then I killed your husband for you and what thanks do I get? You thought you'd escape me, did you?"

Coughing and spluttering, Phoebe cried out in terror while Hugh lunged at Wentworth, raising his heel to bring down upon Wentworth's fingers. The other man just laughed and found another metal spike to hold, slamming Phoebe's head against the side of the landing before dragging it beneath the water once more.

"Watch your whore die, Redding!" he shouted. "And then I'll come after your sister since she knows my secret, too." Wentworth laughed again while Hugh's stomach curdled at the blood that had streaked his beloved's forehead before she'd been pulled under again.

Desperately, he searched about him for a weapon of sorts. Hugh was still holding down Phoebe's head. Time was running out. Every time Hugh tried to deliver a blow to Wentworth's fingers, he deftly moved his hand and bobbed just out of reach to cling to the boat which was secured by a yard of mooring rope.

There was no other way than to do as Phoebe had done and hope he were as lucky in his timing to catch Wentworth by surprise. Hugh was not a strong swimmer but he would rather die trying to save Phoebe than watch her life snuffed out in front of his eyes.

With a great roar of fury he launched himself into the inky abyss of fast-running water.

His speed and accuracy caught Wentworth by surprise and as Hugh's spread-eagled body covered his, he let out a bellow of shocked anger before they all dipped below the murky depths.

21

Blackness swirled about Phoebe's frantically open eyes. She'd accepted long ago that she was going to die.

But she'd not expected it to be by Wentworth's own hand in the icy waters of the River Thames.

Still, she was not going to give in without a struggle, so even though her lungs were fit to burst as he toyed with her, dragging her head up to taunt her before plunging her down again, she kicked and flailed with all her might.

When she caught the back of his hand with her teeth, he hit her head against the side of something hard and what little orientation she had left almost deserted her.

So, this would be it. This would be the moment she'd lose consciousness and it would all be over. She'd go to her maker and he'd pass judgement on her sins.

The fact that it wouldn't be the magistrate, Lord Coulson, influenced by Wentworth's poison, who'd consign her to eternity, was some consolation, though, regardless, she was not yet ready to die.

But then, some large and unexpected object landed in the

water beside her. She felt Wentworth's grip release suddenly at the same time as she was thrust even deeper. Legs and arms appeared to be flailing all around her, the water seething and frothing while her vision blackened.

Yet there was still strength in her.

Struggling, she broke the surface, gasping for air and instantly was swept up by the current, borne swiftly away from her nemesis, the hateful Wentworth, but away, too, from the man she loved, who had saved her and who may this moment be facing his own death.

Phoebe had quite lost all sense of orientation by the time she was brought up short. She was wedged against a large pylon holding up a jetty further down the river, she discovered, as she used her final reserves of strength to cling to the first anchor point that presented itself.

With her skirts and petticoats dragging her down, it was an effort almost beyond her meagre reserves to extricate herself and pull herself onto shore. There she lay, panting with exertion for several minutes, before she staggered to her feet.

At first she couldn't even tell from which direction she'd come. And then, shading her eyes, she saw in the far distance, near the water's edge just where she'd left them, the shadows and frothing waters that indicated two fighting men.

Stumbling towards them, gasping in sustaining breaths and exhaling on chocking sobs, she tripped on a piece of detritus, an old driftwood plank that she had barely strength enough to lift.

At last, she reached the point where Hugh and Wentworth were trying to strangle each other in the muddy waters.

They were well matched, and their snarls and oaths curdled her blood. Summoning up a final burst of energy, Phoebe raised the plank into the air and brought it down hard, crushing the sneering face of the man who had tried so hard to kill her first.

Exhausted, she fell backwards, staring at the sky, until a shadow fell across her face.

Perhaps this was the moment she would die.

Instead, Hugh dropped to the ground beside her and gathered her in his arms.

"By God, you are a remarkable woman," he muttered into her ear before he kissed her.

22

A ferry took them downriver where they transferred to a coach for the journey to the channel. Wrapped warmly in a hooded black cloak and other concealing clothing Hugh had organized, Phoebe surrendered without too many questions to what was being done on her account. Then she'd surrendered to sleep.

Waking up properly in a tiny French town with the aroma of baking croissants wafting into her nostrils, and the cozy enveloping warmth of Hugh's body warming hers as if they were made to be a set, she wriggled closer, though it were barely possible, and opened heavy eyelids.

They'd spoken in convoluted sentences, too exhausted to begin from the beginning and end at the end. Now Phoebe asked another of the disjoined questions that seemed to randomly enter her mind.

"How did you see that I was released into your care?" She touched her forehead, then winced.

Hugh had tended to her medical needs with gentle care but her injuries had been nothing compared with his. Hugh's eyes were black and his face cut and scratched. Yet he treated her as if she were the only one to have suffered injury—and the most precious creature in all the world.

Hugh traced the outline of her lips and smiled."Mrs Plumb's Salon of Sin, where you were deceived and kidnapped, yielded two unexpected allies—including Lord Coulson, in an indirect manner. I was prepared to do whatever it took to save you."

"Lord Coulson? But you *both* believed me guilty." She said it without rancour. "You thought I was guilty because I didn't deny the fact my hand held the weapon," she went on. "That's what the judge determined, and that's why you were so disappointed when we last met. I truly thought I'd never see you again." She frowned at the ceiling, trying to keep the tears at bay, then returned her gaze to Hugh. "You wanted so badly to believe I was nothing like I'd been painted but everything you heard in court bore up the fact that I was a murderess." She gulped. "And then I proved it to you in front of your very eyes."

"Dear God, Phoebe, you were magnificent!" Hugh rose up onto one elbow and smiled down at her. "You did what I was patently failing to do. You struck Wentworth the mortal blow and in so doing you saved my life."

"You were about to lose yours while saving mine," Phoebe pointed out, happy that he was so ready to grasp the distinction between murder and self preservation. She drew in a deep breath. "But come, let's watch the dawn rise over the water. It's the first day of a new beginning for me."

"For us," Hugh corrected her, wrapping the blankets around them both as they stood in the window embrasure.

After some minutes of silence, Hugh admitted softly, "It's true I was dismayed to discover you'd deceived me for the three weeks we'd been together." His laugh was sheepish. "And more than dismayed to discover you were the woman whom the gossips painted as a callous husband killer. I will not lie and say the shock of seeing *you* in the stand in the courtroom meant my head refused to obey what I knew to be true in my heart: that you are the truest, kindest, most blameless woman I know."

He put his arm about her shoulders and pulled her to him, tucking away a strand of hair behind her ear.

Phoebe shuddered at the gentleness. To have such truth and transparency in a relationship was as liberating as it was exciting. He knew the worst of her.

"But the judge declared me guilty and sentenced me to death. How did you persuade him to abet my escape, Hugh?" She shuddered, and Hugh kissed her nose.

Putting his forehead to hers, he whispered, "When I went to the salon where you sought Wentworth's wife, I learned from someone there where I might find Lord Coulson." He chuckled. "He was at Madame Plumb's with a pretty male friend."

Phoebe drew in her breath sharply, and Hugh curled his arm around the back of her neck to stroke her cheek. "You're cold. We should go back to bed and have this discussion while doing something pleasurable."

"Before you return?" Phoebe turned her head away. She shouldn't inject sadness into proceedings, inevitable as a parting was.

"Oh, I'm not going anywhere, my precious."

Confused, Phoebe clung to him. "You know I can never return to England!" She searched his face. "And you cannot sacrifice your future for me. I must forever be on the run with a death sentence hanging above my head. You have assets and a fine future ahead of you in the country from which I must be forever exiled."

His reply was soft and measured. "I shall go wherever you go, Phoebe, my love. The time we spent apart made me realize how dangerous a companion I am when suffering your absence. Just ask Ada."

"But Hugh, you cannot be associated with me. It will be known that you kidnapped me from justice."

"That wasn't justice, and Coulson acknowledged it, too." Hugh grinned. "Lord Coulson had no choice but to give you the sentence he did, but when by pure chance I stumbled upon the means to expose him to the world for his own hang-worthy crime, he was willing to negotiate." He changed the subject, quickly. "You're a widow, aren't you?"

Phoebe was taken aback by his matter-of-fact tone, then outraged when he added, "I mean, you haven't some other secret husband tucked away? You didn't wed during the week before your trial?"

He laughed at her rosy-faced indignation, then swooped to kiss her lips before explaining, "I merely ask so that I might be sure you're in a position to accept me if I made you an offer of marriage." He became suddenly solemn. "I realize you'd be marrying beneath you, which of course is what has made me reluctant to do the honorable thing these past weeks we've been together." He grinned at his poor joke and she swotted his shoulder, her laugh a mixture of joy and disbelief.

"Now, before you say anything, first listen to my complete proposition."

Nervously, she waited. Let him speak first before she revealed the news she wasn't sure was a blessing or a bane.

"Are you attending, my sweet?"

She nodded and he clasped both her hands. A tentative morning sun was gently bathing the room in light, like the light that was filtering through her heart.

Hugh squeezed her hands. "With Wentworth dead, I believe an appeal would go in your favour. The servants were terrified of him but now they can speak the truth."

"The servants had no respect for me." Phoebe hung her head.

"Remember, Phoebe, that they could declare allegiance to only one person if their positions were to remain safe—and that person wasn't you." Hugh spoke reasonably and Phoebe felt a spark of hope. Some of the servants, she believed, had felt sorry for her. They knew Ulrick was an unkind husband and Wentworth a scheming bully.

"It's a risk," Phoebe said, slowly. She sighed and looked up at him. "Perhaps too great a risk when I could just disappear and live the rest of my life in exile. But—" She bit her lip, unsure how to express herself. "Perhaps I'm brave enough to do it if it would benefit...the child I will bear within the next eight months."

She watched the transformation of his features from concern at her response to the marriage proposal he'd not quite put into words, and her shock announcement. Then with a whoop, he swept her into his embrace.

"A marriage and a baby!" he cried. "Why, I must be the happiest man alive!"

Phoebe reached up to stroke his face. "I haven't actually received the marriage proposal, yet, my darling," she reminded him.

When she next looked, Hugh was down on the floor, on one knee, and miraculously, there in the palm of his hand was a glittering diamond ring, larger and more beautiful than anything she'd ever seen, much less owned.

But its material value was the least of her considerations.

She put her hands on his shoulders and stooped to kiss him on the mouth as her blankets fell away to reveal her nakedness. Then before she had time to feel the cold, he whisked her into his arms where she curled against him, fusing her mouth to his in a kiss of sweet, pure passion.

After some moments, he finally broke away and asked, breathlessly, "I take it that's a yes?"

She exhaled on a soft sigh. "Indeed, it is."

EPILOGUE

E*ighteen months later*

PHOEBE CAST A CRITICAL EYE OVER THE ARRANGEMENT OF THE furniture in the blue saloon where the guests would gather prior to the christening dinner. With so many people coming from London and even further afield—many of whom she'd never met from the upper echelons of high society—it needed to be just perfect.

She rearranged a red rose that hung its head amidst an abundant floral arrangement on a side table, turning with a smile of pleasure as the door opened. She'd expected it to be her beloved husband of only two months but it was one of the servants.

"Put the tea over by the window, please, Mrs Withins," she directed. "And ask Mr Withins to keep a watch from the tower for the first of the guests. He's less likely than the footman to be distracted."

"As you wish, Your Grace. Your husband said as he'd be here in two minutes," the servant added with a respectful curtsy.

Despite the circumstances, Phoebe had never detected a hint of disrespect in the attitude of her former nemesis. Naturally there had been shock on both sides when Mrs Withins had been hired by Phoebe's housekeeper to supplement the dwindling staff of the household. Many of the servants—though not James, unfortunately—had deserted Wentworth after he'd taken up residence at Blinley Manor. Phoebe had made sure James was the first to leave under her tenure.

So while Mrs Withins had initially displayed confusion and horror when she'd first been introduced to the dowager duchess, the woman obviously considered that a position as parlour maid at Blinley Manor was a great leap up from working for the miller. Besides, the dowager duchess had been fully exonerated during a sensational appeal some months beforehand and now Mrs Withins was the first to sing the praises of her new mistress.

Mrs Withins knew what was good for her, Phoebe thought, approvingly.

As for Phoebe, her motto was to keep one's enemies close. Or dead.

She thought of Wentworth with a shudder, then returned to examining the room.

The saloon was brighter and more light-filled since the days Ulrick had requested the curtains be drawn to ease his sensitive eyes and when Wentworth had filled it with the noxious smoke from the cheroots of which he was so fond.

"My darling Phoebe, you look radiant! I hope you're not nervous." Hugh swept into the room, putting his arm lightly round her waist and kissing her on the cheek before releasing her. "My sister and her husband are just driving up the avenue as we speak and, I'm afraid, Sir Roderick is right behind."

Phoebe smiled. "With you by my side I can manage *even* Sir Roderick."

"And what creative measures have you employed to manage him this time, dear heart?"

Phoebe put her head on one side and said happily, "The seating arrangement, darling. It was, in fact, Mrs Withins who suggested it. Sir Roderick will spend the evening between Lady Brindle and Miss Smiggle, both of whom—I have on good authority—are as deaf as posts. Which is why I've supplied him with a horn to use when I request that he entertain the ladies, in the drawing room, afterwards."

"Very good." Hugh nodded approvingly, his face lighting up at the sound of an infant's wail. "Ah, and here comes little Lord Cavanaugh, the very reason for this illustrious occasion. Thank you, Mollie," he added, taking his son from the arms of the nursemaid whom Phoebe dismissed so that—for now, at least—it could be just the three of them.

Standing in the window embrasure looking out, they watched as Ada and her husband were helped out of the carriage, before the spider-legged Sir Roderick emerged from his. But Phoebe no longer felt fear and repulsion. She had what she needed to forge ahead with hope and happiness: the wonderful man by her side and an unsullied reputation.

Phoebe turned to watch Hugh making faces at the infant whose wails had turned to gurgles of pleasure. "Are you *sure* you don't mind, my darling?" she whispered, waving her arm vaguely about the room. It wasn't often these days that doubt clutched at her heartstrings.

Hugh's expression, as ever, was unclouded. He glanced up, smiling. "Darling, we've gone over this a thousand times. Why should I mind? Miraculously, I've fathered the future Duke of Blinley. And whereas, some months ago, I was prepared to sacrifice my future prospects to have you by my side when you were the despised murderess, is this not an altogether preferable situation? You have, in fact, elevated *me*. Not only am I now married to the most beautiful woman in all of England, I'm married to one who is famed for having retained her poise and dignity having been shockingly ill-used by the now-discredited male members of her family who tried to frame her for a foul murder." His expression softened. "And now we have young John."

Exactly nine months after Ulrick's death, Phoebe had given birth to a son who was legally Ulrick's heir. The fact that the child was undersized—as it would be at a little more than seven months—had not been remarked upon. Not publicly, at least.

In the few months prior to John's birth, Phoebe and Hugh had been careful to be discreet. The child's future and Phoebe's reputation needed to be protected. And although Hugh had desperately wanted to be with Phoebe during her pregnancy, she'd insisted on a separation of some months. She knew how little it took for tongues to wag.

When baby John had been two months old, she'd gone to Bath to take the waters and there had supposedly met the man who would become her new husband.

What a rapturous reunion that had been. After a whirlwind courtship, Hugh and Phoebe had married in a small and joyous ceremony in the village church and although Hugh was just a mere gentleman, he was well respected in the local district—as Phoebe supposed anyone who wasn't Wentworth, or Ulrick, would be. Increasingly, he was respected on his own merits.

"Mr and Mrs Xavier." Mrs Withins bobbed a curtsey as she introduced the newcomers, and Phoebe crossed the room with outstretched arms to greet her sister-in-law.

"I believe congratulations are in order, Ada," she said merrily, with a meaningful look at the girl's belly. "I'm so glad you were prepared to negotiate the bumps and ruts on that terrible road."

"Nothing was going to keep me away, even though Robert tried," Ada replied, with a fond look at her husband. "Besides, what were a few hours of discomfort in order to celebrate this happy moment? I knew Hugh—and you, I hope—would want us here today."

"You're very right," Phoebe said, warmly.

Ada had been a surprising comfort to Phoebe during Phoebe's separation from Hugh. She'd been ingenious in devising ways in which Phoebe and her brother could meet without the two of them ever formally being connected in any way.

Hugh had, at one time, remarked wryly, that he didn't wish to plumb too deeply into how his sister had developed her frighteningly impressive ability for subterfuge. Phoebe had replied that, sadly, subterfuge was the only recourse for women at the mercy of controlling men.

Ah, but Hugh hadn't liked that until she'd cajoled him into more than just forgiveness.

Phoebe turned as two more guests were announced.

"Sir Roderick, a pleasure to see you again," she said with a small inclination of her head and no smile. "You've arrived at the very same moment as your greatest admirer, Miss Smiggle."

It was indeed auspicious timing that Miss Smiggle was just behind him. The elderly woman's eyes lit up when she saw Sir Roderick. It was well known that she never let an opportunity pass to hound him on his civic responsibilities.

Phoebe lowered her voice as she told Sir Roderick, "Miss Smiggle is keen to let you know her ideas on animal suffrage. She's very fond of her dairy cow, you know. I believe it sleeps in the parlour these days. Miss Smiggle—" Phoebe indicated a cluster of chairs to which she directed Sir Roderick—"do take a seat and entertain our eminent magistrate. Thank you Sir Roderick." She feigned gratitude. "You were always *such* a gentleman."

Phoebe didn't care that he saw the ironic smile she shared with her new husband. She took Hugh's hand and squeezed it, cradling their baby at the same time and lowering her voice to murmur, "What a joy it will be to watch baby John grow into a man of honour and kindness. A duke, yes, but a *real* gentleman of whom I can be proud. *Just* like his father."

As the room filled with guests wishing to bestow gifts and good wishes upon the baby duke, Phoebe's heart swelled with pride. All greeted her with respect and even warmth. With her handsome, generous and honourable husband by her side, Phoebe could manage any number of men like Sir Roderick. Hugh offered her protection and loyalty like Ulrick never had.

And a love that was strong and unquestioning.

"To the mother of the new duke," Hugh whispered in a special toast to Phoebe as he passed her chair to reach his own when the company proceeded from the drawing room to the dining room. He paused to place a kiss upon the top of her head.

"And his father," Phoebe responded, not caring who heard, and not caring who saw the warmth of Hugh's colluding smile as he squeezed her hand.

Because, regardless of right or wrong, the law in this matter was on her side.

THE END

ABOUT THE AUTHOR

Beverley was seventeen when she bundled up her first 500+ page romance and sent it to a publisher. Rejection followed swiftly. Drowning one's heroine on the last page, she was informed, was not in line with the expectations of romance readers.

So Beverley became a journalist.

After a whirlwind romance with a handsome Norwegian bush pilot she met in Botswana's beautiful Okavango Delta, Beverley discovered what real romance was all about, saved her heroine from a watery grave in her next manuscript and published her first romance in 2009.

Since then, she's written more than fifteen sizzling historical romances laced with mystery and intrigue under the name Beverley Oakley.

She also writes psychological historical mysteries, and Colonial-Africa-set romantic suspense, as Beverley Eikli.

With an inspiring view of a Gothic nineteenth-century insane asylum across the road, Beverley lives north of Melbourne with her gorgeous husband, two lovely daughters and a rambunctious Rhodesian Ridgeback called Mombo, named after the safari lodge where she and her husband met.

You can read more at www.beverleyoakley.com

www.beverleyoakley.com
beverley.oakley@gmail.com

ALSO BY BEVERLEY OAKLEY

The Daughters of Sin

The Daughter of sin series is a Regency-set 'Dynasty' that follows the intertwining lives and sibling rivalry of Lord Partington's two nobly born - and two illegitimate - daughters as they compete for love during several London Seasons.

With Hetty and Araminta both falling for men on opposing sides of a dastardly plot that is being investigated by Stephen Cranborne, now a secret agent in the Foreign Office, there's lashings of skullduggery and intrigue bound up in the central romance.

And, just in case you're ever worried that someone doesn't get their happy ending, or just desserts – rest assured that they will do, either in their book, or by the end of the series.

What Readers are Saying About the Series:

"...lies, misdeeds, treachery, and romance. What an impressive story! Ms. Oakley has a unique way of telling her stories, bringing unknown heroes/ heroines into the spotlight, as they navigate a world of espionage, and intrigue, all while trying to survive and find their HEA. Magnificent and mesmerizing!" ~ **Amazon reader**

"Full of secrets, murders, intrigues and you feel you know the characters and want to strangle some of them, especially Araminta!!! I have since read all in the series and can't wait for Book 5... This is a series I will read again and again." ~ **Amazon reader**

Below is the order of the books:

Book 1: Her Gilded Prison Book 2: Dangerous Gentlemen Book 3: The Mysterious Governess Book 4: Beyond Rubies

Book 5: Lady Unveiled: The Cuckold Conspiracy

Below are the five books in the series, in order:

She was determined to secure the succession, he was in it for the pleasure. Falling in love was not part of the arrangement.

**** When dashing twenty-five-year-old Stephen Cranborne arrives at the estate he will one day inherit, it's expected he will make a match with his beautiful second cousin, Araminta. But while proud, fiery Araminta and her shy, plain sister, Hetty, parade their very different charms before him, it's their mother, Sybil, a lonely and discarded wife, who evokes first his sympathy and then stokes his lustful fires.*

ALSO BY BEVERLEY OAKLEY

*Shy, plain Hetty was the wallflower beneath his notice...until a terrible mistake has one dangerous, delicious rake believing she's the "fair Cyprian" ordered for his pleasure. *** Shy, self-effacing Henrietta knows her place—in her dazzling older sister's shadow. She's a little brown peahen to Araminta's bird of paradise. But when Hetty mistakenly becomes embroiled in the Regency underworld, the innocent debutante finds herself shockingly compromised by the dashing, dangerous Sir Aubrey, the very gentleman her heart desires. And the man Araminta has in her cold, calculating sights. Branded an enemy of the Crown, bitter over the loss of his wife, Sir Aubrey wants only to lose himself in the warm, willing body of the young "prostitute" Hetty. As he tutors her in the art of lovemaking, Aubrey is pleased to find Hetty not only an ardent student, but a bright, witty and charming companion. Despite a spoiled Araminta plotting for a marriage offer and a powerful political enemy damaging his reputation, Aubrey may suffer the greatest betrayal at the hands of the little "concubine" who's managed to breach the stony exterior of his heart.*

Lissa Hazlett lives life in the shadows. The beautiful, illegitimate daughter of Viscount Partington earns her living as an overworked governess while her vain and spoiled half sister, Araminta, enjoys London's social whirl as its most feted debutante. When Lissa's rare talent as a portraitist brings her unexpectedly into the bosom of society – and into the midst of a scandal involving Araminta and suspected English traitor Lord Debenham – she finds an unlikely ally: charming and besotted Ralph Tunley, Lord Debenham's underpaid, enterprising secretary.

ALSO BY BEVERLEY OAKLEY

Fame. Fortune. And finally a marriage proposal! Book 4 of the Daughters of Sin series introduces Miss Kitty La Bijou, celebrated London actress, mistress to handsome Lord Nash and the unacknowledged illegitimate daughter of Viscount Partington. Having escaped her humble beginnings, Kitty has found fame, fortune and love, but the respectability she craves eludes her. When she stumbles across Araminta, her legitimate half-sister, on the verge of giving birth just seven months after marrying dangerous Viscount Debenham, Kitty realises respectability is no guarantee of character or happiness. But helping Araminta has unwittingly embroiled Kitty in a scandalous deception involving a ruthless brothel madam, a priceless ruby necklace and the future heir to a dazzling fortune. And when Kitty finally receives an offer of marriage she must choose. Respectability or love?

Kitty has the love of the man of her dreams but as London's most acclaimed actress and a member of the demimondaine, she accepts she can never be kind and handsome Lord Silverton's lawful wedded wife. When Kitty comes to the aid of shy, accident-prone and kind-hearted Octavia Mandelton, her sense of justice leads to her making the most difficult decision of her life: Give up the man she loves for the sake of honour. For Octavia is still betrothed to Lord Silverton who'd rescued Kitty in dramatic circumstances only weeks before. Cast adrift, Kitty joins forces with her sister, Lissa, a talented artist posing as a governess in order to bring to justice a dangerous spy, villainous Lord Debenham. Complicating matters is the fact Debenham is married to their half-sister, vain and beautiful Araminta. However, Araminta has a dark secret which only Kitty knows and which she realizes she is duty-bound to expose if she's to achieve justice and win happiness for deserving Lissa and Lissa's enterprising sweetheart, Ralph Tunley, long-suffering secretary to Lord Debenham. All seems set for a happy ending when Kitty tumbles into mortal danger. A danger from which only a truly honorable man can save her. A man like Silverton who must now make the hardest choice of his life if he's to live with his conscience.

ALSO BY BEVERLEY OAKLEY

Save when you buy the entire box set, available at all retailers here.

The First Three Books in the Series: Her Gilded Prison, Dangerous Gentlemen and The Mysterious Governess. Buy all three as a Box set, and save!

OTHER BOOKS IN THE SERIES

What is Wentworth and Ariane's strange history? You can read about it in **Cressida's Dilemma**, another stand-alone in the *Salon of Sin* series.

A woman who fears her husband is being unfaithful takes an extraordinary and sensual journey to discover an unexpected truth—and helps unravel the mystery of a lost child.

Eight years of marriage has not dimmed Cressida—Lady Lovett's—love for her husband, but the birth of five children has cooled her ardor.

Now rumors are circulating that the kind, dashing and seemingly ever-patient Justin, Lord Lovett, has returned to the arms of his former mistress, and Cressida believes her choices are stark—welcome her husband back to the marital bed and risk a sixth pregnancy she fears will kill her, or lose him forever.

With the astonishing discovery that methods exist to enable the innocent Cressida to transform herself into the vixen of her husband's dreams without expanding her nursery, she seeks to repay the woman responsible for her empowerment...only to discover her unlikely benefactress was, and perhaps still is, her husband's mistress.

Here's a sample of from Chapter One

"The Earl of Lovett has taken a mistress?"

The breathy shock of pretty newlywed, Mrs. Rupert Browne, sliced through the buzz of conversation, lancing its unsuspecting target three feet away and causing a deaf colonel to ask the duchess solicitously if she required a glass of water.

Still choking on her champagne, Cressida, Lady Lovett, strained to hear the response of her cousin, Catherine, who had obviously disseminated this latest shocking *on dit* while she smilingly assured deaf Colonel Horvitt she was quite all right, as if her happiness were not suddenly hanging by a gossamer thread.

She could only hope she was making the right responses to the colonel's monologue. All her concentration was focused on the nearby conversation as she waited desperately for a rejection of the outrageous claim.

"Surely not?" gasped the generally well-intentioned but oblivious Mrs. Browne to Cousin Catherine's whispered reply. "But the earl made a love match. Mama told me he scandalized society by marrying a nobody."

Cressida had to use two hands to keep her champagne coupe steady. The indignity of being described as a 'nobody' was nothing compared with the pain of hearing her husband's amours—real or otherwise—discussed in the middle of a ballroom. She forced her trembling mouth into her best attempt at a smile as the colonel leaned forward and wagged his finger at her, his stentorian tone precluding further eavesdropping. "Your husband ruffled more than a few feathers with his speech in the House of Lords last night, Lady Lovett."

Cressida had once giggled with her ferociously forceful cousin, Catherine, that the colonel used his deafness as an excuse to peer down the cleavage of every pretty lady he addressed. She was in no mood for giggling now. Clearly, Cousin Catherine was disclosing details about the state of Cressida's marriage, of which Cressida, apparently, was the last to know. She straightened and pushed her shoulders back, suddenly self-conscious of appearing the sagging, lacking creature the several hundred guests crowded into Lady Belton's newly renovated ballroom must imagine her, if they were already privy to what she was hearing for the first time. Before her last sip of champagne, she'd considered herself happily married. It was all she could do to remain standing and dry-eyed.

Adjusting the lace of her masquerade costume, she managed, faintly, "Ah, Colonel, you know Lord Lovett and his good causes." She tried to make it sound like an endearment, but the axis of her world had become centered on ascertaining what other tidbits about her marriage Catherine was divulging to Mrs. Browne.

The music swelled to a crashing crescendo, the end of which was punctuated by Mrs. Browne's shocked squeak, "Who is the woman? Madame Zirelli? Was she not once Lord Grainger's mistress? No! His wife? He divorced her? And now she and Lord Lovett—?"

Cressida hadn't wanted to come to Lady Belton's masquerade. Little Thomas was teething, but Justin had been especially persuasive, reminding her that it had been a long time since they'd been out in public, and that, yes, he knew Thomas was cutting a tooth, but there was nothing Cressida could do that Nurse Flora couldn't, just for a few hours that evening.

Searching the ballroom for her husband, she spied him talking to her friend, Annabelle Luscombe, near the supper table. Justin's look was inquiring, as if he were hanging on her every word. Cressida knew he would take equal interest if Annabelle were talking about her latest bonnet or about the Sedleywich Home for Orphans, of which Justin was patron and Annabelle on the committee.

A frisson of longing speared her. Justin had looked at her like that when she'd first met him. So handsome, so determined, so interested and sincere.

The thought that he'd made a special plea for her presence tonight purely in the interest of stilling wagging tongues was almost too terrible to consider.

A mistress? Her kind, beloved, faithful Justin?

As if he were conscious of her from across the room, Justin turned, his dark brown eyes kindling at the sight of her, the warmth of his smile spreading comfort like a woolen mantle. It radiated across the heated, perfumed distance that separated them. Dear Lord, he looked like a handsome prince taken right out of the pages of a storybook, his brown, wavy hair brushed fashionably forward, topped with the laurel wreath required by his costume, his sideburns contouring his elegantly chiseled, high cheekbones. Dressed like a stately Roman senator, he was the stuff of every girl's dreams, yet it was she, insignificant Miss Cressida Honeywell, daughter of a poor country parson, who had won his heart all those years ago.

She'd thought she still had it—had vowed she'd always keep it.

Rallying, she took a step forward, responding to the invitation implicit in her husband's eye, but the colonel began counseling Cressida on the dangers of Justin making speeches about orphans and sanitation when he could better rouse his audience in the Lords if he concerned himself with more important matters.

The look she'd just exchanged with her husband was enough to all but dismiss her fears. Exhaling with relief, Cressida smiled at the colonel who, obviously regarding this as encouragement, closed the distance between them as he pursued his argument. She retained her smile as Justin, from the other side of the room, focused another very warm glance in her direction before attending to the hunchbacked Dowager Duchess of Trentham, whose eightieth birthday celebration this was. Justin had the gift of making every woman feel the center of his especial interest. Clearly something must have been misconstrued...

And yet.

Awareness prickled through her—that she had for some time sensed all was not quite right. Taking a step back, she swallowed past the lump in her throat while making, she hoped, the appropriate responses for the benefit of the colonel. Justin, lately, had not been the contented husband of old. The recent bolstering she'd silently received from him faded upon this acknowledgment and her eyes stung. She knew her behavior had not been beyond reproach—that she had withdrawn and that understandably, he was confused. Some months ago, he'd tried to raise the subject, yet she'd brushed it aside, incapable of putting her feelings into words, unable to entertain that unmentionable aspect of their marriage at the heart of all their problems.

Forcing aside her shame, she turned in the direction of her cousin.

"Catherine? A minute, if you please?" Cressida waylaid the stately, dark-haired young woman dressed as a siren as the colonel—thankfully—responded to his wife's perfunctory summons. With a little intake of breath and a stammered excuse, the recently gossiping Mrs. Browne slipped away while Cousin Catherine betrayed her guilt with a blush.

"Why, Cressy, I did not notice you. How long have you been standing there?"

"Long enough to wonder who Madame Zirelli might be and what she is to my husband," Cressida responded with uncharacteristic harshness.

Catherine's hand flew to her mouth. "Oh, Cressy," she gasped. "I had no idea you— I'm so sorry. But of course, it's only gossip. You know how quick people are to jump to conclusions." But her cheeks were flushed. She knew she was guilty of the charges Cressida made. "You're looking unwell, Cressy. I'll take you home. We'll have a nice, cozy chat in the carriage, shall we? I hadn't expected to see you out this evening, you've been hiding away so long."

Cressida was about to argue that she planned to return home with Justin when Catherine took her arm, saying breezily, "Don't trouble yourself over Justin. He's asked me to tell you he's off to White's with Roddy Johnson. He knew you were anxious to return home to little Thomas."

Was that grim satisfaction she saw on her cousin's face?

It wasn't until she'd gained the darkness of the vehicle that Cressida broke her tense silence. She could barely force out the words, but she would not have Catherine secretly gloating over something Cressida was apparently the last to know about.

"I'd thank you to tell me everything you told Mrs. Browne." Sinking back against the squabs of her husband's plush equipage, she hid her disquiet beneath a veneer of dignified anger. "If she is under the impression Justin has taken a mistress, you apparently did little to disabuse her of that notion, when I know very well it is not true. I'd like to know the source of your information."

Catherine shifted beside her, and although Cressida could not see her face, she could tell she was uncomfortable. "No need to get on your high ropes, Cressy," she muttered, and Cressida could imagine the proud, defiant tilt to Catherine's pointed chin as she defended her actions, just as she had done all through her impish childhood and spirited adolescence. "Like you say, I'm sure there's nothing to it."

Cressida was not about to assume her normally pliant role in order to appease her cousin. Not when her happiness was at stake, and not when it concerned her husband. He was her light, her moon. In steely tones, she asked, "I would like to know, Catherine, how you gained the impression Justin has taken a mistress." This was too important for the tears to which Cressida was sometimes prone, especially lately. With her back pressed stiffly against the carriage seat in the darkness, she felt, ironically, as if some of her own youthful confidence had returned. Justin was the axis of her existence. If her happiness was at risk—though she was sure it was not—she needed to know so she could act.

"Justin appears just as loving toward you as he ever did, my dear," Catherine hedged. "Why, only last week when James and I dined with you, he remarked to me—"

"Obviously, you must have heard something specific. I'm sure you'd not repeat hurtful gossip."

"Really, Cressida, I think you are making too much of this." Catherine halted in the middle of her response, paused, then added in clipped tones, as if she were angry with her cousin, "All right then, if you must know, and since you've all but accused me of being a gossiping jade—though I had hoped to spare you—I'll tell you what whispers are buzzing around the salons in London." In the gloom, her expression was combative. "Justin has been a regular visitor to Mrs. Plumb's Wednesday salons." She gave a self-righteous sniff. "And if you've never heard of her, James says Mrs. Plumb is an actress with literary pretensions. A very vulgar woman, I believe, who paints her face."

Now was not the time to remind Catherine that she herself was not averse to resorting to artifice to enhance her natural charms. Cressida gripped her reticule with trembling fingers and stared fiercely at her cousin. "I take it this Madame Zirelli is also a regular at Mrs. Plumb's. Is it on this flimsy basis that the rumors are circulating regarding Justin's...extramarital amours?" Hurt and anger banished Cressida's propensity to soften life's harsh realities. She rarely spoke so directly to anyone—certainly not to Catherine, who'd taunted Cressida since they'd been children for being 'churchyard poor', but whose respect Cressida had thought she'd gained through her glittering match with Justin. Now, Catherine had seized on the first opportunity to knock Cressida down to size. With dignity, she asked her cousin, "On what grounds am I to believe this? Come, Catherine, it is not like you to be anything but direct."

"If you prefer directness, Cressida," Catherine responded with an air of injury, "do you not think it perfectly reasonable that Justin, like most men after eight years of marriage, feels the need to seek diversion? Is it not perfectly understandable that after so long, you are no longer everything to him? What woman ever is?" she added bitterly.

Cressida gasped as if she had been struck, but her cousin went on, her green eyes glittering as the carriage passed beneath a lamp-post. "He is no different from every other man, but you fail to consider your good fortune, Cressy, for at least Justin is discreet."

"How can you say that?" Deflated, Cressida slumped into the corner, glad of the dimness so she could hurriedly wipe away her tears. Catherine would enjoy her weakness. "You speak as if I am the last to know and that I've brought this upon myself. How would you feel if James—" A sudden illumination stopped her mid-sentence, and she put out her hand, saying before she could stop herself, "James has strayed again? Oh, Catherine, I'm so sorry."

"Save your sympathy for yourself, Cressy." Catherine drew away, as if Cressida's outstretched hand were as welcome as a snake. "I was under no illusions as to James' likely fidelity from the day we wed. He was always too handsome for me—you remember we overheard Mrs. Dooley saying it at our engagement ball?"

Cressida knew Catherine's wounding had been close to mortal all those years ago. Six, she recalled, wondering if by Catherine's calculations, Cressida should consider herself lucky for having retained her husband's loyalty for this long.

Shrugging, as if the matter were no longer of importance, Catherine went on, "James and now Justin are simply conforming to the prescribed role of husbands by doing what society condones within the limits of money and discretion and, like me, you should accept the situation and direct your energies toward the children. Though perhaps in your case—not wishing to criticize—I wonder if that is not at the root of your problem. You dote on those babies and seem to forget Justin has his needs, too. When were you last seen at his side?"

Cressida blinked like one dazed by blinding light. Catherine, whose lack of insight and sympathy was on a par with her lack of tactfulness, had come too close to the bone.

Seeming not to register Cressida's stricken look, her cousin went on. "I mean, have you looked at yourself lately, Cressida? Yes, at twenty-six, you still have that girlish, sleepy-eyed charm that won him over, but must you appear quite so naïve after all those children? As I said, tonight is the first time you've torn yourself from the nursery to accompany Justin anywhere, and whom do you choose to masquerade as? A shepherdess, for God's sake!"

Plucking the black lace of her own daring décolletage, Catherine straightened majestically. "Justin has been your loyal husband for all these years and he loves you. But if you want to win him back from the arms of Madame Zirelli—and yes, I have it on good authority that Madame Zirelli is his new mistress—you'd do yourself more favors parading as something less"—her lip curled —"insipid."

Cressida had experienced Catherine's propensity to lash out when she was feeling vulnerable. Not that this lessened her own devastation. "On whose good authority?" she whispered. "One of your snake-tongued society friends, or someone serving on the Home for Orphans committee?"

Catherine glared at the inherent criticism before saying, "If you must know, it was Annabelle Luscombe—"

[End of Sample]

Printed in Great Britain
by Amazon